ROOM FOR
RENT

NOELLE W. IHLI

Published 2023 by Dynamite Books

www.dynamitebookspublishing.com

ISBN: 979-8-9878455-6-1

First printing, October 2023

Dynamite Books, LLC

For anyone who's survived a roommate from hell.
May you never have to label your food again.

1

..me again: A soft, metallic *clink* on the far side of the

.ya tried to open her eyes, but they were too heavy.

She tried to roll over in bed, but her muscles refused to obey. .ven her tongue felt like it had been glued to the roof of her mouth.

Clink, clink.

Adrenaline prickled through her veins. Her heart hammered in her chest, an impossibly fast tempo while the rest of her stayed sluggish and slow.

Why couldn't she wake up? Why couldn't she move? What time was it?

She managed to force her eyelids open, but it made no difference. She couldn't see anything. The bedroom was pitch dark.

Clink, clink.

Oh, god. She knew the sound now. It was her bedroom doorknob, jiggling back and forth.

He was trying to get into her room.

Again.

The realization moved through her murky b
pery fish. Tiny white dots clouded her field of v
snow, no matter how much she blinked.

Had he drugged her this time?

The panic pulsed harder, pushing her to get out
run. To scream. To do *something*. But all she could d
there, leaden legs tangled uselessly in the sheets.

Was the dresser still pushed against the door?

No. She knew it wasn't.

Was this how she was going to die?

You should've gotten out while you had the chance, b
Jade's voice whispered through her thoughts, sad and solen
Nobody can help you now.

Nya's heart squeezed in her chest. "Help!" The word, mean
to come out as a scream, dribbled out of her mouth in a quiet
splutter.

Click.

She heard the bedroom doorknob turn.

Then the door opened with a *whoosh*.

No, no, no. Oh god, no.

Oblivion was pulling her back under, no matter how hard
she tried to fight it.

Her panicked thoughts skittered just out of reach.

The last thing she heard before the darkness closed in was
the sound of his footsteps, moving toward her bed.

2

TWO MONTHS EARLIER

Nya's pilgrimage from Clearwater, Idaho to Boise was usually her favorite day of the year.

The lonely, five-hour drive sans air conditioning was grueling, and she was never sure whether the old 1995 Honda Civic was going to make it. The bucket of junk dripped oil and was missing its back bumper. The wind whipped through the open windows the whole way, the dry August heat slightly less awful than the alternative of baking alive in a speeding convection oven.

But when the rural county highways finally spilled into the city, she'd find the bustling college town waiting for her with its stately buildings named after beloved professors, treasure troves of books, and throngs of students.

This year was different. This year, a tug of homesickness stayed with Nya while she drove. When a sign that read "Boise, 34 miles" came into view, she was suddenly afraid she might cry. *It's just a semester,* she told herself firmly, blinking away the tears so she could focus on the road. *Suck it up, buttercup.*

No part of the homesickness was for the pristine, rural farmhouse she'd driven away from in Clearwater four hours earlier. Or her parents.

I can't imagine what you've racked up in debt, chasing those worldly ambitions, her mother had said disdainfully that morning before she drove away. Not *I love you.* Not *I'm proud of you for being the first person in our entire family tree to go to college.* Not *drive safe and call us when you get to Boise.* Just a quick, passive-aggressive jab and a tight-lipped frown.

While other parents crowed over their first-generation college students, Nya's parents cried actual tears that their only daughter was obstinately headed back to the den of sin, aka Boise State University, for her final semester to complete her Bachelor of Nursing Science degree. Instead of staying in rural Idaho to farm, worship, and pop out babies like God—and Blood of the Lamb Church—intended.

What she'd really be homesick for this year was Jade.

Jade, with her loud, honking laugh that made no sense with her petite frame and tiny rosebud lips. Jade, who had brought home endless peanut butter malts from the Burger Shack where she worked part-time after classes. Jade, whose quick wit and sharp tongue never lashed out at the people she loved. Jade, who did the best impression of Nya's parents to make her laugh whenever the odd letter full of Bible verses arrived. Jade, who was smart, kind, and empathetic. Jade, who, if Nya was being honest, was her only real friend.

Jade, who had graduated a semester early and was living at her grandmother's house in Indiana, starting her first job as a nurse.

Seriously. Suck it up, Nya chided herself more firmly. Jade wasn't dead. She was just a phone call away. When Nya graduated in December with her own nursing degree, the plan was that she would sell her old Honda—it would never survive the thirty-hour drive—and buy a one-way Greyhound ticket to Indy. Then she and Jade would pick up right where they left off as roommates and, hopefully, coworkers.

The road crested to reveal a distant glimpse of the tree-studded Boise Valley. She'd be there soon.

A quick glance in the rearview mirror made her wince. She'd kept the windows rolled down for the entire car ride to survive the sweltering heat. Now, her long, wild brown hair gave the word *windswept* a whole new meaning. Dark bags rimmed her tired eyes. A red rash of sunburn bloomed across her cheek on the driver's side where the sun had been beating all afternoon. The cheap foundation she'd dabbed on this morning had turned into a cakey, uneven mess that looked more like a skin condition than makeup.

So much for making a good first impression.

Sidney, Nya reminded herself for the umpteenth time. Sidney Holcote. Or maybe Holcomb. The only thing Nya really knew about her was that she was into drum circles. Her Meta profile photo showed a cluster of hipsters gathered on a dirty rug, each holding a small, colorful drum in their lap. The girl in the center of the photo—Sidney—had curly red hair and an ultra-realistic tattoo of a cat on her bare shoulder. Her eyes were closed, her lips partly open in a soft smile, her hands mid-beat on the drum she held.

Sidney was no Jade, but she looked nice enough. Or at least interesting. But the only thing that really mattered to Nya was that Sidney was advertising the second bedroom of a house near campus for half the price of anything she'd seen all summer. And she'd *looked*, scouring the student housing boards and Meta Marketplace.

The housing search had consumed her every break at the Taco Tienda in Clearwater, where she'd worked for the summer. And she'd lost count of how many times she'd hidden in the bathroom stalls at Blood of the Lamb Church to sneak a look at her phone and comb through new listings. Nya dutifully attended services each Monday, Wednesday, Friday, *and* Sunday. Not because she wanted to, but because that was the only way her parents had agreed to let her move back home from college for the summer without tacking on rent.

It was in the church bathroom where she'd finally found Sidney's rental listing. It had been posted just five minutes earlier. Nya had sent Sidney a message on the app right away, shocked when she replied almost immediately with a winky emoji and a message that said, "Can't believe someone else wants to live in this hole. Venmo first month's rent and it's all yours."

The whole transaction happened so fast that when Nya returned to the pew, her parents didn't even realize she'd been in the bathroom longer than usual.

Nya tried to remember the way her stomach had flip-flopped with nervous excitement when she saw that gloriously cheap rental she could actually afford.

Right now, all she could feel were the nerves.

The narrow rural highway abruptly opened up to four lanes, indicating she had crossed into Boise city limits.

"It's going to be fine," Nya told herself firmly, but the sound of her voice was barely audible beneath the rush of hot wind and the rattle of the old car.

3

The rental house was as ugly as it was inexpensive.

Nya had expected that much.

What she hadn't expected was the knot of dread that tightened in her stomach when she laid eyes on it for the first time.

She already knew that the house would be in rough shape from the photos she'd seen. You got what you paid for. But that didn't explain the warning bells clanging in her gut.

Suck it up, buttercup, Nya chided herself as she brought the old Honda to a shuddering stop and stared out the open window. *At least it came furnished. It could be worse.*

Her gut wasn't convinced. The house looked like a project for HGTV's *Teardown Turnaround.* Still, things could always be worse. It was the one life lesson her parents taught her that Nya intended to carry with her out into the world.

The nicotine-yellow rental had peeling brown trim, dusty black shutters, and crumbling cement steps leading to a small, raised porch. One side of the stair railing was missing. Splintered, like something—or someone—had been shoved through the rotting wood.

A rickety once-white lattice wrapped around the bottom of the porch. It might have looked okay if it weren't for a smattering of wide, gaping holes that looked like missing teeth. Had an animal done that? Nya grimaced.

A window AC unit had been wedged crookedly through one of the front windows. Despite the sweltering late-August afternoon, it was silent. With its banged-up, misshapen vents and rusted body crammed into the window frame at an angle, it looked like it had died trying to escape the ramshackle house.

Trickles of sweat dripped down Nya's back. Whether or not that air conditioning unit worked, it had to be cooler inside the house than it was in the car.

Nya clicked off the radio she hadn't realized was still playing beneath the sound of the wind. Then she grabbed her pillow and duffel bag, propped up next to her like a passenger in the front seat. No sense in making another trip back outside to the car in this heat. She could carry everything she owned easily enough.

As she shut the car door behind her, she caught her reflection in the cracked driver's side mirror and winced.

There was no fixing this windblown-bumpkin look without a shower.

You'll fit right in with the house, she scolded the girl staring back at her in the reflection of the dusty mirror.

Half-open mini-blinds covered the narrow window beside the front door. One side of the blinds was compressed, like fingers were holding it down. For a second, Nya thought it might be Sidney peeking out. However, as she got closer, she realized the blinds were just bent that way.

Nya hefted the duffel on her shoulder and picked her way along the short pathway leading to the front door. A graceless mulberry tree hunched over the path, offering a patch of shade. The lowest branches brushed the cement, forcing Nya to duck while she tried to avoid the smears of dark berries rotting on the uneven pavement.

The sticky, splotchy juice looked a little like dried blood. Just a shade too dark.

The image turned Nya's stomach. Blood didn't bother her, but it did make her think about the expensive Advanced Human Anatomy book she'd have to purchase this semester. Three hundred and twenty dollars—and that was *used,* if she could get to the book sale tomorrow before all the pre-owned copies sold out.

Most of her other professors had made the switch to e-textbooks—or offered that option, at least. Not Professor Stern. He'd written the textbook himself—and did not offer a digital version. It was like his name had given him no choice but to become a stick in the mud. A note on the syllabus warned, "Studies show that readers retain information better from physical texts. If you disagree, I encourage you to choose another class session."

There was no other class session.

Everything will work out, she told herself firmly, repositioning the duffel bag onto one hip so she could ring the cracked doorbell of the house. Its surrounding plate was rusted and worn, with chipped yellowing paint flaking from the wall. Did it even work?

Nya hesitated before pressing down on the dingy white button, wishing more than anything that Jade—not drum-circle Sidney—was waiting for her inside the dismal house. The rundown rambler she'd called home for the past three years of college wasn't much nicer than this place. But it didn't matter, because she'd shared it with her best friend.

The plan was that Jade would move out of her grandmother's house as soon as Nya graduated, and put in a good word for her at Interim Health. Then, in a few years, Nya would somehow pay off her crippling student loans, work her way up to day shifts, and never think about Idaho again.

Just four more months.

The doorbell cracked under her finger but didn't ring.

Nya knocked loudly, feeling the beads of sweat drip faster down her back.

When nobody answered, she knocked again, then pressed her ear to the door and listened for any sound from inside. Where was Sidney?

Thump, thump, thump.

It was the soft cadence of a drum, coming from inside the house.

Nya knocked one more time, four hard, loud raps that hurt her knuckles. Then she twisted the doorknob.

The hinges whined in protest but opened, revealing a dark entryway and a glimpse of a kitchen and living room. The steady thumping was louder now and weirdly mesmerizing. The drumbeats were coming from down the hallway. Sidney must not have been able to hear her knocks over the sound of the drum.

A skunky, sour odor lingered in the stale air. Nya wrinkled her nose and coughed. Weed, definitely. But something else, too. Old food? Mildew? The dimly lit kitchen at the end of the entryway was cluttered with dishes, piles of trash, and an old microwave hanging open atop the yellow fridge. That explained at least some of the smell. Sidney seemed like a slob, but Nya could deal with that. Jade wasn't exactly a neat freak.

Anyway, it was a little cooler than outside. That was something. When night fell, she could open a window.

It'll be fine, she told herself again, then gingerly stepped onto the linoleum. The pattern—repeating yellow sunbursts and brown squares—held a sort of vintage charm, despite its peeling corners.

A pair of cheap black flip-flops lay strewn across her path. Nya considered removing her own sandals, but the thought of walking barefoot on the dirty brown carpet was too much.

As her eyes adjusted to the dim lighting, the intricate wallpaper in the kitchen and sitting area came into focus. Nya finally smiled. Like the linoleum, it had a repeating pattern of sunbursts and geometric shapes. With a little elbow grease, the inside of the house could actually be pretty comfortable. Worn-down vintage chic.

The floor creaked with each step as she made her way down the hall toward the sound of the drum. The duffel bag was getting heavy. There was one closed door, kitty-corner from an open door across the hall. At the end was another closed door.

Nya stopped in front of the first door and listened. The drumbeats were coming from inside. This must be Sidney's bedroom. Should she knock? Was it weirder to interrupt the drumming or just start unpacking without saying hello? A quick peek across the hall revealed that the partially-open door was an empty bedroom.

As Nya shifted her weight and turned around, part of the duffel hit the wall with a loud *thunk.* The drum beat suddenly stopped, replaced by unsteady footsteps.

Nya swallowed and repositioned the duffel and pillow to her hip, combing her fingers through her tangled, messy hair. She pasted a smile on her face, ready to offer an apology for not knocking loudly enough earlier.

The bedroom door swung open and the apology died on her lips.

Nya thrust the duffel in front of her protectively and took a hesitant step backward. The person standing in the dimly lit bedroom doorway wasn't a tattooed hipster girl with long red hair.

Instead, it was a tall man with a pair of headphones in one hand. His greasy, rust-colored hair hung limply to his shoulders. His eyes darted back and forth, like a rodent's. Were they actually black, or were his pupils just completely dilated?

"Hey, pretty girl," he slurred.

4

Nya gaped.

The guy wore a frayed corduroy jacket the same color as the carpet. Several buttons were missing, and the T-shirt beneath it was either tie-dyed or stained a mottled orange.

The oversized T-shirt draped nearly to his bare knees. Was he even wearing pants?

She could smell his body odor wafting toward her, even at this distance.

If the house itself were to transform into a human being, like it might in a warped Disney movie, this would be it.

"Is … is Sidney here?" Nya croaked, finding her voice. Did this guy live here, too? Was he Sidney's boyfriend? Had she gotten the address wrong and just waltzed inside this creep's house? She took another step back, ready to beat a hasty exit if he made a sudden move toward her.

The greasy-haired, black-eyed stranger put one hand on the bedroom doorway and scrutinized her closely. "You're *really* pretty," he repeated, somehow drawing out the last word into four syllables.

"Um, thanks," Nya mumbled, immediately hating herself for responding that way. Like Jade always told her, you didn't have to thank creeps for compliments. She clenched her jaw and tried again. "I got the wrong house. See ya."

To her surprise, the guy opened his mouth, threw back his head, and let out a roar of laughter like she'd just made a joke. His teeth were the same shade of pale yellow as the tattered paint peeling from the exterior of the house.

Gross. She wasn't interested in hearing his joke's punchline.

Stumbling against the wall with a painful thud to her elbow, Nya hurried back down the hallway toward the entryway.

Erratic footsteps thudded after her.

Holy shit. He was actually following her? Nya grabbed the handle to the front door, no longer caring about the blast of heat waiting for her outside.

Before she could yank the door open, she heard something that stopped her cold.

"Nya, wait."

Heart racing, she turned to face the beady-eyed, glazed-over man wearing the corduroy jacket. He was leaning against the wall at the end of the hallway, holding his hands palm-up as if in surrender.

"Call me Sid," he slurred.

Nya stared at him in silent shock, still processing what she'd just learned. Sidney—*Sid*—was a dude.

He continued holding his hands palm up toward her, like he was waiting for her to accept whatever he was offering.

Her stomach churned.

He wasn't just some random creep.

He was a very specific creep.

This wasn't the wrong address.

This was the right address.

And Sid was her roommate.

What the hell was she supposed to do now? The only thing she knew for sure was that she had to get out of here and think. Call Jade. Drive away, somewhere, anywhere. Get away from this guy and regroup. Right this second.

Pulling her duffel bag and pillow to her chest, she left him standing in the hallway. Then she pulled open the battered front door, slammed it behind her, and booked it back down the walkway, terrified he'd follow.

When she was almost to the Honda, Nya shifted the duffel bag to her other hip and hazarded a glance behind her to see if Sid was watching through the squatty front window. The crease in the mini-blinds was more exaggerated now. His squinting eyes were just visible through the reflection in the glass.

Nya gasped as one of the mulberry's low-hanging tree branches skittered across the bare skin of her arm. When she moved to dodge the branch, her left foot hit a crack in the uneven walkway. She managed to avoid a faceplant onto the concrete, but the heavy duffel bag flew out of her hands and hit the mulberry-covered pavement with a thump. She scrambled to scoop it up and kept going, not bothering to wipe the glaze of crushed berries that clung to the bottom. They squished through her fingers.

With shaking hands, Nya opened the car door, shoved the duffel bag and pillow into the passenger seat, then twisted the key into the ignition. The Honda let out a high-pitched, strained whine while the engine struggled to turn over then finally caught, grumbling to life and lurching forward. She could still feel Sid's eyes on her, but she refused to look at him as she pulled away.

Her mind spun while she drove through the neighborhood at a snail's pace. What the hell was she going to do now? Classes started tomorrow. Where was she supposed to go? She was out of gas. Fully in the red. So wherever she went, it had to be close. The last thing she needed was to spend money on a tank of gas. Her budget was razor-thin, and it didn't include escape fuel.

She ticked through the possibilities, eliminating them one at a time. Jade wasn't *technically* her only friend. The past three years held a handful of study buddies, dates, and acquaintances, but nobody she'd feel comfortable calling at the last minute to beg for a couch to sleep on.

Don't spiral. Just find somewhere cool you can walk around. Call Jade. Figure it out, Nya told herself. It was too hot to think in the car. Even with the windows rolled down and a breeze streaming inside, the car was scorching.

The lava-hot steering wheel burned her hands, but she gripped it hard anyway. *Shit, shit, shit.* Sweat trickled down her forehead. When she wiped it, she noticed that her fingers were stained red. She stared at them in shock for a moment too long, finally realizing it was from the damn mulberries from the sidewalk in front of the rental house.

Nya slammed on the brakes just in time to avoid hitting a group of pedestrians crossing a few feet away. The three blonde girls, dressed alike in adorable matching denim cutoffs and pink tank tops, glared at her. One of them, the closest to Nya's car, lifted her middle finger before hustling away.

Nya cringed and mouthed *sorry.* The girl yelled something unintelligible and lowered her middle finger. Then she stood at the edge of the crosswalk and squinted at Nya through the dirty windshield. Her angry expression suddenly morphed into pity and concern.

Nya hit the gas and looked away. A quick peek in the rearview mirror revealed that she'd inadvertently wiped grimy reddish-purple streaks down her face from the mulberries on her fingers. It probably looked like she was driving away from a crime scene.

She swallowed down the sticky lump in her throat and forced herself not to sneak a glance back at the three perfect blonde girls in the rearview mirror. From the looks of it, they were headed somewhere fun. Maybe an end-of-summer party.

Nya pulled out of the neighborhood, scanning streets that felt equally foreign and familiar after being away for the summer. Walmart was close by, she remembered. She could go there and hang out until she figured out what to do. There would be a drinking fountain, bathrooms to wash her face, and air-conditioning there. Plus, she could call Jade.

Jade would know what to do.

Jade had always been the smart, savvy one.

Nya, on the other hand, had been under the impression that babies came from kissing until her junior year of high school. That was the year the Estradas had moved into a rental down the street from Nya's family in Clearwater.

On the first day of junior year, Nya had hurried past her new neighbors' house, curious but wary. The Estradas weren't members of the tiny Blood of the Lamb Church, which meant that no matter where they'd come from, they were worthy of suspicion.

It was a ten-minute walk to the bus stop and a twenty-minute ride after that to get to the high school. To Nya's dismay, she'd found Jade patiently waiting at the bus stop. Nya had managed to keep her distance that morning, carefully allowing her to get on the bus first so she could choose a seat on the opposite side of the nearly empty vehicle. But there was no avoiding the girl with the wide smile and the tight, springy curls on the way home.

As soon as Nya got off the bus, a loud voice behind her said, "Hey, wait up. Aren't you hot?"

Nya bristled but held her tongue. The late-August day was indeed boiling, despite what she was wearing.

Why was this girl trying to make conversation, Nya had wondered. The other kids at school weren't exactly dying to hang out with the girl who wore floor-length skirts and high-necked, long-sleeved blouses. They'd reached a sort of stalemate that they wouldn't make fun of her, and Nya's mother wouldn't show up at their parent's houses with a tongue-lashing and a Bible.

"I'm fine," Nya had responded, tight-lipped.

Jade had just shrugged. "Right on. The pattern on your skirt is bitchin'. Do you want to come over to my house? I could use a friend."

Nya swallowed hard. Outsiders were dangerous. Especially outsiders who used the B-word. She'd been warned about kids like this when she entered the public school system in Clearwater her freshman year. Some of the other parishioners at Blood of the Lamb raved about the Ancient Languages program that allowed their children to appreciate the Bible in its purest forms: Latin and Greek. There was also the promise of a Home Economics class that would help Nya learn the skills she needed to be a good homemaker and mother.

But when she looked at Jade's smiling, guileless expression, she couldn't help thinking, *I could use a friend, too.*

When Nya asked permission to visit Jade and her family, she told her parents she was witnessing. To prove it, she tucked a fat Bible in her backpack. And that was that.

The vibrant house down the street became the refuge Nya didn't know she needed, and Jade became the best friend she didn't know she'd been waiting for. The Estradas' home radiated color, sound, and personality from the vibrant blue-and-yellow bedspreads and curtains, to the eclectic knickknacks and dishes that adorned the shelves. The polar opposite of the buttoned-up farmhouse where Nya had grown up. Most intriguing of all, they went to the doctor when they got sick.

There were just four people living in the Estradas' home—Jade, her mother, her father, and her sister, Berta. However, the sounds of lively chatter and laughter were constant, mingling with the smells of something mouthwatering and spicy that Jade's mother was endlessly preparing.

Nobody seemed to care about Nya's strange, ultra-modest clothes or the fact that she'd never seen the inside of a doctor's office or that she went to church four times a week. They just folded her into the bustle and fed her delicious things that made her laugh with delight—or sputter when Jade's mom cooked with ghost peppers.

Jade's family moved away to Indianapolis just a year after they'd arrived in Clearwater, as soon as their lease was up. Jade's grandmother Tita had dementia, and it was getting worse. So they picked up and drove across the country to be closer to her. But by the time they left town, Nya had started borrowing some of Jade's clothes and makeup to wear to school each day, so she could change in the bathroom. It was exhilarating to trade the long skirts and high-necked shirts for short sleeves and jeans.

When she saw her face with eyeshadow for the first time in Jade's mirror, she gasped out loud. She didn't feel a dark presence like she'd been warned in Sunday School. Instead, she just felt pretty.

Nya's parents were outraged when they found out she'd been "corrupted" right before Jade moved away, but by then, the damage was done. Jade had helped Nya secretly apply to Boise State, where Jade had already been accepted. To her surprise, Nya even earned a partial scholarship and a book stipend that would help offset the fact that her parents made it very clear they wouldn't be offering any kind of monetary support if she continued on her "path of destruction."

Not that they had much to offer in the way of financial help. Despite her parents' meager income, every spare dollar went to Blood of the Lamb.

They'd barely even agreed to sign the FAFSA. Not just because they hated the fact that she was going away to college—instead of settling down in Clearwater and building her world around agriculture, babies, and Blood of the Lamb Church—but because she was going into debt to do it.

In her parents' eyes, Nya's life was basically a seven-layer dip of sin.

5

The Walmart a short distance from campus was busier than Nya had expected. The parking lot teemed with students driving a rainbow of clunkers. Baby-faced freshman accompanied by parents striding toward the entrance to pick out the perfect comforter for their new dorm room. Frat bros hauling out cases of cheap beer, chips, and frozen pizza for the parties they would throw to kick off the year. Roommates looking for a perky plant, a bean bag chair, or a funky glowing neon sign to glam up their new apartment.

They all looked happy. Eager. Nervous. Tired. Giddy.

What would it be like to be just another college student preparing to graduate?

Nobody else had the words *desperate* and *afraid* painted across their face—along with smears of mulberries.

"Okay, Little Match Girl," Nya muttered to herself, staying in the roasting car a little longer to dab her face with a napkin. The sticky residue had dried, so she licked her finger and rubbed at it furiously for a few seconds before giving up. Gritting her teeth, she shoved her phone into the back pocket of her shorts and made sure the car door was locked tight. The last thing she needed was for somebody to take the few possessions she had to her name.

Keeping her eyes on the blistering blacktop, Nya tucked her chin to her chest and made a beeline for the entrance. The bathroom would be right inside. She could clean herself up, gather her composure, and browse the store with the rest of the back-to-school crowd, pretending she was just another carefree student.

"Welcome to Walmart, honey," an elderly greeter wearing a blue vest said so sweetly that Nya almost looked up. The *honey* part came dangerously close to bringing the tears burning back to her eyes. Nobody ever called her *honey*. It was a word that other people's moms and grandmas used.

Nya forced a smile and rushed to the bathroom.

It was full of the usual suspects: a woman with bottle-red hair trying to push her cart full of merchandise into the end stall, an overflowing toilet clogged with a bloated maxi pad, and a dripping sink smeared with a pale orange substance that looked like spray cheese.

It was air-conditioned though, and the cool water from the sink felt like heaven compared to the hot car.

Nya scrubbed at her face with a paper towel until the dark mulberry streaks disappeared. She ignored the curious side glances from two teenage girls at the sink next to her. When the woman with the shopping cart full of merchandise finally exited her stall, Nya darted inside and locked the door behind her.

While she peed, she pulled up Sid's Meta profile, wondering how the hell she'd gotten into this situation. Had Sidney intentionally pretended to be female, so he could lure some unsuspecting girl into sharing the rundown rental with him? Why would he do that? Did he really think she was going to move in after he'd tricked her like that?

The app crashed twice before it managed to open, and Nya realized that her phone battery had already dropped to twenty percent since she'd unplugged it from the car charger less than an hour earlier. The elderly phone worked—but barely. Jade had joked that as far as smartphones went, it was solidly at the bottom of its class.

The app finally loaded, and she navigated to her messages and then Sidney's profile page.

Her heart picked up its pace when the drum-circle photo popped up on her screen. There, in the middle of the photo, was the cool hipster girl with long auburn hair and the tattoo of a cat. Absolutely not the guy in the rundown rental house.

But wait. Nya squinted. The photo wasn't quite centered, like she remembered. The hipster girl was definitely the primary focus of the photo—but she wasn't the only person in the frame, after all. Next to the redhead in the drum circle was a skeevy-looking, skinny man, banging on a drum. His chin was tilted upward, and his eyes were closed like he was feeling that drumbeat all the way down to his greasy toes.

Nya clicked on the photo and zoomed in as far as she could.

It was hard to tell without seeing those dilated black pupils, but she was almost positive the guy next to Tattoo Girl was Sid.

He *was* in the profile photo after all.

Nya swallowed hard. *Fuck,* she thought, feeling a phantom ping of guilt at the curse word. Maybe *she* was the idiot.

Someone rattled the bathroom door.

"Occupied," Nya choked, her eyes still on the zoomed-in photo next to the words "Sidney Holcomb." She scanned through the rest of his barebones profile, looking for anything else, aside from the misleading profile photo, that would indicate he was trying to pass himself off as a girl.

He didn't specify his gender. However, he also didn't specify his birthday, hometown, relationship status, or interests. His profile was really just a blank slate with a few sporadic posts about drum circle events dating back a few years. For all Nya knew, the hipster girl in the photo was his friend. Or his girlfriend.

It wasn't like he could help his name. Boys could be named Sidney. Just like girls could be named Blake or Taylor.

Uncertainty crept through the lingering panic. This wasn't a *Dateline* episode. This was a low-budget sitcom, and Nya was the butt of the joke.

The bathroom door rattled again, harder, and Nya gritted her teeth. *"Occupied!"*

What was she supposed to do now? Pinpricks of doubt cooled the fear she'd felt earlier. How much of her reaction to the fact that Sid was a boy came from the way she'd been raised? If her parents knew she had a dude for a roommate, even a platonic, greasy dude who had about as much sex appeal as an old broom, they wouldn't speak to her again. Ever. If you lived with a boy, you were living in sin. End of story.

Nya blew out a breath and considered this thought. The closer she got to graduation, the freer she felt from the strict way she'd been raised. She no longer bought into her parents' ideas of "sin." Still, some of that old wiring ran deep.

There was also the fact that, as much as Nya hated to admit it, her parents were still her emergency lifeline. They'd allowed her to live at home over the summer, despite the fact that she wore tank tops and sat stone-faced through each and every church service. If she were starving, they'd definitely feed her. If she were destitute, they'd take her in—as long as she attended church services. It wasn't much, but it wasn't nothing, either.

And that lifeline wasn't unconditional. The soft-shun could easily turn into a hard-shun if her parents found out she was breaking one of the foundational rules that had been drilled into her since childhood: cohabitation before marriage was a serious sin. There were no exceptions.

Fuck, she whispered again. It wasn't *just* the fact that he was a boy, was it? The way Sid slurred his words when he called her a "pretty girl" echoed in her brain like a warning bell.

She ignored the third rattle of the bathroom door and tried to remember everything he'd said and done. He was clearly high on something when she met him, but Jade took the occasional edible too, and she wasn't a creep.

The pinpricks of doubt widened into cracks. Maybe the combination of the ramshackle house, his greasy appearance, and the initial shock that he wasn't a girl had sent her into panic mode.

Were any of those issues really that bad? Dealbreakers?

The situation wasn't ideal, but it also wasn't a crisis. *You're overreacting.* Her brain nudged, even while the curdled-milk feeling in her stomach sloshed as violently as ever.

Out of the bad options available—living in her car, tucking her tail between her legs and abandoning her final semester of college, or living in the ramshackle rental with the greasy but probably harmless stranger—what was the best option?

The greasy stranger seemed like the clear choice. As long as he was, in fact, harmless.

Was he? The image of those glazed, beady eyes wouldn't fade.

Jade would know what to do. Nya tended to trust Jade's gut far more than her own. But she couldn't call her from inside the bathroom, with the constant echo of flushing and worse.

The bathroom door rattled yet again, and this time Nya unlatched it and yanked it open, glaring at a middle-aged woman wearing a crocheted sweater vest.

"I thought maybe you needed help in there," the woman said in a twangy, saccharine sing-song that was clearly a *fuck you.*

Nya bit back a snarky response. There were two empty stalls on either side of her—but both more than likely had clogged toilets. Nya muttered an apology, quickly washed her hands, then hurried into the main store.

Outside the bathroom, the chaotic swell of students, parents, and shoppers was comforting in its own way. You could hear everyone's—and no one's—conversation. The tantalizing smell of french fries from the McDonald's at the front of the store wafted through the air, and Nya's stomach growled so loudly she nearly laughed. Her bank account was ridiculously low, but if there was ever a time to splurge on a dollar menu, it was right now.

Then she'd call Jade and figure out what to do.

6

"*Bebé!*" Jade's bubbly greeting was the thing that finally made Nya's stomach unclench a little.

"I'm so glad you answered. You have no idea how good it is to hear your voice."

"Of course I answered, silly! Hold on, I'm just getting into my car. Grandma Tita's making *pozóle* tonight. It's everyone's favorite, but it's spicy as fuck. It'd make you cry. I've told Tita so much about you, she said she already loves you and wants you to visit for Thanksgiving. Can you come for Thanksgiving?" Jade asked, finally pausing to breathe.

Nya swallowed hard, and her stomach growled again, this time chewing its way through the hamburger she'd wolfed down. Nothing sounded better than a home-cooked meal with the Estradas. But November might as well have been a million years away—even if she could afford the $200-dollar bus ticket to Indianapolis.

If she laid out just how bad things were financially, Jade would tell Mama Estrada—and Grandma Tita. Then Mama Estrada would be calling Nya's phone, offering to purchase a Greyhound ticket with money the Estradas didn't have to spare and trying to convince Nya to skip her last semester of college. She could live with them in Indianapolis. Get a job at a diner or a bowling alley nearby. Figure things out from there.

If Nya was being really honest, she was worried she would give in and say yes.

But then the mountain of student debt she'd racked up, the summers at Taco Tienda scrimping and saving, the four-times-a-week church services in exchange for a roof over her head during the summers, the shitty on-campus night-shift janitorial jobs during the school year. What had all of it been for?

She was enrolled in a whopping twenty-seven credits this final semester so she could graduate early. It had taken some finagling—and written permission from the dean of students—along with a promise that she wouldn't work a job her final semester. It was a ridiculous course load.

Just one more semester. Four months. Then she'd have her degree. Then she could swallow her pride and maybe even let Mama Estrada buy her a bus ticket—that she'd repay with her first paycheck at her first real job.

"I'll probably have to wait until Christmas," Nya said carefully, then quickly pivoted to, "Hey, can you tell me if I'm being weird about something?"

It was a question she asked Jade regularly, after slowly coming to the realization that everything about the way she'd grown up had been weird. Sometimes, it was hard to trust her reactions to the world at large.

"Always, *bebé.*" Jade never made fun of these questions, some of which sounded ridiculous even to Nya.

Careful not to sensationalize anything, Nya told her about the dirty rental and the unsettling surprise roommate waiting inside. She left out the part about the mulberry smears. And about the house being her only real option aside from living in the Honda.

Jade was poor, but not Nya's kind of poor. Not the kind of poor that teetered on the edge of homelessness. Admitting how bad things really were—even to her best friend—felt too shameful. So, Nya didn't.

She also left out the part of the story where Sidney called her a "pretty girl" the second he met her. Jade didn't like pushy guys. The last boy who catcalled her in the hall the final week of junior year had ended up in the nurse's office, and Jade had ended up in detention.

Jade was uncharacteristically quiet for a few seconds when Nya finished the story.

"I'm being weird, right?" Nya started. "I think I just reacted that way because he's a boy, and you know how my parents are about that kind of thing. I knew the house was going to be shitty. Just like our rental was." She forced a laugh. "It's just one semester, right? I'll be at the library most of the time, anyway."

It was true. Her course load was so intense, she'd have to spend nearly every free moment studying.

The tuition she'd save by shaving a semester off her last year would be worth it. At least, Nya hoped so.

She could hack it. As long as she had somewhere to live. Would it really be that bad living with Sid, just for one semester?

"I don't think you're being weird. I think you should trust your gut, *chula*." Jade's voice was soft for once. Worried.

"To be fair, my gut likes to eat Oreos for breakfast," Nya said, forcing another laugh. "It's not exactly trustworthy. Seriously, he wasn't that bad. I think it's doable."

The words felt clunky and awkward in her mouth, like stale gum. She'd hoped that Jade would reassure her she was overreacting. Tell her that she was freaking out over nothing, like the time she'd drunk her first beer freshman year and cried on their ratty plaid couch, sure she was now on the path to alcoholism, addiction, and life in the gutter. Or when she finally kissed a boy for the first time and had to ask Jade if she could get AIDS from touching his mouth.

Both of those times—and so many others—Jade had gently reassured her that the panic was an old reflex. The world wasn't nearly as scary as she'd grown up believing.

But Jade wasn't reacting that way now.

"*Chula,* listen to me. Why risk it? You can find another house, right? Crash on somebody's couch until you find something else?"

Nya swallowed the bitter bubble of desperation that rose in her throat. There was no other house. There was no couch to crash on. There was only Jade on the other end of the nearly dead phone in her hand and the searing-hot Honda waiting for her in the parking lot.

"I made it sound worse than it was," she said halfheartedly, hating the fact that she was lying to Jade. "I just need to suck it up and deal. The semester will be over in no time."

Jade took so long to respond that Nya checked the phone to see if it had died. Just ten percent battery remained, but the call was still connected.

Finally, she said, "Okay, *bebé.* But if your gut tells you to get out of there, you listen, okay? I know you don't think you can trust your instincts, but you have to. Get some pepper spray, at least, please?"

Nya forced a smile onto her face, hoping Jade would hear it in her words. "I will. It'll be fine. I love you, okay? But my phone's about to die ..."

The sentence petered out with that last word. She'd been meandering the aisles and had ended up in the housewares section. A display of welcome mats showed cheerful, peppy phrases like, *Hooray! It's You!* and, *Come in!* However, the shaggy welcome mat at eye-level was the one that drew her attention,

It had a barbed-wire border circling one word: *Leave.*

It was definitely a joke. A silly, tongue-in-cheek welcome mat. But she couldn't shake the feeling that it was a directive.

Leave.

Run.

Keep out.

"Nya, you still there? What happened?"

Two girls with long brown hair, both snapping gum, reached past Nya and snatched up the *Leave* sign. "This one is great," one of them said gleefully. "Jen will hate it, but it's fucking perfect."

"Sorry," Nya told Jade. "The store is super busy. I love you. Tell Grandma Tita and everybody that I love them and I wish I could try the *pozóle.* Call me tomorrow?"

"Abso-fucking-lutely. I love you too. Please, be careful."

7

Nya stood in front of the pepper spray so long that she started to worry that the gallon of milk in her cart would get warm.

The option with the black container was $9.99. Its identical, neon-pink counterpart with curly font that read "Keep 6 Feet Back" was $13.99, discounted to $9.99 Why in the world was the pink version four dollars more expensive at full price?

Buying the pepper spray seemed like a no-brainer. It was the smart thing to do, even if it was the same price as two gallons of milk. Plus, she'd promised Jade she would.

Even so, each time Nya reached her hand out to put the pepper spray into the cart next to the milk, off-brand Wheaties, instant coffee, granola bars, and ramen, she drew her hand back. Buying it meant that she'd decided to go back to the rental house.

Back to the red-purple smears on the sidewalk.

Back to countertops piled high with rotting food.

Back to Sid.

Why risk it?

Jade's words circled round and round in her head, along with the answer to the question: *Because it's the best of your bad options.*

When the phone in her pocket had died a few minutes earlier, the time was eight p.m. Despite the perpetual fluorescent daylight in Walmart, the sun was going down outside. Thankfully, night meant the temperature would finally drop. It also meant darkness.

Nya did not want to go back to the rental house in the dark.

She didn't want to go back to the house at all. But sometimes, you had to do things you didn't want to do, to get where you wanted to go.

Suck it up, buttercup, she repeated to herself for the umpteenth time that day. She'd seen the phrase on a T-shirt at the mall once, with Jade. A stolen afternoon when Nya's mom thought they were studying—and maybe having a heartfelt conversation about the Book of Revelations. Nya and Jade laughed about the shirt all day, imagining how Nya's parents would react if she came home wearing it. They hated the word *suck* with a passion that defied logic. It was like they didn't know how many other swear words existed.

Nya reached for the hot-pink canister of pepper spray, pulled it off the shelf, and tossed it into the cart next to her box of granola bars.

"Keep 6 Feet Back." That would be her line. Six feet. And as long as Sid didn't push that boundary, she could suck it up and get through the semester to graduation.

She probably wouldn't need the pepper spray.

At least, she hoped she wouldn't.

8

The sun sank past the tall poplar trees lining the streets off-campus, throwing the neighborhood into a soft gray pre-darkness. The temperature had mercifully dropped at least ten degrees by the time Nya pulled back up in front of the ugly rambler.

The Honda rattled hard as she turned the ignition, like it might have eked out its last iota of gas just as she shifted into park on the street in front of the rental. It didn't matter. She couldn't afford gas anyway.

Nya pushed the depressing thought away, took a deep breath, and gathered her nerve.

Through the open passenger window, she could just make out the soft, distant thump of Sid's drum coming from inside the dark house. The little rectangular window beside the front door glowed orange, flickering a little with a passing shadow.

The hair on the back of her neck prickled with a sense of foreboding and déjà vu. Sid was still in there, drumming away, high on whatever made his eyes so red and his pupils so dilated. Of course he was still in there. He lived there. He would be there for the next four months.

Nya's eyes were red and grainy by now, too. All she wanted was to lock herself into her bedroom, take a shower, and fall into a deep, undisturbed sleep. The used-book sale tomorrow was her one and only chance to get her copy of the Advanced Human Anatomy textbook at a price she could remotely afford. That meant setting her alarm for the buttcrack of dawn to get in line with the other unfortunate souls who needed to scrape by. After that, she'd have a full day of classes and could easily spend the day on campus studying in the library.

Could she just walk inside and lock herself in her room for the night without talking to Sid again? She shook her head. Regardless of whether he was partly to blame for the misleading profile photo and his off-putting introduction, Nya bore at least some blame for starting things off badly. She'd basically slammed the door in his face and then run away.

He couldn't help it that his name was Sidney.

A new disturbing thought tingled in the back of her head.

What if he wouldn't let her back in?

What if he thought she was too unhinged to share a house with?

The idea was ridiculous. Probably. He most likely didn't even remember the details of their interaction earlier, he was so high. However, the possibility that she might not be welcome back sent a fresh shiver of fear down her spine.

Nya gritted her teeth. She'd properly introduce herself. *Then* she could lock herself in her bedroom and avoid him like hell for the rest of the semester.

Carefully balancing the duffel bag, pillow, and groceries in her arms, Nya started up the walk again. She managed to avoid the mulberry branches, the mess of berries, and the weedy cracks in the walkway this time too.

Something rattled against the dirty lattice wrapping the front porch.

Nya froze and stared at the dark diamond pattern behind the broken lattice. It shuddered briefly, then went still.

Just a possum. Maybe a raccoon. Breathe.

The spot where she'd dropped her duffel bag on the sidewalk earlier looked like a crime scene in the semi-darkness. Smears of mulberry juice alongside a perfect, purple-dark handprint.

Breathe.

Nya clutched her belongings tighter and tiptoed through the last of the mess.

Before she could shift the duffel to her shoulder to knock, the door creaked open a few inches. Then a few more. She could just make out Sid's silhouette behind the door. He'd seen her coming this time.

Smile. Be friendly.

Nya forced her cheeks to rise and her lips to curl upward, but no matter how hard she tried for *genuine*, it felt like a grimace.

Sid opened the front door wide, backlit by the dim light flickering in the kitchen. It took her a second to realize he was now wearing nothing more than a pair of dingy white briefs hanging much too loosely around his hips.

Oh my god. Seriously?

Was she being a prude? Or was this every bit as weird as it seemed?

He was taller than she remembered. At least six-foot-three. His bare chest, eye-level for Nya, was covered in a thin fuzz of hair. His nipples were tiny and dark, almost black. Small and beady, like his eyes. If Jade were here, she would have laughed about this. Nya, on the other hand, quickly raised her eyes to his face.

He kept one hand on the inside doorknob. He used the other hand to scratch at an angry-looking rash that spread from his neck to his collarbone. What the hell was that? Her brain flipped through everything she knew about drug side effects. None of them caused a rash like that.

Sid followed Nya's eyes as she sneaked a glance at his rash then moved back up to his dilated eyes.

"I wondered if you'd be back," he muttered, studying her stained duffel bag and groceries. "Gonna move in after all?"

Nya darted her eyes around the room, focusing on that cheery wallpaper. Once she cleaned things up, the interior of the house wouldn't be so bad. Maybe Sid would turn out to be the same. Rough on the outside, less scary on the inside.

She forced her grimace-smile wider, still wishing she'd opened the pink canister of pepper spray instead of leaving it in her grocery bag like an idiot. Why wasn't he wearing more clothes? Who answered the door like this? Why did his eyes look so messed up? Amphetamines? Ketamine? Could she really live with this person?

She didn't know. And she wouldn't be asking Jade for advice this time. She already knew what Jade would say: *Get the hell out of there.*

Nya set the duffel bag on the porch at her feet. Her hands were shaking so hard she was about to drop it. *Suck it up. Six feet is your boundary. If he even lets you in the door.*

Sid scratched at the rash then crossed his arms over his chest. He was clearly waiting for her to say something.

Nya decided he looked a little like Spike from *Notting Hill*—the pantless, eccentric roommate who turned out to be harmless, even lovable. The movie was old news by the time Nya watched it with Jade, but it was the first rated-R film she'd ever seen.

"I—I'm sorry for how I acted earlier." The words came easily, even though they tasted like battery acid. If there was one skill she'd mastered growing up, it was how to meekly apologize for just about anything.

The muscles in his jaw relaxed slightly, and he opened the door a hair wider. She was right. He definitely wanted an apology.

Forcing her eyes to stay on his face instead of the dark, peach-fuzz nipples, the rash, or the too-loose briefs, she continued. "I didn't recognize you from your profile photo. That's all. I thought I had the wrong house, and then I freaked out. I—I looked you up after, and it was my mistake. I'm an idiot. Can we start over?"

He laughed, an uneven, jarring sound like a broken garbage disposal. "I figured that's what happened."

Not, *I'm sorry I scared you.* Not, *No need to apologize. My photo does mostly show a pretty girl with a cat tattoo.* Not, *Oh hey, let me go put some clothes on so you don't see my junk flopping around.*

Just, *Figured that's what happened.*

Then, he finally added, "Come in."

9

Sid turned into a surprisingly chatty tour guide as soon as Nya lugged her stained duffel bag through the door and set it down on the sunburst linoleum.

Apparently, she was here to stay.

There was a sliver of relief in that. But only a sliver.

Sid didn't put a shirt or pants on. From all appearances, he felt completely at home in those dirty white briefs. However, he did lead the way into the kitchen, waving an arm at the mess of dishes and debris covering the countertops. "Sorry it's messy. Been living here by myself for a while."

Nya forced a laugh and held her breath. The kitchen wasn't just messy. It was an absolute disaster of old food, trash, and dishes covering every surface. The sink was filled to the brim with cheap plastic cups and plates coated in moldering residue. The table—a rickety fold-out card table—was covered in crumbs and something yellow that had spilled and dried. An empty pizza box sat open on one of two metal folding chairs at its side.

"I'll try to be less of a slob, now that there's a girl here." He threw her a smile over his shoulder and leaned on the counter, hiking up the back of his briefs, which were inching their way lower on his hips.

One of his hands rested inches from an oily puddle of grease.

Nya tried for a smile. The pungent, rotten smell near the sink made her eyes water. But she forced herself to focus on the retro, multi-colored Tiffany light fixture above the table. The lightbulb was flickering, but it just needed to be changed. Someone had put a lot of love into this house, once.

Breathe. Just not right now. With a little elbow grease and some hot water and soap, the kitchen could be salvaged. She didn't have the energy to do anything about it tonight, but maybe tomorrow. Sid *had* said he'd try to be less of a slob. She couldn't imagine how he could stand living like this, but the last thing she needed was another confrontation. "No worries, I get it," she managed, trying not to breathe in too deeply. "Okay if I put my milk in the fridge?"

He made a weird little flourish with his hand, indicating the squat yellow refrigerator. It had rounded corners and looked like something out of *That '70s Show.* "You have to twist the handle sideways," Sid instructed, smiling slightly while he watched her try to open it without success.

The grimy handle hung loose on the refrigerator door. When she followed Sid's instructions and twisted it to the left, the door opened, revealing bare wire shelves. To her relief, it was cleaner than almost anything else in the kitchen. The light inside flickered, casting a strobe over the sparse contents: a half-empty gallon bottle of kombucha, yet another pizza box, a lone shriveled apple, and an enormous bag of string cheese.

Nya carefully set the gallon of milk on the far side of the fridge, away from everything else, wishing she'd thought to buy a Sharpie to label it. It probably didn't matter. From what she could tell, Sid didn't make much use of the fridge—except for string cheese. She shuddered, then suppressed a laugh, imagining him scurrying around the dank kitchen like a rat, gnawing on all that mozzarella.

She decided she'd keep the granola bar and non-perishable food in her room. Until the kitchen was in better shape, anyway.

Mercifully, the small house meant that the rest of the tour was short. "My room. Your room," Sid said, waving his big hands around in the narrow hallway. "We each have a bathroom. That's the utility closet." He indicated a narrow door next to her room, then brought his hand back to his neck to scratch at that rash. The skin was red and inflamed, with blotchy raised patches. It looked awful.

"Are you okay?" she asked, unable to stop the words from tumbling out her mouth. She'd never seen the rash's equal.

He shot her a confused look and stopped scratching. "Yeah, I have eczema," he muttered defensively, dropping his hand to his side. "It's not contagious or anything."

Nya nodded, deciding now wasn't the time to reveal the fact that her course load last fall had included a class in Immunology and Infectious Diseases. That rash absolutely wasn't eczema. She'd have to poke around on the internet later. Until she knew what it was, it was just another reason to stay six feet away from him.

She was tantalizingly close to her bedroom door now. Not wanting him to follow her inside, she peeked her head into the empty room she'd glanced in earlier and smiled. Her first real smile. The carpet was the same brown shag in the hallway. A smaller version of the Tiffany light fixture hung in the center. It was old, dusty, but welcoming. And empty. Best of all, the bedroom door had a lock. The enormous, silent air-conditioning unit sat wedged at a crooked angle, blocking most of the window frame.

"Does that work?" she asked on a whim.

To her surprise, Sid nodded and then shrugged. "Yeah. I think it still works. I don't mind the heat, but do whatever floats your boat." He grinned like he'd made a joke, revealing startlingly straight, white teeth.

He wasn't on meth, apparently.

"Great, well, I'm just going to unpack." She nodded at the heavy duffel making her shoulder ache. "I don't mean to be anti-social, but I'm completely dead."

He smiled when she said the last part, like now she'd made a real joke.

Nya's fingers itched to lock the bedroom door and shut him out, but he was saying something else about the air-conditioning unit. "... old roommate left it when he moved out. It's loud as fuck, but he had the nerve to complain about *my* drumming. He ran that thing nonstop. Then he nearly fucking broke it before he moved out."

That explained the A/C unit's bedraggled appearance. Sort of. Why would he have broken his own air conditioner before he moved out?

"Oh," was all Nya could think to respond. It sounded like a long story, and she felt exhausted down to her bones in a way she hadn't felt since the night her parents found out about the extent of her friendship with Jade and the Estradas. The night they'd learned she sometimes secretly wore shorts and T-shirts to school and went to the mall once in a while. The night they kept her up until dawn, first raging about her deceit and corruption then demanding she repent.

Nya flashed Sid the grimace-smile, hoping he'd go away now. Instead, he tucked his hands into his briefs like he was some kind of cowboy, and leaned against the bedroom door frame. "Last thing," he began.

Thank god, Nya thought.

He shifted on his bare feet and indicated the door at the end of the hallway. "Don't go down there."

Her stomach rolled uneasily. She'd assumed it was a storage closet. "What do you mean?"

He smiled again, revealing those perfect, pearly white teeth tucked behind chapped lips. "That's the basement."

"The basement?" Nya repeated. She hadn't realized there was one.

Sid shrugged. "It's not finished. Total shit show."

That didn't explain why she couldn't go down there. "Okay ..."

His eyes glinted like he was enjoying her discomfort. She took a step into the bedroom, itching to lock the door behind her. As long as there wasn't an actual monster behind that door, she didn't really care right now.

Sid tucked his thumbs deeper into the waistband of his underwear. "The landlord—my cousin, Rick—keeps all his storage shit down there. Some of it's valuable. Doesn't want tenants messing with it."

Nya nodded and reached for the door handle. "Oh, makes sense. Hey, I have to wake up really early, so I'd better—"

Sid continued like she hadn't said anything. "Rick thought he was gonna make like, a shit-ton of money when he bought this place so close to campus. Got it for cheap. It hadn't been updated since it was built in the 1930s—maybe you can tell?" He laughed. "He wanted to add two more bedrooms in the basement and make a ton of money on renting it out to students. So he tore up the carpet down there, hired contractors, started framing and everything. He knew he'd have to make the windows egress, but he figured that'd be no big deal."

Sid paused dramatically. "But ... somebody tipped off the city that he was doing the reno without a permit. Long story short, they screwed Rick over and fined him up the ass."

"Oh. That sucks," Nya said feebly. She didn't care about Rick or his grand plans to renovate.

Sid kept going with his long story about the basement. "Turns out, there's lead paint galore in the whole goddamn house. So Rick couldn't rip out the old windows or walls or remodel anything—unless he planned to basically gut the whole house. It would have cost a ton."

Nya frowned. "So there's lead ... everywhere in here? Is it safe?"

Sid slapped his bare, hairy thighs and made that laughing, barking sound. "Yeah. Unless you're planning on eating it."

She made a mental note to verify this later. "Great. I won't go into the basement." *Or anywhere else in this trash house, until I have a chance to clean up,* she added silently. "Does ... Rick visit very often?" she asked.

Sid chuckled again. "Nah. He lives in Oregon. Never stops by. Only thing he cares about is the rent being on time. You can pay that to me, by the way. Cash, by the last day of the month. Don't be late."

Nya shrugged. "Sure."

He nodded, apparently satisfied.

Taking it as a signal that the conversation with this half-naked man was finally over, Nya started to pull the door shut.

"Hey, uh, you want a beer? Or some pizza?" he asked hopefully.

Nya's stomach had the audacity to gurgle. "Um, no thanks. I'm really, really tired."

Before he could respond, she pulled the bedroom door shut behind her, locked it, and sank down on the bare—but mercifully clean—mattress. It squealed in protest.

Soft footsteps, followed by a quiet creak, came from the floor in the hall outside her room.

Nya stiffened. The dim lighting in the bedroom shifted slightly as a faint shadow moved underneath the doorway. Sid must still be standing right outside her door. The idea of him hovering there in his underwear was enough to send a shudder down her back. But after a few long seconds, the quiet footsteps receded and the door across the hall shut with a hollow *clunk*.

Nya let out a long sigh.

Six feet. As long as he stayed that far away, she was safe in this house.

Safe-ish, anyway. It was the best she could do for now.

NOELLE W. IHLI

10

The window A/C unit roared to life when Nya pressed the power button, sending a delicious blast of cold air into the stagnant room while she unpacked her duffel of belongings.

Sid had been right: The A/C unit *was* loud. But something about the white noise made her feel safer. Even if Sid was standing right outside the door, he wouldn't be able to hear what she was doing in the room.

"Thanks, old roommate," she whispered and patted the flaking, silver behemoth. One part of the control panel was cracked, revealing some of the machine's guts. The narrow gap running along the top of the window frame had been stuffed with grungy-looking socks that Nya decided not to touch. The air conditioner worked, and that was all she cared about.

It only took her a few minutes to unpack everything she owned. The mulberry-stained duffel was bulging at the seams, but most of the space was taken up by her faded blue bed sheets and the soft quilt her mom had made for her when she was a freshman in high school—to remind her to stay strong in the faith. The squares were carefully, lovingly embroidered with vaguely threatening and cherry-picked scriptures. *I know your deeds. God opposes the proud. Do good and suffer for it. God cannot be mocked. Do not be deceived. A man reaps what he sows. Keep watch, lest you be tempted.*

Nya loved and hated the quilt. It was a butter-soft jersey. And it reminded her that, once upon a time, her mom wanted to wrap her up and protect her from the world—even if the dangers she saw included tank tops, pop culture, and modern medicine. But at the end of the day, she kept it because it meant she wouldn't have to buy something else to keep her warm when the weather turned cold.

When Nya was finished making the bed, she opened the closet and hung up her jacket and the one dress she'd brought with her.

The closet was strangely enormous for the small room. It had mirrored gold doors on tracks that clattered softly when Nya slid them open. She cringed when she noticed her reflection in the mirror. There were dark pit stains underneath her arms, and her hair was stringy and damp with sweat. Sid probably thought she was just as disgusting as she thought he was.

A couple of bent metal hangers clanged together in the center of the pole that ran the length of the long, narrow closet that seemed to go on forever.

Finally, she tucked an armful of T-shirts, socks, a sweatshirt, and underwear into the squatty dresser that doubled as a nightstand next to the bed. The mid-century dresser was made of solid wood and the drawers glided smoothly. Besides a few scratches and dents on its surface, it was kind of cute.

The last item Nya pulled from the duffel was a little, three-legged wooden horse. It had been painted with intricate swirls and dots in vibrant blue, pink, green, and yellow with green accents. An *alebrije*. Jade's grandfather carved and painted the fantastical creatures. Each one was unique. And each one was supposed to protect and watch over its owner. Grandpa Estrada had sent it, along with its matching twin, through the mail for Jade to give to Nya right before Jade moved from Clearwater to Indianapolis. One for Nya, and a matching horse for Jade. Something to hang onto until they reunited for college at Boise State. Nya had never gotten a gift before. The closest thing was the scripture quilt. The church didn't celebrate holidays. Sure, there were longer church meetings on Easter and Christmas, but that was the extent of the celebration. She considered the three-legged painted pony one of her most prized possessions. A reminder of Jade, of the Estradas, and all the good things waiting for her when she finished her degree and moved to Indianapolis. She'd never been to Grandma Tita's house in Indy, but she already knew it would feel like home. Especially after the horrible rental.

Nya had tried gluing the *alebrije's* missing leg back in place several times, but it never stayed.

Her parents had found the painted horse tucked inside the Suck it Up Buttercup T-shirt she'd hidden under her bed after the Estradas moved away.

Her father had hurled the *alebrije* at the wall.

Nya set the horse on top of the short dresser and positioned it so the missing back leg was hidden. The intricately carved head pointed toward the locked bedroom door, like a sentinel.

She peeked into the bathroom, scanning the grimy blue tub and lime-coated showerhead. It would have to be another cleaning project for another day. Now that the room had cooled down a little, the idea of going to bed early and taking a quick shower in the morning seemed like the best option.

After placing the granola bars and other meager groceries in the bottom drawer of the dresser, Nya set the pink canister of pepper spray right next to the wooden horse.

Between the three-legged *alebrije* and the pepper spray, she finally felt safe enough to close her eyes and drift off to sleep.

11

Nya jolted awake.

For a moment, she couldn't figure out what had woken her.

Then it came again, a sporadic sound coming from somewhere nearby. It was definitely coming from somewhere inside the house.

The hallway maybe? Was that the house settling? Her bleary eyes opened wide in the dark room, trying to pinpoint the source of the sound.

Bam.

A soft thud broke up the creaks.

Nya clutched the scripture quilt tighter, as if it could protect her from whatever was moving through the house.

Her eyes followed the faint shards of moonlight glowing between the cracks in the air-conditioning unit. The light glinted off the mirrored closet doors in haphazard patterns, reflecting slivers of brightness that looked like stretched-out stars.

Creak. Shuffle. Thump.

One of the slivers of light on the mirrored doors trembled in a faint strobe.

Her heart sped up, pumping blood through veins and arteries, funneling oxygen to her legs so she could run. An image of the human heart she'd dissected with Jade two years ago in a biology class, bloody and unbeating, popped into her mind.

The slivers of light on the mirror shook in time with the next soft *thud.*

The sound was definitely coming from somewhere inside the house.

Nya stayed frozen in the double bed, afraid that if she moved, the creaky mattress springs would give away the fact that she'd woken up. Those had to be footsteps, but they seemed to be getting fainter.

Everything's fine, she told herself, willing her heart valves to stop their panicked pumping and let her fall back asleep.

It must be Sid moving around the house, but why the hell was he awake at this ungodly hour of the night? He had a bathroom in his room, just like she did. Was the insomnia a side effect of the drugs he was using? Was he headed over to the nuclear disaster in the kitchen for a midnight snack?

Trying not to make the mattress groan in protest, Nya slowly rolled over. She reached for her phone, lying on the carpet, then unplugged it from its short charger to check the time. It felt like she'd been asleep for barely fifteen minutes, but her phone told her otherwise.

It was solidly the middle of the night: two thirty-six a.m.

She tucked the phone under her pillow and listened hard.

The noises had stopped.

Nya closed her tired eyes and tried to relax, but the silence felt wrong. Like someone was waiting for her to make a move. Was Sid standing outside the door right now? Should she check?

No. The house was so quiet, he'd hear her get out of bed. And if, God forbid, he was standing outside the door right now, the last thing she wanted to do was unlock it.

A thought floated to the front of her exhausted brain. *The air conditioner.*

Nya's eyelids fluttered open.

The crooked hunk of metal wedged into the window frame was now silent, even though Nya hadn't turned it off.

So that was the reason it felt so eerily quiet in here. The unit must have turned itself off automatically once the tiny room finally cooled down.

Nya closed her eyes and tried to slow her breathing.

After just a few seconds, a soft clicking sound from the far wall drew her attention.

What was that? Even as she asked herself the question, she tried to push the worry away. Old houses made noises. She had a weird roommate who liked to stay up late. She just had to get used to it all.

She almost got out of bed and padded across the floor to turn the A/C unit back on, but the room was at a comfortable temperature now. Even though the loud, erratic white noise was soothing, the idea that it might obscure soft footsteps moving toward her made her heart beat fast again.

She'd keep the air conditioner off. For now.

Creak.

Another sound came from somewhere in the bowels of the house. So soft, it wouldn't have woken her if she had been asleep.

Creak.

There. This time, there was no question that the sound had come from the hallway.

Creak. Shuffle.

Her heart rate, which had just started to settle, revved up again. The fog of sleep was completely gone, but not her exhaustion.

Creaaaak.

Nya squeezed her eyes shut. Someone was in the hallway, standing outside her bedroom door. Of course, it wasn't just someone. It was her roommate. But whatever Sid was doing out there, he was doing it *out there.*

He can't bother you out there, she told herself firmly. *He's just a weird creep.*

Taking a deep breath, she finally swung her legs over the side of the bed. The mattress squealed in protest, loud and harsh in the quiet room. Then she grabbed the pepper spray, padded to the door, and listened.

Nothing. No heavy breathing. No more creaks. No hint of movement on the other side.

With trembling fingers, she reached for the doorknob and twisted. Just to be sure.

Of course, it was still locked.

Before getting back into bed, Nya hit the power button on the old A/C unit, to bring the rumbling machine back to a dull roar. If the room was silent, she'd be on a hair-trigger listening for more noises for the rest of the night. It was just the house settling—or Sid being Sid.

You're safe, she told herself. *Go to sleep.*

However, the part of her brain that had jolted awake to the sound of footsteps wasn't so easily convinced.

Each time she felt herself drifting, lulled by the promise of much needed rest before her alarm rang—a mental image of Sid's coal-black eyes appeared in her mind's eye.

12

Sunlight hit the mirrored closet doors, burning into Nya's closed eyelids.

So bright.

Nya groaned, first in annoyance then panic.

Shit, shit, shit.

Her eyes popped open and she blinked away the red and green shapes floating in front of her retinas.

Her alarm should have woken her up, not the sunlight. What time was it? It had to be later than six a.m. So why hadn't her alarm gone off?

The answer hit her like a slap. She'd unplugged the phone when she checked the time in the middle of the night.

Shit, shit, shit.

Nya reached under her pillow for the phone, already knowing it wouldn't light up when she pressed the power button. It was dead.

Had she missed the used book sale altogether? *Shit.* Her first class of the day? *Shit.*

Nya jammed the phone back into its charger and hit the power button again and again. But like the crotchety elderly piece of technology it was, it would take its sweet time waking up no matter how much she cajoled it.

Abandoning the phone, she jumped out of bed and threw on the cutoff shorts she'd worn yesterday, along with a fresh but wrinkled Def Leppard T-shirt that she'd found at Savers with Jade last year. Turning to face the closet mirror, she saw that her hair looked even worse than it had yesterday, wild and tangled with sleep and old sweat. There wasn't time for a shower anymore, though. So much for good first impressions.

The air conditioner had turned itself off again at some point, and the room was already heating up. It was going to be another sweltering day.

The phone finally turned on with a beep, and Nya snatched it off the dresser. Eight a.m. The used book sale had been going on for an hour.

She swallowed her disappointment. Any used copies of the Advanced Human Anatomy book were almost surely gone. Her first class didn't start for an hour though, so if she rushed she could still make it in time to check for a miracle—and grab whatever other books she could find.

The sounds of the neighborhood coming to life floated through the poorly positioned window unit. Snatches of distant laughter and conversation as a trickle of students walked toward campus for early classes or the book sale.

The same jealousy she'd felt yesterday at Walmart enveloped Nya like a prickly blanket. She shook it off and focused on brushing her teeth and wiping the sleep from her eyes.

You'll figure it out, bebé. You always do.

That's what Jade would say. Nya whispered the words to herself while she tugged on socks and sneakers, successfully drowning out the less encouraging voice. The one that came from deep down in her gut. The one that never seemed to shut up.

The wicked will get what she deserves, having built a life of sin.

The scripture in Proverbs said *he*, not *she*, but her parents wanted to make sure Nya knew they were speaking directly to her on the Sunday before she left for her freshman year of college. It was their last attempt at an intervention. It was also the most memorable. Because back then, Nya still cared what they thought of her. Still hoped that maybe they could love her anyway.

"Shut up," Nya muttered. Most of the time, she was proud of how far she'd come since she trudged to the bus stop in her high-necked dress and met Jade that fateful day in Clearwater. She no longer believed that the devil himself was the architect of modern medicine. Or that science was a clever ploy to lure true believers away from relying on the Lord. Or that getting an education was in direct opposition to being godly.

At least, most of her didn't believe those things.

The voices she'd listened to all her life were still stitched into her DNA. Unraveling them felt like unraveling part of herself. Impossible and painful. When bad things happened, she sometimes still wondered if it was because she was a bad person who deserved bad things.

Nya grabbed her purse from where she'd left it in the bathroom last night, double-checked to make sure her wallet, pepper spray, phone, and charger were in there, and threw everything into her backpack along with a granola bar.

She hesitated before unlocking the bedroom door, listening for any sign that Sid was awake.

She pressed her ear to the door crack.

Nothing.

Bracing, she carefully twisted the lock and eased the door open.

The stale, hot air from the hallway was there to greet her, smelling like rotting food and mold from the kitchen. Nya wrinkled her nose and held her breath, grateful to the air conditioner and the old roommate for the umpteenth time.

To her relief, Sid's bedroom door, right across the hall, was closed. The house was quiet.

This, at least, was a win.

She quickly examined the outside of the doorknob, relieved to see that there was no keyhole, pinhole, or slot that could easily be opened with a penny or screwdriver from the outside. The round brass doorknob was rubbed and worn, revealing dull bronze patches beneath the gold veneer. There didn't appear to be any way to pick it from the outside.

Before Nya pulled the door quietly shut behind her, she scanned the sparse, sunny bedroom she'd be calling home for the next few months. In the daylight, with its textured, seafoam-green walls bathed in light reflecting off the mirrors and the colorful quilt, it looked almost homey. Brown shag carpet notwithstanding, it was kind of cute—if you didn't think too hard about the amount of poison the paint contained. She made another mental note to verify what Sid had told her about the relative safety of the lead locked into the walls.

As she hurried out of the room, her eyes landed on the carved wooden horse she'd placed on the dresser.

She frowned and stopped in her tracks.

The little horse's head was no longer pointed toward the door, looking at her as she stood in the frame. Instead, it was facing the bed, like its bright blue eyes had been watching her sleep instead of standing guard.

Had she unknowingly brushed the figurine, turning it around when she grabbed her phone in the middle of the night?

The dresser was too tall for that—the reason she'd been forced to lay her phone, with its too-short phone charger, on the carpet instead of on top of the dresser.

So why was the horse facing the bed?

She shrugged off the question for now. There wasn't time. Trying to be as quiet as possible, she tiptoed down the hall toward the entryway. The carpeted floor wasn't nearly as creaky as she'd anticipated, but a few spots elicited a soft whine of protest that sounded just like the noises she'd heard in the night.

Nya shook her head. It wasn't a crime for Sid to be in his own hallway in the middle of the night. Just weird. Then again, everything about Sid was weird.

She rolled her eyes and kept holding her breath, unwilling to take a lungful of air until she was outside on the porch. Cleaning up the kitchen was a priority, as soon as she had a spare moment.

Right now though, she had bigger problems to tackle.

13

Nya managed to make it to the campus bookstore in just fifteen minutes at a jog. Aside from the fact that she didn't have gas to burn, she knew from past years that trying to find a parking spot any closer to campus would be fruitless—and expensive. All the lots surrounding campus were paid parking—an expense that was so far down her list of priority spending it was laughable.

Her underarms were dripping sweat by the time she walked through the doors of the air-conditioned building.

A cluster of shiny, smooth-haired girls breezed past on their way outside. One of them glanced at Nya then leaned over to her friend and said something that drew a muffled laugh.

Nya ignored it and breathed in the whoosh of icy air that smelled like new books and learning. The campus bookstore welcomed her like a friend, year after year. Despite her exhaustion and the nightmare of the last twelve hours, being here felt so good.

The bookstore was her favorite part of campus. She longed to consume every one of the shiny, thick stacks, stuffing her brain with every single thing she might have missed growing up.

Nya had hated everything about public school—at first. The stares, the teasing over her hair and clothing, the blur of confusing information that told her she was far behind her peers in every way. But after a little while, the puzzle pieces started to click into place in her brain. She realized, to her complete astonishment, that she was smart. And that there was much more to learn than she'd ever considered. By the time her freshman year ended and her world once again shrank to the size of the little farmhouse down the dirt road on the outskirts of town, she was earning straight A's in all of her classes.

Nya took the steps two at a time to the upper level of the bookstore. Thirty minutes until her first class of the day—Advanced Human Anatomy, of course—started across campus.

Thankfully, half of her classes this semester didn't require a textbook at all. Just lab work and writeups. She just needed four books in total—all in the sciences section.

Genetics. Public Health. Ethics in Medicine. Advanced Human Anatomy.

She found the first two books almost immediately. Both had beautiful, scuffed-up covers and that gorgeous orange USED sticker.

There was just one copy of *Clinical Ethics* left, tucked partially out of view behind a biology textbook. It was new, but the price was a pleasant surprise: $59.99. It was more than she'd spend on groceries this month, but it was a steal for a physical textbook.

There were plenty of copies of Advanced Human Anatomy left.

All of them new.

All of them full price.

Nya swallowed. She'd been bracing for this, but seeing the ridiculously high number on that sticker still knocked the wind out of her.

There was no way she could justify spending that much money on a single textbook, even if it was for the most important class of her final semester. That was nearly all her rent and grocery budget. What other choice did she have, though?

Suck it up, buttercup. Nya hovered a hand over the glossy cover that showed a close-up of the human heart. Was there any way her budget could stretch without dipping her checking account into overdraft territory?

Maybe she'd mule drugs for Sid. It was what her parents thought she was doing at college, anyway. Sex, drugs, drinking, showing her shoulders and ankles. Visiting the doctor's office whenever she had a cold. She sighed and rolled her eyes. Things were bad, but they weren't *Breaking Bad*. Shaking the dark thoughts away, she left the Advanced Human Anatomy book on the shelf and bit her lip, trying to think.

Maybe there was a pirated copy online somewhere. And if not, maybe she could cobble together the information she needed to know from her old pal Google. It wasn't ideal. Professor Stern, his name staring back at her in enormous block letters on the textbook cover, had made a huge deal about having a physical book. Maybe it would be enough to get her through the semester, though.

All she had to do was survive.

Story of her life for the next four months.

Nya tore her eyes away from Professor Stern's blocky name and drew in a calming breath, wishing she'd had time to brew a cup of instant coffee.

This was Sid's fault. If she hadn't been up half the night stressed over him, she would have woken up on time to get to the used book sale before all the good stuff was gone. And she wouldn't be standing here with bedhead and a fuzzy brain on her first day of classes.

While Nya waited in line to buy the other books she'd found, she imagined telling Sid in no uncertain terms to stay away from her bedroom door—and put some damn pants on when she was in the house. Clean up the kitchen while he was at it.

The verbal beat-down in her head was so satisfying that she didn't realize she was at the front of the bookstore line—and moving her lips silently—until a deep voice behind her said, "I hope you won the argument, because you're next."

Nya blinked and glanced sideways at the cute, lanky guy standing next to her in line. His pale cheeks flamed red, and he smiled sheepishly like *he* was the one who had just been caught having a savage mental argument with himself. "Oh, uh, thanks."

He smiled and shrugged. "Pour some sugar on me."

Was that some kind of weird pickup line? She raised an eyebrow at him. He was definitely cute, with his bright blue eyes and close-cut curly dark hair, but what the hell?

The color in his cheeks burned brighter. "Def Leppard song. I like your shirt."

Now it was Nya's turn to blush—and rush forward as the student cashier waved her to the available register impatiently. She didn't actually know a single Def Leppard song. Had forgotten she was even wearing the shirt. Jade loved a good eighties band though, and gushed over the T-shirt when Nya tried it on at Savers their freshman year. So Nya bought it.

To her relief, the lanky guy with the curly hair was gone by the time she finished at the register and rushed to her first class.

14

The day passed in a feverish blur of notes, syllabi, study groups, lab hours, and assigned readings. But that was just what Nya wanted. The idea of a twenty-seven-credit semester was slightly terrifying, but it was just one semester. And besides, she'd be able to throw herself into her studies fully without the time commitment—or income—of a part-time job.

For the past three years, she'd worked early morning janitorial to keep up with her mounting expenses. It wasn't that bad. Lots of chilly, quiet walks to campus as the sun blinked over the horizon. Lots of empty, echoing hallways waiting to be mopped clean of the endless dirty sneakers that would shortly reappear. Never-ending battles with the leaky cleaning cart that refused to roll straight, banging into every single stall door and leaving a little trail of mop water behind wherever it went. Still, she could listen to whatever music she wanted. Even sing, if she felt like it. And the job came with a key that let her inside the sleeping campus buildings before anyone else. For a few hours, it was all hers.

This final semester, the hours she'd spent scrubbing sinks and emptying feminine hygiene boxes could be spent with her nose in a book. She finished the day's readings just in time, as the library announced its final call for students to exit the building.

Her eyes were bleary, her mind was full. But so was her heart. She'd gotten through her first day, even with the sleep deprivation.

It had taken her twice as long to do the homework for Advanced Human Anatomy as it should have, trying to decipher the syllabus and the corresponding readings without the actual textbook and charts she was supposed to have. However, she was confident it was doable. Regardless of how disappointed Professor Stern might be, she could get through the class without the physical textbook. That was a huge win for the day.

By the time Nya started the walk back to the rental house with her full backpack, it was dark, past ten o'clock. After spending so many hours in the air-conditioned library study area wearing only a T-shirt, the warm night air felt good on her skin.

As she exited the library, she found herself thinking about the cute guy she'd run into at the bookstore that morning. Looking back, she wished she hadn't been so quick to jump to embarrassment. He was just making conversation. Maybe even flirting with her.

Nya had managed to fully charge her phone on a wall outlet while she studied. Out of habit, she took the scratched-up, cracked rectangle out of her bag and hit the power button to call Jade. She always did this on her way home from the library at night. At this hour, campus was mostly empty except for a few stragglers at the library. The pathways leading between the buildings were well-lit, but as soon as she reached the edge of the manicured landscaping and stately buildings, the floodlights disappeared, giving way to dark, off-campus neighborhood streets.

When the phone blinked on, she saw she'd missed a call from Jade and had at least fifteen unread texts—all from Jade. Nothing from her mom or dad. Not that she'd expected anything else.

Jade's first message was a meme that said "First day of work, didn't cry once." Nya smiled. Jade was a tough cookie, but she was sensitive and cried easily if she was overwhelmed. The other texts were just a string of questions about the weird roommate situation, the first day of classes, the rental house. A final text simply said, "Call me already."

Nya hesitated with her finger over the CALL button. It was two hours later in Indianapolis, so nearly midnight for Jade. She pressed the button anyway—and laughed out loud when Jade answered on the first ring.

Her voice was sleepy. There was no doubt she'd woken up out of a dead sleep and lunged for the phone, but there was no trace of annoyance in her exclamation.

"*Chula!* I thought I was gonna have to send out a search party. It's late, but tell me everything. Are you okay? What the hell happened with your roommate?"

"Everything is okay," Nya said. Because right now, at this moment, it was. "I was just at the library. It's earlier here, remember?"

"Not *that* much earlier," Jade teased. "Are you gonna make me ask all my text questions again?"

Nya shifted the heavy backpack and hurried across the street, wishing that Jade was waiting up for her in their old rental with fresh popcorn and reruns of *Parks and Rec* on the Estradas' borrowed Netflix account. The nostalgia made her stomach hurt with longing.

She started with the story about her embarrassing encounter with the cute guy in the bookstore and Professor Stern's ridiculous textbook.

Just then, an enormous shadow darted out in front of her. Nya gasped and froze on the sidewalk, still holding the phone to her ear. The shadow moved again, just behind a bush.

Sid, was the first thought that blazed into her mind. It didn't make any sense. Why would it be Sid? How would he even know to find her here? Besides, the rental house was still another five blocks away. The panic blazing through her veins didn't care, though. For a moment she imagined that he'd been watching her. Following her. Waiting for her to come home to—

"Nya? What the f—"

The shadow moved again, then came into focus.

It wasn't Sid. It wasn't even a person. A long-legged doe stood just a few feet in front of her at the edge of a brambly hedge where it had just emerged from someone's yard. The deer stared at Nya, wide-eyed, looking just as surprised as she was.

Nya let out a bubble of shocked laughter. The deer darted across the street and into another dark front yard. With the foothills and the Boise River so close to campus, wildlife sightings weren't unusual. Especially at night.

"Sorry. It was just a deer," she told Jade, trying to catch her breath. "Scared the shit out of me." She needed to calm the hell down. Recalibrate. Sid wasn't following her. He hadn't done anything to her. Nothing bad had actually happened.

"You're okay, though? Like, really okay?" Jade yawned loudly. "Girl, I love you, but I gotta be awake at six tomorrow. Just tell me everything's all right at the rental house with that weird-ass dude? Boy-Sidney? I've been worrying about you all day."

Nya's relief shriveled a little at the edges. "Oh, yeah. It's actually kind of cute on the inside. And Sid is … weird. He reminds me of Spike from *Notting Hill.* I locked my bedroom door and he left me alone." *Sort of.* "The kitchen is pretty gross, but … not the end of the world. I'm basically living at the library this semester anyway." *Sid has a weird rash. He's totally high on weed and who knows what else, and I'm pretty sure he was wandering the house in the dead of night. The house is filled with lead paint and a mystery basement. I couldn't sleep at all. I miss you. I hate this.*

"Spike?" Jade laughed. "Oh, god."

Nya forced a lighthearted laugh in response. She hated not telling Jade the whole truth. A small part of her wanted to blurt out the frantic thoughts. But no. That was selfish. Nya refused to make Jade worry more than she already was. Not when Jade was hundreds of miles away and couldn't do a thing about any of it.

Jade would be pissed when she found out that Nya had knowingly kept so much from her, but she'd understand. Jade would do the same thing if the situation were reversed.

"Get some sleep, silly," Nya said. "Or you're definitely gonna be crying on the job tomorrow. I love you!" She did her best to make her voice believably bright.

Jade yawned again, then asked, "Are you home safe yet?"

Nya braced herself to end the call. "Yep, home safe and sound," she said confidently, picking up her pace. "Talk to you soon." Just one more block. Close enough.

The call disconnected, and Nya ran the rest of the way with her book-filled backpack bumping against her spine. Some of the windows she passed blazed with light and muffled voices from other student renters. Laughter. Squeals of delight. Blaring music. Other windows were dark, quiet, and tucked in for the evening. The old neighborhood was a disjointed blend of long-time local residents and college students.

Would anyone come running if she screamed right now? *Probably not,* was the easy answer. There was always somebody shrieking, blasting music, or making strange noises near campus. Both the neighborhood residents and students had little choice but to grow a thick skin when it came to bumps in the night.

She was breathing hard by the time she stood in front of the rental with the tall mulberry tree. Her skin felt damp and sticky. Her hair, when she touched it, was an awkward blend of limp locks and static. Maybe tomorrow would be the glorious day when she didn't sweat through her T-shirt or run wherever she was going in a mad rush.

The house was as unsettling as ever in the darkness. She noticed, for the first time, that the way the roof dipped down in front made it look like an upside-down, grimacing mouth.

Gathering her resolve, Nya picked her way down the dark, uneven walkway and up the steps. From the porch, she could hear that same familiar drumbeat, uneven and erratic. Louder than yesterday.

The key Sid had given her clicked in the lock, and the door opened without a fuss.

The drumbeats suddenly stopped.

A whiff of skunky weed, combined with something rancid, hit her nose as soon as she opened the door and took a breath. She gritted her teeth, determined to make at least a little progress on the disgusting kitchen before she went to sleep. If she was really feeling bold, maybe she'd make Sid help her do it.

Nya shut the door behind her and felt for a light switch.

She bit back a scream when the orange glow of the light illuminated the entryway, and her eyes settled on the pale figure seated at the card table in the dark kitchen.

Sid cocked his head and smiled, then let his raised palms slap down on the surface of the drum he held between his knobby, bare knees and hairy legs. Once again, he wasn't wearing a shirt. Or pants. While it was impossible to tell from the position of the drum, he appeared to be in his underwear again. Either that, or he was naked.

Nya mumbled a greeting and averted her eyes. Then, without waiting for him to reply, she rushed down the hall and into her bedroom.

She shut the bedroom door behind her and locked it.

"Creep," she whispered.

Cleaning the kitchen could wait.

NOELLE W. IHLI

15

Nya stood in her bathroom, staring at the powder-blue tub while the water level rose a little at a time. Between the loud rattle of the air conditioner and the waterfall from the faucet, she couldn't hear the drumbeats anymore. Was Sid still out there? *You're safe,* she told herself. *He's weird, but he's harmless. And you're being a prude about the underwear.*

When the steaming water reached the little silver knob at the top of the bathtub, she turned off the water and looked around the small bathroom. All she wanted to do was strip off the Def Leppard T-shirt and cutoffs and sink into the hot bath, letting it wash away all the stress-sweat. But the idea of taking off her clothes, even in the privacy of her own bathroom, suddenly made her skin crawl.

She spun in a slow circle, scrutinizing every inch of the tiny bathroom. There were no cabinets. Nowhere to put her toiletries except the toilet tank. The only window in the bathroom was a narrow rectangle just above the bathtub.

He can't see you, she told herself. *He's out there. Everything is okay.*

So why did she feel like a wary gazelle right before it dipped its head to drink from a crocodile-infested watering hole?

She shook her head and focused on the cheery pattern of the water-damaged linoleum. It had the same intricate, retro sunburst and squares as the entryway. The heavy, chipped mirror hanging on the wall was actually really pretty. So was the pedestal sink. These details comforted her, reminding her that the house had been loved once.

Nya listened for the drumbeats again.

Nothing, except the drone of the window A/C unit. She couldn't decide whether to keep it on while she slept or not. Was it better to drive herself crazy listening to whatever Sid was doing at night? Or was ignorance bliss?

For tonight, ignorance won.

Pushing the image of Sid's beady eyes and hairy legs out of her mind, she undressed and stepped into the bathtub.

Like the rest of the bathroom, the tub itself was painfully small. Nearly all of the pale blue tiles running along the rim of the yellow tub were chipped. The grout was missing in a few spots, leaving dark, linear gaps growing mold and cobwebs.

So it wasn't exactly Club Med. Not that Nya had been there, either. But when she eased herself back and pulled up her knees, she could get most of her body underwater.

The hot water felt so good she wanted to cry.

She stayed that way, eyes closed, for so long she might have fallen asleep if it weren't for the rapidly plummeting temperature in the small tub.

Step. Pause. *Step.* Pause.

Nya felt more than heard the soft thud of footsteps beneath her head on the dirty porcelain lip of the bathtub.

Her breathing sped up. It was hard to tell, with the sound of the air conditioner on blast, but it sounded like the footsteps were coming from the bedroom.

She held her breath, trying to listen over the noise of the A/C unit and the pounding in her chest.

It wasn't possible that someone was in her bedroom. She was sure she had locked the door. Absolutely, one-hundred percent positive.

Which meant that either her mind was playing tricks on her —and the footsteps were actually coming from the hallway—or that Sid had a way to get into her room.

Trying to make as little noise as possible, Nya sat up in the bathtub and listened, keeping her eyes on the closed bathroom door.

Step. Pause. *Step.* Pause.

The soft footsteps landed between long pauses, like the person was taking purposeful steps. Like they were trying to be very, very quiet while they moved.

Step. Pause. *Step.* Pause.

If her mind wasn't running away with itself, the person connected to those feet was standing right outside the bathroom door.

Nya sat forward a little more, so she could see the crack beneath the door more clearly. A soft orange glow from the light in the bedroom shone through one side. But the other side was dark. Like something was blocking it. Standing there. Waiting.

Her chin trembled, and her teeth threatened to chatter as the tepid water swirled around her knees and stomach from the slight movement she'd made when sitting up. Had she left clothes in a pile by the door? There had to be a reasonable explanation—other than Sid standing in her room on the other side of the bathroom door right now.

Her eyes snapped to the interior doorknob. She hadn't locked it. Why would she, when she'd locked the bedroom door?

She imagined the doorknob turning. Imagined herself face to face with a mostly-naked Sid, his eyes greedily taking in her fully naked body in the bath. Was there anything she could use as a weapon if he came in here? Her cell phone was on the bed, far out of reach.

The best option she could see was the flimsy shower rod running overhead. A cheap plastic curtain hung from it, the weight making it bow a little in the center. There was no way she'd do any kind of damage with that.

Her heart hammered harder. *Get out of the damn tub,* she told herself. *Start by doing that.*

Finally giving in to the adrenaline pumping through her veins, she stood, careful not to slip, and snatched the ratty beach towel she'd left hanging on the grab bar beside the tub.

Her own footsteps on the tub floor made a flurry of soft *booms.* The water sloshed, making it even harder to hear what was going on outside the bathroom door.

She darted one hand forward, locking the bathroom door.

Instead of turning with a satisfying *click*, the lock spun. It was broken.

She gasped and twisted it again, but it was no use.

If her eyes hadn't been fixed on the crack beneath the door, she would have missed it.

The shadow moved a few inches.

So Nya finally screamed.

16

The moment she'd screamed, the footsteps had scattered away from the door, followed by a quiet *thunk.*

She stood dripping with her ear to the door for several long minutes, breathing hard, until she was certain that the only sound she could hear was the rattle of the air conditioner.

By the time she dried off, wrapped the towel around herself, and gathered the courage to open the bathroom door a crack, she was shivering violently. She'd left her pajamas in the bedroom, a mistake she'd never make again.

When she finally eased open the bathroom door, she let out her breath in a rush. The tiny room was empty. Nothing out of place.

Nya hurried across the room and tried twisting the bedroom doorknob. Still locked. For good measure, she knelt and peeked underneath her bed. The sparse metal frame was low enough to the ground that she doubted an adult human could fit underneath it, but she had to see for herself.

Steeling her nerves, she looked in the last spot someone might be able to hide: the closet.

The mirrored door slid along their tracks then hit the end with a quiet *thud*. Was that the sound she'd heard when she screamed?

She gritted her teeth and kept her eyes on the closet while she put on her pajamas as quickly as she could. Then she opened the mirrored doors and peered inside.

Empty, except for the clothes she'd hung up last night.

Relief, mixed with confusion, drained the adrenaline. *What the hell just happened?*

The scripture quilt lay in a twisted bunch at the bottom of the twin mattress, where she'd left it that morning. The little painted *alebrije* horse on the dresser was still facing the bed, unmoved.

Her mind spun with questions. Had Sid been in her bedroom just now? Was there some other simple explanation for the noises she'd heard? What the hell was she supposed to do now? She could put up with a lot, but this was crossing a line.

The skeptical voice in her head piped up in answer. *What exactly was crossing a line? There's nobody in here.*

Fear dissolved into annoyance.

This was the last thing she needed to be obsessing over.

Where was Sid right now? In the hall? Still drumming away, basically naked, in the kitchen? Had he been home all day? Doing what? Was he a student? Did he have a job? Had he been in her room while she was gone during the day? Who the hell did he think he was? A wave of angry shivers prickled down her back in sync with the droplets of chilly water from her wet hair.

Nya's body and mind were a tangle of jockeying, contradictory needs.

Anxiety, humming through her veins, keeping her frozen and listening at the door.

Anger, prompting her to storm into the hall and confront him right this second.

Exhaustion, promising that if she just kept the air conditioner on and fell asleep, it would all work out. She could push the dresser up against the door while she slept, for extra reassurance that Sid definitely couldn't get in without her knowing.

Hunger, growling in her gut, nudging her toward the cereal and milk in the disgusting kitchen.

Fear, demanding she keep the door locked and stay in the bedroom, no matter how much her stomach begged.

For a while, Nya lay down on the bed and tried to fall asleep, but it was no use. No matter how tired she was, the anxiety kept her awake like a strong cup of coffee.

In the end, it was a combination of anger and hunger that finally made her push the door open. It was nearly eleven o'clock at night, but she hadn't eaten anything all day.

Pepper spray in one hand, Wheaties box in the other, Nya tentatively stepped into the hall. She'd been keeping all her non-perishable food in the bedroom, given the disgusting kitchen. She could eat the cereal dry, but was she really going to let him stop her from drinking her own milk?

The musty hallway was dark and quiet. No more drumbeats, no Sid. His bedroom door was shut.

Nya almost knocked to confront him. However, the knowledge that he was shut away inside his own room was good enough for the moment.

She walked down the dark hallway and into the kitchen. The Tiffany light still flickered above the dirty, cluttered card table, bathing the room in soft orange light.

Despite the hunger pangs, the smell in the kitchen made her nauseated. The blinking green time display on the microwave read ten fifty-two. If she spent just twenty minutes cleaning up the worst of the mess, she could enjoy her bowl of cereal on a clean table and still be in bed by eleven-thirty.

It wasn't her mess, but it *was* her problem. And the idea of purging some of Sid's nasty garbage and reclaiming the space as her own in some small way was undeniably appealing.

Plus, it would give her something to do with the adrenaline still begging her to run.

* * *

Nya scrubbed, rinsed, and scoured the horrible kitchen. The experience felt a little like popping a giant zit. Disgusting, satisfying, and painful all at once. Once she started, she couldn't stop until she'd squeezed every last bit of pus from the wound she'd opened.

She found a handful of wadded-up trash bags under the sink, a dirty sponge, and a nearly empty bottle of Windex. Not caring how much noise she made anymore, she tackled the trash on the countertops, then the piled-up dishes in the sink.

Anything that stank went into the trash bag, including a few plastic baggies filled with unidentifiable contents.

When she went to clear off the card table, she found a collection of mail underneath the greasy pizza box. The white envelopes were stained with yellow spots.

She picked them up gingerly and flipped through. Some looked like utility bills, addressed to Sidney Holcomb. Others were addressed to Rick Holcomb. The landlord—and Sid's cousin —Nya remembered. A handful of spam mailers displayed unfamiliar names that must have been previous tenants. Alison West, Tiffany D. Sigliotti, Reese Cumberland. Mostly girls. Nya frowned, suddenly wondering if she wasn't the first woman who had been drawn in by Sid's confusing profile photo and cheap rent.

At the bottom of the pile was a thick envelope from the Collections Department at St. Alphonsus Hospital, addressed to Arlo C. Hunter. It was postmarked nearly a month ago, despite the red PAST DUE in big red letters on the front. Whoever poor Arlo was, Sid clearly wasn't going to forward his mail.

The words "PAST DUE" set Nya's heart pounding hard again. The idea of debt accumulating, spiraling out of control with late fees and penalties, was one of her worst nightmares.

She tossed out the spam mailers, stacked Sid's mail on the counter in plain view, and then tucked Arlo's envelope into her back pocket. She'd drop it into the mail on campus tomorrow with "No longer at this address" on the front. It was the least she could do.

* * *

By the time Nya finally finished cleaning the airless kitchen, the microwave clock read twelve forty-nine, and her clean-bathed skin was now covered with a fresh sheen of sweat and grime.

At least Sid hadn't made a peep. Was he asleep by now? Or just high out of his mind?

She saved the mostly bare fridge for last. When she'd put the milk inside it yesterday, it had been mercifully clean—aside from the pizza box, beer, and massive amounts of string cheese.

She poured a small serving of Wheaties into a freshly scrubbed bowl then tugged on the broken latch of the old yellow refrigerator. The door squeaked open, letting out a puff of cold air. She reached for the milk carton and frowned.

Some of the milk was gone.

It had been completely full last night, when she got home from the store.

Which meant he'd already drank her damn milk.

The adrenaline and anger she'd tried so hard to dissolve for the past two hours flared hot again. The gallon was still mostly full, just a couple of inches missing from the top. Jade had drunk her milk sometimes. The offense was nothing compared to what had just happened in the bathroom. But the sight of it made her see red. That was a meal he'd taken away from her. That was money straight out of her pocket.

Without stopping to think, she slammed the refrigerator door shut and marched back down the hall.

Then she pounded hard on his door.

No response.

She pounded again, glad the hollow-core door amplified the sound far louder than it needed to be. Unless Sid was dead, which was too much to hope for, he had to hear the sound.

When he still didn't respond, she reached for the knob of his door—then caught herself. *No.* She wouldn't invade his privacy like that, even if he was awful. She wouldn't stoop to his level.

Finally, on the third set of knocks, she heard an angry "What the fuck?" Then the sound of stumbling and footsteps on the other side of the door.

She backed up and squared her shoulders, pepper spray clutched tight and lowered next to her hip. If he tried anything, she'd spray it right into his eyes and call the police.

He flung the door open hard, sending the knob smashing into the wall. Nya flinched, already wishing she could rewind her choice to confront him. The anger slipped a little, replaced by fear.

Sid had clearly just dragged himself out of bed. His hair and beard looked wild, and his eyes were squinty and blinking. He'd traded the dingy white briefs for a pair of low-slung flannel boxer shorts that slunk dangerously low on his hip bones.

He stared at her with undisguised rage. "What the fuck?" he repeated. "What could you possibly need right now? It's like, one a.m."

Nya gaped at him. He had the audacity to tell *her* it was late? The anger came roaring back.

His hand went to his neck to scratch at the rash, which seemed to be spreading to his chest. Nya had spent a few minutes of precious study time in the library examining close-ups of common rashes online, and so far she hadn't found an explanation for it. It was raised and puffy in small sections, like a mosquito had taken its time wandering back and forth across the skin. The hall light above Sid's door revealed that there were yellowish patches mixed in with the red.

It was truly disgusting.

She shivered and took a step away from him. "You drank my milk," she said, wishing her voice were steadier.

He blinked and scratched the rash again. "You woke me up to bitch about *milk*?"

She hesitated. "And … you were in my room. While I was taking a bath. I heard you in there."

He cast a glance down to the hot-pink canister of pepper spray in her hand. "What the fuck are you talking about?" Then he had the nerve to raise an eyebrow and look at her like she was the crazy one.

The barest hint of a smile tugged at his lips, and she had the distinct impression that he was imagining her in the bath.

"Don't touch my food, don't come into my room, and pick up after yourself for God's sake," Nya demanded in a rush, finding her anger again. It felt good to let it out.

He stared at her for a few seconds in silence. When he spoke again, his voice was lower. "Sorry. I'm not used to having a girl around." The sliver of a smile returned when he said the word *girl*. Nya kept her finger on the pepper spray trigger.

"And I didn't drink your milk," he insisted. "I have my own food."

She made a scoffing noise. Just because he didn't remember drinking it didn't mean he *didn't* drink it. He probably didn't remember anything he did while high. Although, he didn't seem high right now. His pupils looked normal, and he wasn't slurring. But he'd definitely been high yesterday. Probably this morning. "You have your own food? You mean the rotten takeout on the counter?" she said.

He rolled his eyes. "Some of it's still good."

Nya shook her head. "I tossed anything sitting out on the counters. The kitchen is clean now."

She expected a grunt of thanks. Maybe just a nod. Instead, his eyes narrowed and he suddenly pushed past her into the hallway and marched toward the kitchen. She followed close on his heels, heart pounding.

"What the hell?" he said incredulously when he saw the clean countertops and sink. "You threw everything away without asking me? And then you knock on my door at fucking one in the morning to rip me a new one about your fucking milk?"

A trickle of doubt wormed through Nya's indignation. Had she made a mistake?

He spun in a circle, scanning the countertops and muttering to himself in disbelief. "What about the baggies? Did you at least save the goddamn baggies?"

"No," Nya mumbled, taking another step back into the hall. "They were gross."

"You just threw out like $300 worth of shrooms," he spat. "Where's the trash bag?"

When she didn't reply right away, he took another step toward her. "Where the fuck is it?"

"It's on the front porch," Nya said quietly. "It—it stinks."

He marched to the front door. She watched in horror as he knelt on the porch and ripped open the top of the trash bag.

Debris and food piled up on the concrete steps as he pawed through the contents of the trash bag with his bare hands. Nya watched in stunned silence.

After a few minutes, he held up the baggies. They were covered in some kind of brown liquid.

He stood up and glared at her. "Don't touch *my* stuff," he barked.

Then, baggies in hand, he stumbled back down the hall and slammed the door to his bedroom.

17

Nya couldn't stop replaying the confrontation with Sid while she tried to fall asleep.

She rewound each interaction, trying to decide whether he'd really been in her room, whether she'd crossed a line by throwing away his stuff, whether she'd been the jerk to bang on his door in the middle of the night.

It was the rattling hum of the air conditioner that finally lulled her into a troubled sleep.

Her eyes popped open in the dark when it clicked off after a few hours, just like the first night. At first, she thought it was the sudden silence that had woken her.

But no, it was something else.

The sound made the sweaty, damp baby hairs on the back of her neck prickle.

She was almost positive it was the sound of someone breathing.

Not a raspy, out-of-breath gasp. Just a steady in, out, in, out, coming from somewhere in the darkness. Toward the door.

She stayed frozen where she lay, eyes roving. She'd pushed the dresser tight against the door before she fell asleep. Even if

Sid *did* have a way to unlock the door, the dresser would have toppled over with a loud bang when he tried to push it.

Like before, she'd left her phone charging on the floor beside the bed. The pepper spray canister sat beside it, within easy reach.

She felt, rather than saw, something move in the darkness by the door.

Not *outside* the door.

Inside her room.

Shit, shit, shit. Move, she screamed at her frozen limbs. *Grab the phone. Grab the pepper spray.*

Something Jade told her once came screaming back to her. "When you gotta make yourself do something, you just count to three. And then you do it. No exceptions." Jade was talking about jumping into the pond after school, the first time Nya had ever gone swimming. She wasn't talking about unfreezing her body so she could pepper spray her roommate.

Maybe it would work the same, though.

Step, stop. The barely audible sound of footsteps.

Her blood rushed so loudly in her ears that she couldn't hear anything else. *One, two, three,* she screamed mentally.

Then she felt herself rise up on her elbows, as if her brain were directing the movement via remote control. The mattress squeaked. The pulse pounding in her head rose to a roar. For a few seconds, she thought she might pass out.

She flung her body partway over the side of the bed, grabbing the pepper spray with one hand and the phone with the other, fumbling to get it free from its cord.

"Get out!" she screamed, panting and scrambling back against the wall. The soft glow from the phone screen sent shadows flying over the walls. Her eyes darted around, looking for the source of the breathing, the footsteps.

Then she saw it.

The bedroom door, which she'd so carefully locked tight and barricaded with the dresser, was wide open. The dark rectangle was just a slightly different shade of black than the inky room. The dresser sat parallel beside the open door, like it had been ever so carefully nudged there.

She couldn't see anything past the rectangle of blackness in the hallway, except the edge of Sid's bedroom door.

She held her breath as she took a few steps forward. squinting into the shadows.

His door was open too. Just a few inches, but definitely open.

A soft clicking sound in the walls floated toward her. What the hell was that?

The sound sent a hard shiver down her back. A reminder that it was impossible to know which sounds were innocuous pipes tapping, floors settling, water dripping—and which sounds might be more sinister.

She imagined Sid standing just behind the slitted black crack of his doorway. He must have slipped away as soon as the bed creaked and she fumbled for her phone. Was he looking at her right now?

On shaky legs, Nya moved toward her open bedroom door. She held the pepper spray in front of her, ready to fire off a shot of the burning liquid without asking questions. He had definitely been inside her room. What did he want? How long had he been watching her sleep before she woke up?

Her eyes stayed fixed on his door crack across the hall, watching for any sign of movement. What would she do if he suddenly flung open the door and rushed her? The pepper spray felt silly and inadequate. It probably wouldn't stop him if he really wanted to hurt her. It would just slow him down.

She considered darting down the hall and out the front door to her car, calling the police or Jade, or even her parents when she was safely locked inside.

However, that would require walking right past Sid's door. It was the middle of the night. She glanced quickly at her phone screen. It was four-thirty a.m., to be exact. Jade was already at work. Her parents probably weren't awake yet. The police would answer, but what could they do? She couldn't prove Sid had been inside her room. He hadn't actually hurt her or threatened her.

She already knew the silence that would follow if she told the police that she'd seen a shadow and heard breathing in her room. *Maybe you heard noises from the street. If you're uncomfortable living in the house, I recommend you move out.*

That's more or less what they'd said when Jade called the cops late one night two years ago, when someone kept banging on their back porch.

Sid's door didn't open any wider. After a few minutes, the sound of deep breathing—and a soft snore—drifted through the quiet air.

Nya stared at the door crack incredulously.

He was asleep.

After all that, he got bored and fell back asleep.

Not sure what else to do, Nya relocked her bedroom door and pushed the old dresser back in front of it, cringing at the sound it made. Wondering what good it would do, but unable to stop herself from trying all the same.

She got back into bed and wrapped herself in the soft scripture quilt, angry tears springing to her tired eyes.

Morning was just two hours away. She was exhausted and terrified. She couldn't spend the semester like this, but what else could she do? Where else could she go?

Anywhere, a voice that felt like Jade's insisted. *Anywhere, flaca. Get out of there as fast as you can. We'll figure it out.*

She squeezed her eyes shut and tried to fall asleep, but it was no use. She couldn't stop imagining someone lurking in the shadows of her bedroom, able to reach her whether or not she barricaded the bedroom door. Couldn't stop imagining the sound of breathing in the darkness.

Her parents would say it was demons: fallen angels who rebelled against God and were cast out of heaven. They were tormenting her because of her sinful choices. She'd given them power over her.

The concept of demons had terrified Nya as a child. The idea of dark beings feasting on human sin and suffering was horrifying. Even now, she shuddered. But she didn't believe in demons anymore. They were the stuff of bad dreams. They weren't real, and they couldn't hurt her.

She couldn't say the same for nightmares made of flesh and blood.

18

When the opening chords to "Try Everything," by Shakira blared through Nya's phone, her wakeup alarm at six a.m., she barely reacted.

The song usually made her smile. Shakira was the first pop artist she'd ever listened to.

But this morning, her eyes felt like salted slugs, dry, gritty, and slow. Her body protested when she sat up and surveyed the bedroom in the faint morning light.

The dresser was still pushed against the door.

She was still alive.

But she felt awful.

Her head hurt worse than any hangover, and her limbs were leaden and uncoordinated. Her brain, already struggling to get by on the meager servings of granola bars and Wheaties, was full of static. Sleep, she knew from every biology class she'd ever taken, was absolutely essential for the brain and body to function.

If you didn't get enough sleep, you slowly wasted away.

If you didn't get any sleep for long enough, you actually died. The body and brain needed it that badly.

So if Sid didn't kill her, the lack of sleep might.

She couldn't spend the semester like this. If this was what two days of no sleep felt like, there was no way she'd be able to keep up with her classwork for the entire semester.

"Suck it up, buttercup," she whispered to herself, bleary eyes still locked on the bedroom door. But instead of giving her the boost she needed to get out of bed and throw on something cleanish to wear, the words made her feel like crying. How the hell had Sid gotten into her room last night? What would have happened if she hadn't woken up when she did and grabbed the phone?

And, even more terrifying: What would happen tonight?

The idea of sleeping even one more night at the rental house filled her with a rush of slick, hot dread.

Today's class schedule was grueling. It started in an hour and didn't end until six p.m.

Maybe sleeping in her car at the Walmart parking lot was her best bet after all. The idea filled her with fresh horror at the new terrifying possibilities that living in her car would bring.

Tears brimmed over her lashes and slid down her cheeks. She couldn't think about that yet. Right now, she needed to get dressed and get to class. She'd figure out what to do after that. Until then, she had to focus.

Keeping her eyes on the closed door and wiping the tears away, she forced herself to get out of bed. She'd kept the air conditioner off for the rest of the night, and the musty old house was already heating up.

Nya padded to the door and listened until she was sure there was no movement from the other side. Sid was probably sound asleep after staying up all night getting high and breaking into her room. The mental image made her blood boil.

She ran a comb through her hair and dabbed on concealer in a futile attempt to hide the dark circles beneath her eyes. Then she pulled on the same pair of shorts from the day before and a fresh T-shirt—an oversized, soft v-neck she'd borrowed from Jade and never given back. She quietly collected her things, dragged the dresser back beside the bed, and listened at the door one more time. The only sound she could hear was the birds chirping brightly outside the window, welcoming the dawn.

Her hand was clammy and slippery on the doorknob, but she twisted the lock and eased the bedroom door open.

Sid's door was fully closed. The hallway was dark and silent.

Gritting her teeth and clutching the pepper spray, she quietly shut her door behind her. Then she rushed down the hall, not stopping until she made it outside.

* * *

Between the sleep deprivation and her growling stomach, the day slipped away in a blurry haze. No matter how hard she tried to focus on what the professors were saying, she couldn't translate the lectures into notes that made sense. And the task of wading through the day's assigned reading and homework was excruciating.

She stayed in the library until closing again, only half-focused on the computer screen in front of her. It was impossible to concentrate. Each minute that ticked by was one minute closer to the moment she'd have to walk back to the rental house. Then, she'd either have to pack up her belongings in the Honda and try to sleep in the Walmart parking lot, or lock herself into the bedroom knowing that Sid would still be able to find a way inside.

She opened a new browser and combed through the off-campus housing boards and social listings for the umpteenth time.

The prices were even worse and the options were even slimmer, now that classes had begun.

She couldn't afford a single one.

She'd even messaged the two homeless shelters in Boise. Both were full for the night.

In desperation, she sent a message to her lab partner from spring semester, Reese. From the little green dot next to her name, Reese was online right now. *Hey, long time no see! I know this is a random message, but I'm in a weird situation and wondered if you had a couch I could sleep on for a while?*

Nya cringed but hit send anyway, then stared at the screen until the word "seen" appeared beneath the message.

The green dot next to Reese's name disappeared. *No longer online.*

"Attention: The library will be closing in five minutes," a perky female voice chirped over the loudspeaker when the clock showed nine fifty-five p.m.

Nya looked longingly at a wall of well-worn couches a few feet away, wondering if there was any way she could evade security and fall asleep on one of them for the night.

She closed her eyes and let herself get lost in the fantasy of crouching on top of a toilet, pulling her feet up onto the lid in the bathroom stall until security had finished their evening check. Then curling up on the soft cushions and closing her eyes without fear.

It wouldn't work. She'd get caught. If not tonight, then tomorrow or the next day. And if she got caught, she'd get in trouble. Maybe lose her scholarship or face academic consequences.

So what the hell am I supposed to do? The thought circled in her head, around and around like a revolving door moving too quickly to dart through any opening.

Jade had texted a string of emojis and memes an hour earlier, telling her to call when she left the library, while she walked home for the night. Nya had sent back a fib, telling Jade to go to sleep, because she was studying with a lab partner until late. She wouldn't be able to hide the exhaustion and the terror in her voice. Not tonight.

Jade would see through the facade and demand to know what was going on.

"Hey, are you okay?"

Nya's head snapped up at the closeness of the deep voice beside her. She must have fallen asleep at the computer for a few minutes.

She blinked in surprise, recognition slowly dawning. It was the tall guy with the blue eyes and close-cropped, curly hair. The one she'd seen in line at the used-book sale yesterday. The one who had commented on her Def Leppard shirt. Her cheeks flushed hot, and she scrambled to log out of the library computer and pack up her things. Another announcement, indicating that the library was now closed, was playing on the loudspeaker.

"Um, yeah. I'm fine," she lied, stuttering. As soon as the words left her mouth, her stomach erupted in a long, mortifyingly loud growl.

He bit back a smile. "Your stomach begs to differ."

Heat rose in her cheeks. "Yeah ... I forgot to eat dinner." *And lunch. And breakfast.*

He looked at her intently. To her surprise, there was a blush on his cheeks, as well. "I actually studied through dinner, too." He reached into his backpack, an old black Jansport, and pulled out a crumpled paper sack. He shrugged. "Maybe this is weird, but I have a peanut butter and jelly sandwich in here and a few other things. If you want half, it's all yours."

She stared at the paper bag, unable to keep her mouth from watering. A stranger offering her a bag of delicious food was the last thing she'd expected right now. Would it be a terrible idea to say yes? Should she decline? Would it be any more reckless than going home to glassy-eyed Sid?

He lowered the bag to his side like he was going to put it away. "No pressure. I promise I'm not a creep or anything. My name's Curtis. I saw you at the bookstore yesterday." Red splotches bloomed on his cheeks again. "I was trying to get up the courage to ask you out for coffee yesterday, but I ruined it with the dumb Def Leppard joke."

This finally made her smile. She tucked her belongings into her bag and stood. Security had already lowered half the lights, a pointed signal for any remaining students to get out. "No, pretty sure I'm the one who dropped the ball on that one. I actually don't know any Def Leppard songs."

"Not even one?" He laughed, a deep comforting sound.

Nya raised her hands. "Not even one."

She walked next to him, heading for the library exit. Out of the corner of her eye, she studied him more closely. He walked with a hunch, like he didn't want to overwhelm anybody with how tall he really was. His nose was a little crooked, but it suited him. His wide eyes were the clearest blue she'd ever seen. His curly hair was short and tightly cut, but up close she could see that it was a little uneven, like he'd done it himself. His clothing bore the same vaguely unstylish, scuffed, well-worn hallmarks of the thrift store that hers did. Those details, plus the fact that he was inviting her to share a peanut butter and jelly sandwich instead of inviting her to grab something to eat at the late-night food truck lot, told her plenty. He still held onto the brown paper bag in one hand.

He wasn't really her type. Cute enough in a nerdy way, but there was a quiet intensity about him that made her slightly uncomfortable when he held her gaze with those big blue eyes for too long.

Still, the idea that he might be just as poor as she was endeared him to her immediately. That, and the fact that she was nearly delirious with hunger and wasn't in any hurry to get back to the rental house.

Why not say yes?

So when they reached the metal detectors at the library exit, she shrugged. "If you're still offering, I'd love to share your dinner. I'm Nya, by the way."

His head snapped up and his eyes went impossibly even wider. He darted forward to hold the exit door open for her as they walked into the warm, dark evening. "Nya. That's really pretty. And yes, definitely. Let's eat." He darted his eyes around and pointed at a bench a few feet away. "This spot okay?"

Nya nodded. "Great." If her luck was bad enough that she'd managed to find a second psychopath this early in the semester, the bench was close enough to the library exit that one of the security guards or janitors would hear her scream.

19

"Did you make this?" Nya asked in disbelief when Curtis unwrapped the layers of plastic around the enormous sandwich, thick with peanut butter and dripping with strawberry jam.

He hesitated. "No. My roommate works at Albertson's. He brings home some of the stuff they're going to toss in the dumpster." He shrugged, but his cheeks turned red again.

"That's brilliant," Nya rushed to say, not wanting him to feel embarrassed. "I wish I had that kind of roommate ..."

He looked at her intently with those wide blue eyes, waiting for her to elaborate.

She changed the subject. Sid was terrifying and ominous and she'd have to deal with him soon enough. He didn't get to ruin this lovely moment. Her stomach rumbled happily as she took a bite of the sandwich. It was absolutely delicious. "I don't care how old this is. It tastes like heaven."

The anxious expression on his face broke into a wide smile. He dug back into the bulging paper sack. "I've got chips, too. They're expired, but you'd never know it. And some grapes and a brownie."

She stared at him in disbelief as he produced item after item of perfect-looking food. "Magic," she whispered. "Thanks for sharing with me."

He glanced at her and gently placed a bag of chips into her hand. "Thanks for eating with me."

By the time the picnic was over and the food was gone, the last lights shining through the glass windows of the library had been replaced by the bluish glow of the metal detector columns inside.

"I'm so full I think I might pass out," Nya said, holding her stomach and crumpling the empty brownie wrapper to place it inside the paper sack. With her belly finally full, the idea of slipping into an uninterrupted sleep was all she wanted.

With that thought, the food in her stomach roiled with anxiety. That wasn't likely to happen tonight, or anytime soon.

It was time to face the music. Or the drumbeats, more like.

Curtis nudged her knee with his. "Are you okay? You've got that same look on your face that you did in the library."

She hesitated, keeping her eyes on her hands. It was getting really late. Just past eleven. She was going to have to deal with the shit show at the rental house, one way or another. She absolutely had to get some sleep tonight. Tomorrow was her first lab, and she needed to be alert.

She looked up at Curtis, sizing him up. He met her gaze and waited. Not prying, but clearly eager to offer a listening ear.

The truth was, she was dying to ask someone else what they thought. To spew out the whole truth of the terrifying situation with Sid. She desperately wanted that person to be Jade, but Jade wasn't here. And Jade would freak the fuck out.

Curtis was here, right in front of her. The fact that he'd just shared an expired meal with her made her feel like maybe he'd understand her dilemma. He was clearly navigating some of the same difficulties she was as a dirt-poor college student.

"Which direction are you headed?" she finally asked him. "I'm that way. Just a few blocks off campus." She nodded between the dark buildings and dimly lit pathways to their right.

"Same," he told her, standing and hefting the black Jansport backpack over his shoulder. "Talk while we walk?"

She stood and fell into stride beside him. "You sure you want to know? It's kind of a long, depressing story."

He laughed. "I'm sure. Tell me everything."

* * *

She told him more than she'd intended.

A *lot* more.

The story about stumbling onto the cheap rental house somehow bled into the backstory about her parents, Blood of the Lamb Church in Clearwater, Jade, the Estradas, and even the three-legged *alebrije* she kept on her dresser.

By the time she finally finished word-vomiting the whole saga of Sid, they had circled the dark neighborhood block five times, giving the rental house a wide berth.

Curtis listened in silence the whole time they walked, letting her go on and on. He finally stopped walking and turned to face her on the dark sidewalk. His thick eyebrows were furrowed in either concern or horror. Oh, god. What was he about to say?

"I'm sorry," she apologized again. "It's so late. I'm basically sleep-drunk. I should let you go home. You don't even know me. I just ... I just really don't know what to do." Her voice broke on the last word, and for a horrifying moment, she was afraid she was going to cry.

He winced and her heart sank. She should have kept some of the details back. It was way too much for a first date—if eating a day-old sandwich on the library bench counted as a date, anyway.

He clearly liked her. At least, he had before she spilled her guts all over him at midnight. She knew she sounded unhinged. She'd probably scared him—and his supply of day-old food— away, just like that.

The thought sent an uneasy twinge of guilt through her full stomach. He was nice, and kind of cute. But he gave her friend vibes more than boyfriend vibes. Still, what was the harm in being friends? She needed a friend right now. Desperately.

She was about to say sorry again when he held up a hand. He kept his eyes on his shoes, like he was embarrassed for her. "Stop. You don't need to apologize. I understand why you were zoning out in the library now."

He shoved his hands into his pockets, looking uncomfortable, still not making eye contact. One foot inched backward, like it was getting ready to sprint away from her. The adrenaline rush Nya had felt while she blurted the story out faded, replaced by an overwhelming sense of regret. What was she thinking, telling him all that? This was her problem, not his.

He glanced down the street, where the rental house—all its windows dark—sat tucked behind the tall mulberry tree with its spidery branches just visible through the moonlight.

Nya frowned. Was he looking at the rental house? *Her* rental house? It sure seemed like it, but she hadn't told him which house it was—or the address.

"How do you know that's where I live?" she asked softly. The fine hairs on the back of her neck and arms prickled.

He looked at her sharply, and she knew instantly that she'd guessed right. He *did* know which house it was. But why?

Curtis finally met her eyes. "I—kept debating whether to tell you when I realized you were talking about the Gore Shack."

"The *Gore Shack?*" Nya repeated, wondering if she'd misheard him.

He shrugged. "Yeah, a lot of people call it that. Because of all those nasty berries on the sidewalk. They look like blood."

Nya tilted her head, waiting for him to continue. The temperature was still plenty warm outside, but she wrapped her arms around her middle, suddenly fighting the need to shiver.

Curtis sighed. "You should probably know ... about what happened there. With your roommate Sid."

"What?" she prodded, desperate to know what he'd been holding back.

He looked at his feet, like telling this story pained him. "The guy who lived there before you—his name was Arlo—"

"Yes," Nya rushed to say, kicking herself for interrupting. "I saw his name on a piece of mail."

Curtis glanced up at her and studied her expression. "Yeah. I don't know all the details about what happened, but I know enough. I live just a few streets that way." He pointed north, farther away from campus.

"What happened to Arlo?" Nya prodded.

Curtis eyed her carefully, as if unsure how much to reveal. Finally, he shook his head and began. "Sid and Arlo hated each other's guts. I heard them fighting a couple of times, when I was walking to class. About food, about the A/C, about Sid's drug habit."

Nya hugged herself harder, hanging on every word.

"Apparently Sid's cousin owns the rental and keeps some of his stuff in the basement." He looked at Nya for confirmation. She nodded mutely.

He continued. "I guess things finally boiled over. One day, they got in a huge fight and ..."

"And what?"

Curtis shook his head. He was quiet for a few moments. Finally, he said, "I was walking home from class when I saw the ambulance pull up in front of the house. There was a big group of students gathered around. I walked over to see what was going on. That's when I saw ... the blood. At first, I thought it was the mulberries. But then I saw him."

Curtis shoved his hands deeper into his jeans. In the silence, they made a faint rattling sound, like he had brushed against a Tic Tac bottle.

"Who did you see?" Nya whispered.

"Arlo. He was lying facedown on the front walkway, underneath the mulberry tree."

20

Nya felt her vision narrow. Curtis was still talking, but his voice sounded like it was coming from underwater. *Ambulance. Arlo. Facedown.*

For a moment, the only other thing she could hear was the rattling sound from whatever he was fiddling with in his pocket. Had Sid … killed Arlo?

No. Nya pictured the letter she'd stumbled upon while cleaning the kitchen. The one she'd tucked into her back pocket. It was still in the jean shorts she'd stripped off when she finally got into bed late last night and re-worn this morning. Dead people didn't get letters, did they?

She forced herself to pay attention.

"I was sure he was dead," Curtis was saying. "He *looked* dead. There was blood coming from his mouth, and his face was kind of … gray." He looked at her, like trying to decide whether he should keep talking. When she didn't say anything, he kept going. "Sid messed him up pretty bad. Had to stay in the hospital for a while."

Nya nodded. "I think I have one of his medical bills," she mumbled. "What happened then?"

Curtis took his hands out of his pockets and crossed his arms. "I don't know this for sure. There's a lot of rumors about what happened, but there are some pretty consistent details ..."

"Just tell me," Nya insisted. "Tell me everything you know." She didn't feel tired anymore. She felt like a cold bucket of water had been poured over her head.

Curtis nodded. "While Arlo was in the hospital, I guess Sid told his cousin—the landlord—that he'd caught Arlo stealing stuff from the basement. The landlord believed Sid. So on top of everything, Arlo got kicked out of the rental."

Nya's head swam. "Are you fucking serious?" she breathed. "But didn't Arlo press charges against Sid? For sending him to the hospital and everything?"

Curtis shrugged. "Like I said, some of the details are hard to pin down. But apparently Sid told the police that Arlo hit him first. And that he pushed Arlo out the front door in self-defense. Sid said he had no idea Arlo was hurt, so he just shut him out of the house to cool down. Police ultimately said it was Arlo's word against Sid's."

The look on Curtis's face told her that he still knew more than he was telling her. "What else?" Nya whispered.

Curtis's mouth was set in a grim line. "A buddy from one of my classes told me Arlo's version of the story. He said Sid went into a rage about something. At one point, he kicked Arlo in the stomach. Said afterward, Arlo begged Sid to call an ambulance. Knew he was hurt bad. Couldn't find his phone. Sid left Arlo on the floor and shut himself in the bedroom. Poor Arlo finally managed to crawl outside to get help, then passed out under the tree, where the students found him and called an ambulance."

Nya hugged herself tighter. It was worse than she'd thought. She could imagine the terror Arlo must have felt while he lay there on the peeling kitchen linoleum, begging for help. Maybe they'd been fighting about the same dirty dishes and trash she'd just cleaned up. Or maybe it had been a fight over the constant skunky smell in the house, or the shrooms in the disgusting baggies.

She imagined the look in Sid's beady black eyes when he shrugged and walked away, leaving his roommate on the floor, pleading for an ambulance.

There was no longer any question in her mind: Sid was a violent psychopath who had nearly killed his previous roommate. She couldn't sleep in the same house with him tonight.

The hot sting of tears pressed behind her eyes. When this conversation with Curtis was over, she would sneak inside the rental, grab her things, then spend the night in the Honda. She would figure the rest out later—somehow.

Or maybe she would just call Jade. Come clean with the full truth of how scared she was. How Sid had been standing in her room while she bathed. How she'd awoken in the middle of the night to her bedroom door hanging wide open. How she couldn't sleep. How she'd just learned that he'd nearly killed his roommate. She could be on a bus to Indianapolis in the morning.

No. She pinched the soft skin on her inner arm to push the tears back. She'd worked so hard to finish college. She couldn't give up. Not now. Not when she was so damn close.

Curtis was looking at her with a mixture of pity and concern in his eyes. "I'm really sorry. Are you mad I told you?"

Her eyes widened, letting a trickle of tears spill down her cheeks. "I'm not upset that you told me. I'm upset that I either have to sleep across the hall from him or ..." Her voice hitched and she backed down from finishing the thought. "I'm just going to find a hotel—or something—tonight." *Or something,* she thought to herself bitterly.

A look of panic crossed his face, like he was the one responsible for the fact that she'd have to flee her home in the middle of the night. "I'd let you crash at my place ... but it's not my place." He ducked his head, clearly embarrassed. "I'm sleeping on my buddy's couch for a while," he mumbled. "Housing is so expensive."

Nya nodded. The fact that he would have offered at all made her feel grateful and embarrassed all at once. When he drew her in for a tentative, awkward hug, she didn't resist.

His clothes had a lived-in, slightly fuggy smell, like they'd been worn one too many times between washes. Her nose wrinkled, but she knew she had no right to judge him. There were never enough quarters for the laundromat. She knew her clothes probably smelled pretty much the same. She was just used to her own funk.

After a few long seconds, he pulled back. The panic on his face had faded, replaced by a thoughtful expression.

"There might be another way," he said slowly. "I mean, if you have somewhere else to go tonight, you should probably do that ..." He said each word carefully, like he knew full well she had nowhere else to go. Maybe it was the way she'd wolfed down her half of the food he'd shared with her. Maybe it was the fact that she was already living in the "Gore Shack." Maybe he'd smelled the same telltale smell on her clothes that she'd smelled on his. Maybe he just knew what desperation sounded like. Either way, she hung on the possibility of whatever he was about to say next.

"There was a video that got passed around after what happened to Arlo."

Nya stared at him in disbelief. "A video of what?"

"Well, the thing is ... Arlo wasn't stealing the cousin's stuff from the basement. But Sid *was*. And Arlo took a video that proved it."

Nya stared at him. *Sid* was the one stealing from his cousin. That tracked. She remembered what he'd told her the day she moved in. *Don't go into the basement.* Was there even lead in the paint down there? Or did he just want to keep her from seeing what he was doing? That he was stealing.

"Do you have the video?" she asked.

Curtis frowned. "It's been a couple months, but I think I can find it in my texts. I'll send it to you, if you want."

"And then what?" Nya whispered.

Curtis looked thoughtful. After a moment he said, "Tell Sid that if he bothers you again, you'll send the video to his cousin."

Nya felt the blood drain from her face. The idea of confronting Sid—blackmailing him—was terrifying. From what Curtis said, he'd put his old roommate in the hospital over run-of-the-mill roommate squabbles. She could only imagine how he'd react to Nya threatening to nark on him about grand theft.

At the same time, did she really have a better option?

No.

There were no good options tonight. It was only getting later. The night was only getting darker. The desperation rising in her chest was only getting harder to push back down.

Curtis pulled his phone out of the Jansport: a cheap-looking flip phone. He tapped on the tiny screen a few times then scrolled in silence for a few long minutes.

Finally, his face lit up. "Found it."

She squinted and moved in closer to see. There, on the screen, was Sid standing on the porch of the rental house, talking to a blonde woman wearing navy blue sweats and a tank top. He was handing her what looked like a leather biker jacket. She reached out to stroke it appraisingly before hefting it over one arm and handing him a wad of cash.

The person holding the phone—Arlo—was close enough to the porch that you could see every second of the transaction in perfect detail. The camerawork was shaky, *Blair Witch* style, but there was no question of who was in the video and the fact that a transaction was taking place.

The blonde woman beat a hasty retreat from the porch to her car, clutching her new treasure. Sid held the bills in his hand. He didn't count them. The camera stayed on his face as his leering eyes followed the woman to her car.

"Why didn't Arlo send that video to the cousin himself?" Nya asked.

Curtis pursed his lips and zipped the phone back into his backpack. "Dunno. As far as I know, nobody's heard from Arlo since right after he got out of the hospital," he said with a shrug. "He had nowhere to go after he got discharged. Big old pile of medical bills. Had to drop all his classes."

Nya furrowed her brows. That explained the collections letter from the hospital. Her stomach clenched when she thought about how easy it was to ruin someone's life. Especially someone who was already hanging on by their fingernails, scraping to get by, and willing to live in the "Gore Shack."

"You really think that's the cousin's stuff Sid was selling?" Nya asked. For the first time since she'd rolled up to the rental house, she felt something other than powerless panic. The desperation had hardened into something new: A flicker of determination. She wouldn't let Sid push her out—or ruin her plans—like he'd done with Arlo.

She wouldn't cower. She'd hold her ground.

She had nowhere else to go.

But what if he holds his ground? Jade's voice whispered from somewhere in the back of her mind. *What if he does the same thing to you that he did to Arlo? Or worse?*

Curtis hesitated. "That's what I heard," he said slowly.

"And how do I know Sid won't go postal on me, too?" Nya asked slowly. "What if the reason they got in the big fight was Arlo threatening to show the cousin the video he'd taken?" It made sense. The camera angle on the video had been coming from *inside* the rental house: from the bedroom Nya now occupied. That meant Arlo had made the video right *before* he ended up in the hospital.

Curtis's gaze burned into hers, a tight smile on his lips. "You're going to do it smarter than Arlo. Tell Sid you got the video from a friend. Make sure he knows it's not the only copy," he told her sternly. "And that if anything happens to you ... the video will go straight to the cousin. I've heard he's a scary piece of shit with a temper. Sid was apparently terrified of him finding out he was stealing his stuff."

"Why don't I just send the video to the cousin right now? Maybe he'll kick Sid out," Nya said hopefully.

Curtis raised an eyebrow. "But what if he doesn't? What if he slaps Sid around and makes him pay back the missing stuff, instead? Then you've lost your leverage. Just play it cool. I think it'll work."

Would it, though? Could it really be that easy? She'd just tell Sid she knew about the video and then he'd leave her alone to finish the semester in peace?

Don't risk it, flaca. *Get the fuck out of there. It's not worth it,* Jade's voice insisted, before it was drowned out by the thumping in her chest.

You have to try, she told herself firmly. *This could actually work.*

"Send me the video," she told Curtis softly.

21

Nya's hands shook as she fumbled with the door key. It was nearly one a.m., and the Gore Shack—as she now thought of it —was dark and silent.

Curtis had walked her as far as the drooping branches of the mulberry tree. When she felt the key click to unlock the door, she glanced over her shoulder. She could still see him standing there in the shadows among the spidery branches.

Her hands shook as she pushed open the door and slipped inside the dark entryway. The stuffy, warm air in the house was an unwelcome contrast to the cool night air. It was at least twenty degrees warmer in here.

The black flip-flops that usually greeted her—they seemed to be the only shoes Sid ever wore—were conspicuously absent. Was he out of the house?

Nya frowned. The plan was to confront him tonight. No waiting around to find out whether he'd come into her room again.

The only other alternative was locking herself in her room until morning, knowing that somehow even this wouldn't stop him.

A noise from the basement drew her attention.

So Sid was home after all.

She tiptoed across the linoleum, glancing at the kitchen. It was just like she'd left it. Airless, stifling, but mostly clean. At least he hadn't managed to trash it again already.

When she reached the carpet in the hallway, she hesitated.

The hall light was off. But a faint, watery yellow glow was coming from the partially-open door that led to the basement.

"Asshole," she whispered to herself. A fresh wave of anger bubbled up inside her when she saw this with her own eyes. From the soft rummaging sounds coming from the basement, he was looking for something else to sell from his cousin Rick's stockpile.

She had the video pulled up on her phone in case Sid didn't believe she had it. Curtis had promised he'd wait just outside, until she texted him that she was okay. If she screamed, he'd be able to intervene right away. This time, he'd call the police. Nya couldn't let herself think through that possibility in too much detail, but she took comfort in knowing that Curtis was out there in the dark all the same.

She padded down the hallway, taking slow careful steps so the old floorboards wouldn't creak beneath the carpet. Then she eased open the basement door.

The smell of mildew and dust met her as she crossed the threshold and took a first tentative step onto the stairs. The light Sid was holding—a flashlight? His phone?— was flickering a little as he held it out in front of him.

Nya took two more steps down, finally able to see the basement floor at the bottom of the landing. As her eyes adjusted, the shadows came into sharper focus. Exposed pipes ran along the ceiling. The concrete floor was cracked, bare where Rick had pulled up the carpet and never replaced it. The walls were coated with that same thick, uneven paint as the upstairs. But what caught her eye were the piles of stuff that began at the bottom of the stairs.

Electronics, skis, a lamp. Some of it looked like junk, but some of it looked like it was worth a good amount of money.

She took another step down.

One of the boards on the unfinished stairs let out a groan.

Shit.

The shadowy figure standing in the sea of boxes swung his light—she could see it was his phone now—to the top of the stairs, where Nya stood frozen.

She squinted in the bright light but didn't retreat.

He slowly lowered the phone to his side and stepped out from behind the nearest pile of boxes.

For once, he was wearing both pants and a T-shirt—ratty and oversized with an image of some band. He looked at her like he'd been caught with his hand in the cookie jar. In the exaggerated shadows of the phone flashlight he held, his features twisted from shock to dismay to anger.

"I told you not to come down here," he muttered, moving one hand behind his back. The shadows shifted, and he set something down behind him on a precariously balanced pile of boxes.

Nya's mind went blank. Sid took a step toward her, and she imagined him lunging for her, grabbing her foot, and pulling her down the stairs.

He'd say it was an accident.

She had to do what she came here to do before he came any closer.

"I know you're selling your cousin's stuff," she blurted out.

He swung the phone flashlight toward Nya, blinding her again for a few seconds. She blinked and retreated a step, back up the stairs.

Then, without warning, he charged.

A box tumbled to the floor beside him with a hollow thunk as he leapt forward. Most of the stuff in the basement was pushed up against the walls. The remaining objects Sid had been sorting through in piles created something of a haphazard obstacle course that he neatly maneuvered as he rushed toward her.

Nya considered screaming. Instead, she raised her voice and called, "And I have a video. I can prove it."

He stopped walking, the phone flashlight in his hand sending rays of light bobbing erratically around the room. "You little bitch."

To Nya's surprise, his words didn't send her running the rest of the way up the stairs. She stayed where she was and held up her own phone, so he could see the proof she held in her hand: a still frame from Arlo's video. "I'm not going to send it to your cousin," she said, proud that her voice wasn't shaking this time.

Sid stayed where he was on the basement floor, studying her. He was breathing heavily, like he'd just finished a run. Was he so angry he could barely breathe? Or was he that messed up from the drugs he was using?

It didn't matter. How he reacted to what she was going to say next mattered.

She balled her hands into fists by her side and watched him carefully for any sign he was going to charge her again. "I won't tell Rick—as long as you leave me alone."

He made a low, growling sound.

"I want to be crystal clear about what I mean. Do *not* come into my room. Do *not* touch my things. Do *not* touch my door-knob. Do *not* touch my food."

He started to protest. "I haven't—"

She held up her hand. "Shut up. I'm not finished. If anything happens to me—like what happened to Arlo—that video still gets sent to your cousin. And the police."

The second she said the name *Arlo*, the look on Sid's face shifted to pure hatred. "How the fuck do you know about Arlo?" he spat. "That guy is a piece of shit." He cocked his head to the side and gestured to the walls of boxes and stacked items in the basement. "He's the one who had the idea for stealing some of this stuff in the first place. I just went along with it ..."

She stared him down while he babbled on about how Arlo was the real mastermind. While he spoke, he scratched his neck so hard that dark dots of blood appeared beneath his fingernails.

Nya shook her head in disbelief. Everything Curtis had told her was true. This confirmed it. "Well, you're the one in the video," she said calmly. "And you should know I'm not the only one with a copy. I sent it to my friend for safekeeping. She's in Indianapolis. If she doesn't hear from me every single morning, she'll send that video to Rick and call the police," she lied. It was better if Sid thought the other person involved in this wasn't living in the neighborhood. Who knows what he'd do if he found out Curtis lived just a few streets away.

Sid shook his head in disgust. "Seriously? You are the most paranoid bitch I've ever met." He made a sort of laughing, hacking sound. "And I told you I didn't drink your stupid milk. I have better things to do than snoop around in your bedroom—"

"Like, snoop around down here?" she clapped back.

The muscles in his jaw twitched. He lifted a hand to scratch at the welted skin near his neck again, his eyes like glassy black marbles rolling back and forth while he studied her.

Nya clenched her teeth, waiting for his move. Would he back off, or would he charge again? And if he charged, could she get out of the house fast enough?

He shuffled his feet, still standing at the bottom of the stairs. "Whatever. I'll stay out of your way, you stay out of mine. Fucking roommates," he mumbled.

"I'm still not finished," Nya said, gathering her courage. Maybe he genuinely didn't remember drinking her milk. Maybe his drug use had something to do with the memory lapse. Maybe they even drove him to the late-night prowling. Opioids, weed, and a whole host of other drugs caused sleep disturbances and memory lapses when taken in high doses.

"No more drugs," she insisted, feeling like a total killjoy.

His eyes widened in disbelief. "The fucking nerve—"

"I'll be out of here in four months. Then you can get as high as you want."

He sighed like she was asking him to give up one of his limbs. Then his shoulders drooped and he kicked at a box. "Fine," he muttered.

Surprised he'd actually given in, she pressed a little further. "And you have to wear clothes when you're not in your bedroom," she added quickly, scooting back to the top of the stairs away from him. "All your clothes. Not just the underwear."

He rolled his eyes. "Whatever. Fuck you." But there was no venom in it.

She'd won.

Her phone pinged, and she glanced at the screen in her hand. It was Curtis: *You ok?*

She needed to let him know she was okay, and quickly. Otherwise, he'd be bursting through the front door she'd left unlocked any minute. The plan had worked so far. There was no need to poke the bear anymore tonight.

Without bothering to respond to Sid, she turned on her heel and ran the rest of the way up the stairs. She slammed the door shut behind her. Then she marched down the hall to the kitchen, retrieved one of the rickety chairs around the card table, locked her bedroom door, and propped the chair up underneath the knob.

She still wasn't sure how Sid had unlocked her door, let alone bypassed the dresser. The wooden dresser wasn't particularly heavy, but it wasn't light either. How long had it taken him to push that blocked door open, inch by inch, without sending the dresser toppling to the ground with a crash?

However he'd done it, she wasn't taking any chances tonight. He seemed to take her threat seriously, but would he follow through on the not-getting-high part? That was TBD.

Her phone pinged again. Another message from Curtis.

I'm getting worried. Text me?

A smile tugged at her lips. The idea that he was out there in the middle of the night, watching over her, was comforting. Like he was some lanky guardian angel. She quickly texted him back. *Yes, all good. It worked. Thank you.*

Text me in the morning? he replied.

Definitely, she wrote back. *Night.*

Nya moved to the window and stood on her tiptoes to look past the air-conditioning unit. She lifted her hand in a tentative wave. He should be able to see her waving in the dim orange light of the bedroom, even if she couldn't see him. Then she clicked the air conditioner on, wishing she could just open the window a crack to let in the cool night air. The bulky body of the A/C unit had been wedged into the opening, filling it completely. The wood molding surrounding the window frame was cracked at one corner, straining to accommodate it.

The unit rumbled to life, sending a blast of cool air into the stagnant room. Nya looked at her nearly dead phone, cringing when she saw the time.

Just a few more hours until she had to be awake for classes.

She needed to spend those hours asleep. Not lying awake terrified, waiting to hear footsteps coming from the shadows.

Still, she pulled up the video Curtis had sent her to re-watch it. She let the whole thing play through twice, her stomach curdling each time Sid flashed that slimy smile to the woman buying the stolen coat. Out of curiosity, she hit the three little dots at the bottom of the video to see the metadata. June tenth, two-thirty p.m. Right in the middle of summer semester. The incident with Arlo had happened just two months before she'd moved in.

Where was Arlo now?

Still too wired to sleep, Nya typed Arlo's name into a Google search.

The first result that popped up promised to reveal his phone number and address and other juicy details for just twenty dollars. Nya rolled her eyes and kept scrolling. No social media presence she could find. Nothing in the news about the assault.

Arlo was a ghost.

If she had his birthday she could search for him in the Idaho repository, but she didn't know how she'd get that information.

Nya finally let out a shaky sigh and closed the web browser. She'd done everything she could to put Sid on notice. And if, God forbid, something happened to her tonight, Curtis would come through for her. At the very least, someone would know that Sid had done something awful.

Her body wouldn't stay hidden in the basement for long.

She plugged in her phone and set the pepper spray next to the *alebrije* on the dresser. Then she flicked off the light and pulled the scripture quilt tight around her body, not bothering to brush her teeth or even get undressed.

Now I lay me down to sleep ...

The words her mother had made her recite so many times came unbidden to her mind. She pushed them out, squeezing her eyes shut. But not before the line that had secretly terrified her as a child slipped through.

And if I die before I wake ...

22

Shakira's lyrics filtered into Nya's dreams, playing all the way through the chorus before she managed to blink her eyes open and realize that her alarm was going off.

She'd been dreaming. Which meant she'd actually been sleeping.

Bright curls of sun shone through the windowpane above the A/C unit, bathing the upper half of the little room in light.

A wave of excitement and relief cut through the fuzzy edges of sleep still trying to coax her to stay in bed. She'd made it through the night. Four hours of uninterrupted sleep. It wasn't much, but it was more than she'd had in days.

Nya sat up and stretched, listening to the birds chirp outside the window. The air conditioner was silent, having clicked itself off sometime during the night as usual. The shadows her hands made danced across the still-locked door with the chair propped underneath the handle, like she'd left it.

But she'd gotten sleep.

Sid hadn't tried—or succeeded—at breaking into her room last night.

Which meant Curtis's plan had worked.

Her first class was near the edge of campus. Fifteen minutes to walk, without rushing. She'd have plenty of time to shower and eat breakfast before she left this morning. The warm water would feel so good on her skin, washing away the grime and the stress-sweat from yesterday. Just what she needed.

This time, she locked the bathroom door, keeping one ear trained for any sound that indicated Sid had broken their tenuous agreement.

But there was nothing.

Even the vibe in the room felt different. Safer, somehow.

Nya turned the knob all the way to the right, not caring whether she used up all the hot water, and stood in the stream until the mirror steamed up and her skin turned pink. The shampoo and conditioner she'd brought with her from Clearwater wasn't fancy, but it smelled incredible. Like green apples. She rinsed out her hair, watching the bubbles slip between her toes then down the drain.

Before she hopped out of the shower, she spun the knob all the way to cold and stood in the bracing water for a few seconds. It was a trick she'd learned her freshman year with Jade, when she had a six-a.m. class. Extra hot, followed by extra cold woke you up even more effectively than coffee.

Shivering, she toweled off and put on one of her last remaining clean T-shirts and a lightweight blue maxi skirt that swished when she walked and always drew compliments. Another Good-will score. Then she applied a little mascara, dabbed on some lip gloss, and twisted her hair into a bun that would give her curls for tomorrow when it dried.

She studied herself in the mirror and tried on a smile.

Her freckles stood out more starkly than usual, sprinkled cinnamon on her pale skin. She looked worn down, like she'd just gone through the wringer with the flu. The makeup and shower definitely helped, though. So did the promise of a full night's sleep tonight, and the flicker of hope that maybe she'd make it through this semester alive after all.

After gathering her things for the day, she eased the folding chair out from under the doorknob, careful not to make a sound. Sid's door was closed. The house was dark and quiet.

Nya's stomach growled, reminding her of the Wheaties and milk within reach in the kitchen. She hesitated, not eager to spend any more time inside the house than she absolutely had to. But she needed to eat, and the cereal sounded good.

Besides, this was her house, too. For the semester, at least. She'd stood her ground last night and claimed her space. If she was going to get through the entire semester living here, that was the kind of energy she had to bring every day. *Take that, buttercup,* she thought with a smile this time. Then she poured herself a big helping of Wheaties and milk and stirred up a cup of instant coffee. When she put the milk back into the refrigerator, she used a pencil from her backpack to draw a line across the jug to mark the level.

She waited until she'd closed the front door behind her and picked her way across the mulberry gore on the walkway before she sent a quick text to Curtis.

Still alive. Got a few hours of sleep.

It wasn't even seven o'clock yet, so she wasn't expecting a reply. However, as she started walking down the road toward campus, her phone pinged.

Happy to hear that. Have a great day.

She grinned, drawing in a big breath of morning air and letting herself savor the sun warming her skin.

Thumbing through her texts from the night before, she saw the fib she'd sent Jade about studying with a lab partner. A pang of guilt twisted uncomfortably in her stomach. She wanted to tell

Jade the whole story about Curtis and the late-night picnic, what he'd revealed to her about the rental house—*the Gore Shack*—and how she'd stood up to Sid last night and finally got some sleep.

But she couldn't. Not yet. Jade would be frantic with worry about the major details that Nya had kept back. She'd also be hurt that Nya had lied to her.

She'd tell Jade everything in Indianapolis at the end of the semester. For now, she just wanted to feel good. To feel proud of herself. To turn over a new leaf. To get the semester back on track.

She knew Jade would already be at work, but she dialed her number anyway and smiled when she got Jade's new voicemail recording.

Sorry I can't come to the phone right now. I'm either causing trouble or sticking somebody with a needle. Maybe both. Hasta pronto!

Nya laughed into the phone. "Are you that bad at drawing blood? Hey, I know you're at work, I just wanted to say hi on my way to classes." She hesitated, trying to remember how much she'd told Jade about Sid. Enough to worry her, but not enough to send her into panic mode. "Things are good here," she said slowly. "The roommate situation is under control. He's a total douche, but I can handle him." She smiled, finally believing it. "I also met somebody. I mean, not *somebody*. Just a friend. He's no Jade Estrada, but he's really nice. And he shared a really, really good peanut butter and jelly sandwich with me at the library." She giggled, knowing that when Jade got this message she'd blow up Nya's phone with requests for more details. "Anyway, this voicemail is already too long. Hope you have a good day at work. I love you. I miss you."

When she hung up, she saw that another text from Curtis had come through:

Late night picnic + walk you home tonight?

Her smile widened. *Definitely.*

* * *

Nya's first class was a lab for Advanced Human Anatomy. To her relief, the readings she'd found online to compensate for the missing textbook had given her plenty of preparation for this morning's lab. "Suck it, Professor Stern," she muttered under her breath.

She peered through the eyepiece of the microscope, struck by the intricate network of blood vessels and lymphatic channels in the slice of live, diseased spleen. It was strangely beautiful. The healthy red blood vessels, bright bobbing balloons, swarmed the damaged sections where the blood vessels turned dark and sickly, breaking them down as fast as the disease corroded them.

While she observed, she kept one ear tuned to the lecture Professor Stern was giving. "The spleen doesn't get a lot of credit, but it's a vital organ. It traps bacteria and other foreign bodies, produces white blood cells, and fights infection. While it's true that life without a spleen is possible, thanks to modern medicine, it's far from ideal. A flu bug that might put you out of commission for a few days is a matter of life or death to someone who's had their spleen removed."

Nya sat back and let her lab partner observe the tissue sample, turning her gaze to the enlarged still frame on the screen at the front of the class. Professor Stern continued. "See that white pulp there? Around the arterioles? That's where the magic happens to keep the immune system running. Over here, you can see the splenic sinusoids, which recycle old red blood cells and recycle the iron for fresh cells."

Nya jotted down notes, feeling the same thrill of excitement that she always did when she was in class. The information was overwhelming, but it made her feel alive. Like her brain was lighting up in a way it never had a chance to back in Clearwater. She knew what her parents would see when they looked at this tiny slide of diseased spleen: A crass, bloody bit of flesh, separate from the miracle of life God had so artfully created. What was the point in studying it, or in leaning on the "learning of man" when faith was the answer, and God would provide? Modern medicine was a "graven image, an idol before God."

"The prayer of faith shall save the sick, and the Lord shall raise him up." Her mother had quoted the verse in the book of James when Nya was in middle school and her fever reached one-hundred and five.

Nya wasn't sure what she believed anymore when it came to God and faith and all of that. But she did know that when she peered into the intricacies of the human body, it was the closest she'd ever come to seeing a miracle.

* * *

There was no time for a lunch or dinner break, even if Nya had the spare cash to grab something in the food court. The day passed in a blur of lectures, labs, and study sessions between classes to scan the readings.

When her last class ended at six, she made her way to the library to start on the homework that had piled up. Her stomach rumbled loudly as soon as she sat down at the computer—the same one she'd sat at yesterday when Curtis came up to her. He hadn't texted again, but she assumed he'd find her here when he was finished with classes for the day.

She ignored the protests from her stomach and dove into the readings and homework for the day, letting herself get lost in the new things she was learning and sleuthing out the right images and diagrams to replace the Advanced Human Anatomy textbook.

The hours ticked by, and when the first announcement came that the library would be closing in half an hour, Curtis was still nowhere to be seen. She tapped her phone again to see if he'd texted. There were at least ten texts from Jade, asking for all the details about Curtis, but nothing from Curtis himself.

She typed out a quick text to Jade, promising to call soon. Then she packed up her notebook and got ready to leave. She'd managed to finish almost all of her homework, and the rest could wait until tomorrow.

When she looked up from her backpack, she saw a familiar lanky frame standing next to her computer. His big blue eyes crinkled into a smile when she startled. "Sorry to scare you. And sorry it's so late. I was studying down in Periodicals."

When she raised an eyebrow he added, "Ground floor. I was hoping I'd find you here, but I knew you'd distract me if I came up any earlier." His cheeks flushed red and he hurried to keep talking. "You still up for a picnic?" He gestured to the bulging backpack slung over one arm.

Nya felt her cheeks redden, too. She'd distract him? The thought sent a little thrill down her spine. She still wasn't sure how deep her feelings for Curtis ran. All of this was uncharted territory, given that she'd never had a boyfriend. But he made her feel safe and wanted—and fed. And she needed all of those things so much right now.

Her stomach piped up with an enthusiastic growl. Nya clamped an arm around her waist and laughed. "Obviously, yes."

Curtis smiled. "I promise it'll be worth the wait. My room-mate got some incredible stuff last night. Come on." He nodded toward the exit. "Let's go. And I want to hear more about what happened with Sid Vicious."

When Nya gave him a quizzical look, he laughed and said, "Lead singer for the Sex Pistols? Another music reference. Sorry."

Nya shook her head with a wry smile. "I definitely wasn't allowed to listen to anything by bands called 'The Sex Pistols' growing up." She left out the part that she'd never even listened to the radio until she met the Estradas, who kept the radio station on either Rumba 100.3 or 80's 104.3 nearly all the time. She had a better appreciation for Shakira, Cristian Castro, and Maná than any current American pop star. Nya didn't want to talk about her stilted upbringing right now, though. She just wanted to enjoy the rest of the night with him.

He took her hand and led her through the library and into the warm night air. Her body felt nearly as exhausted as it had the day before, but everything else was different about tonight. The late-summer evening felt more magical than sinister now, and she was dying to know what was in Curtis's bag.

Crickets chirped from the immaculately landscaped campus flowerbeds, and the air smelled like freshly cut grass. Nya breathed in and threaded her fingers through Curtis's as they walked, feeling brazen and brave. This was what college was supposed to feel like.

Tonight, Curtis didn't stop at the bench outside the library. Instead, he led her toward a hilly spot next to the engineering building, where a streetlamp shone on the grass like a spotlight. He took off his jacket and lay it on the grass, then motioned for her to sit beside him.

She smiled and sat down next to him, close enough that his arm brushed against hers. She studied him more closely while he unzipped the black Jansport and pulled out a full, wrinkly paper bag. She couldn't tell whether she was falling harder for him or the food. Both, maybe? It was still new.

All she knew right now was that this picnic, under the velvet summer sky, was one of the best moments she'd had in months.

23

Nya's eyes widened when Curtis pulled out a full container of potato salad, a greasy plastic clamshell filled with cold fried chicken, and even a half-smashed sleeve of mini donuts. She clapped her hands in delight. They were the same ones Mrs. Estrada had once bought for her and Jade as an after-school treat. Her mouth watered when she imagined tucking into the powdery white rings that sent a puff of sugar to the top of your mouth with each bite. "Are you serious right now? Your roommate gives you this stuff like, all the time?"

She looked up to see him shrug with a smile. "Yeah. Honestly, it's a lot of food and I hate to see it go to waste. I'm glad to have someone to share it with now." His voice dipped low, like he was letting her in on a secret.

She snuck a glance at the expired-by date on the side of the potato salad container as she opened the lid and took one of the plastic spoons he'd handed her. Just one day past its best-by date. As far as Nya was concerned, that barely even counted as expired. "Thank you for sharing," she said, her heart bursting with gratitude. "This looks even better than Chicken Chick."

It was a minor exaggeration. The swanky bistro on the south side of campus catered to the students whose parents set them up in the posh apartments that had hot tubs and covered parking. Nya herself had never eaten there for obvious reasons, but the scent of sizzling fried chicken sandwiches carried all across campus when the breeze was right.

While they ate, she gave him a play-by-play of exactly how everything had happened with Sid the night before. The standoff on the stairs. How she'd insisted he stay clean until she moved out. How she hadn't woken up a single time all night. "I still can't believe it worked," she said gleefully.

She expected him to break into a grin that matched hers, or maybe offer a high-five. Instead, he nodded seriously and took another bite of chicken. A little crumb stuck to his upper lip. "I'm glad," he said. "Just, don't let down your guard, okay? It took me so long to fall asleep last night. I was worried about you."

A rush of warmth filled her chest, cooled slightly by a chaser of guilt. She felt bad that he was worried, but the idea that he'd been thinking about her long after he left her at the Gore Shack made her feel indescribably happy.

"I won't," she promised. "I think I really put him in his place, though." She shuddered, remembering those button-black eyes looking back at her in disbelief from the dark basement. "He was down there, rummaging through stuff, when I came home." She shook her head. "At least he was wearing pants this time."

Curtis narrowed his eyes. "What a piece of shit."

Nya nodded and reached for a donut, relishing the feel of the powdered sugar on her fingertips. "Yeah. It looked like maybe he was sorting some of the stuff into piles."

Curtis chewed for a moment without responding, his expression a mix of disgust and annoyance.

"Enough about Sid, though. And enough about me," Nya said. "I'm pretty sure you got my entire life story last night. Tell me about you."

His eyes widened a little, enough that his piercing blue irises were momentarily ringed by a flash of white. It was like nobody had ever asked him this question before. Especially not a girl. He came across as the type of guy who had been teased in high school—maybe for his gangly legs, maybe for braces—and still thought of himself as the odd one out. Nya understood that feeling well, and it made her want to boost his confidence a little. It was the least she could do.

He laughed nervously. "Um ... I'm from out east."

She cocked her head and looked at him curiously. "Like, New York?"

"No." He laughed, a throaty warble that made his Adam's apple bob up and down. "Eastern Idaho. Shelley, but nobody knows where that is."

She'd heard the name, but Idaho was chock-full of tiny rural towns. "Tell me more," she prodded.

He looked away. "Shelley was ... well, Shelley. It wasn't the easiest place to grow up. My mom packed up and left the day after I turned thirteen. And my dad's mean streak turned into ... a mean chasm, I guess?"

He tried for a halfhearted smile, and Nya pursed her lips to keep the pity-frown contained. Most of the time, pity felt worse than hardship itself.

"I mean, I get it," he said. "He worked construction in Rexburg. Shitty jobs, shitty pay, and just a useless teenage kid to come home to." He stared off into the darkness beyond the street-lamp.

"I'm sorry," she breathed, unable to keep from saying something. "And I bet you were a cute kid."

His face reddened. He shrugged off her comment and continued. "Thanks, but you didn't see me in high school. Anyway, that was a long time ago. He never calls. Last time I tried him a couple years ago, I got a 'this number has been disconnected' message." Curtis laughed sadly, a softer warble this time. "I actually thought I would impress my dad when I told him I was studying construction management. Follow in his footsteps, I guess. I think his exact words were, 'Good luck with that.'"

Nya winced. *Ouch.*

He shot her a quick glance. "I don't usually tell people that. Especially girls I just met ... but after what you told me about your family last night, I just thought ... you'd get it."

She nodded to show him that she most definitely did. What he'd just told her was incredibly sad, but it made her feel closer to him. She'd never met anybody who understood what it was like to be rejected by your own family. "Did you stick with construction management?" she asked.

He shrugged. "Yeah. It got me through college sooner than any other major. Less artsy-fartsy electives."

"When do you graduate?"

He played with a piece of fabric that was coming loose at the hem of his shirt—a dingy gray crew neck that was too big for him. "End of this semester."

"Me too," she exclaimed. "God, I can't even think about my student loans without feeling sick." The bite of donut she'd just swallowed stuck in her throat even as she said the words.

He smiled sadly. "Yeah, same."

They ate in silence for a few minutes, polishing off the rest of the donuts and the chicken. When Curtis had tucked the wrappers back into the wrinkled paper sack, he sighed and lay down in the grass. "Let's not think about student loans or how deeply we've disappointed our parents, though. Look at those stars."

She laughed and scooted over so that she could lay her head next to his on the jacket. He was right. If you didn't snatch these pockets of happiness for yourself once in a while, what was the point?

Even with the lights glaring from campus, the stars popped like diamonds on velvet. A hint of the Milky Way was visible tonight, a wisp of smoky white. She closed her eyes, letting the little green after-image dance along her eyelids while she breathed in the warm air. "Will you text me in the morning?" Nya whispered. It was getting late. Time to walk back to the rental house and find out whether the fragile ceasefire with Sid would hold.

She felt his fingers, skinny and calloused, awkwardly lace with hers.

Nya ignored the subtle twist in her gut that warned she was headed into uncharted territory with Curtis.

So what if she was?

She tried to convince herself that all of this was simply new. After all, she'd never really had a boyfriend before.

Still, she couldn't help thinking of the summer she turned sixteen. The summer her mom made her clean up the church building with Brother and Sister Conde every Wednesday evening. The Condes' son, Joseph, was two years older than Nya and could rattle off all the Scripture Mastery verses. It was no secret he was looking for someone to court. Someone to cook his dinners and stand behind him in a high-necked dress.

Nya had dutifully dusted the baseboards next to thin-lipped Joseph, doing her best to make a good impression. But the feeling Nya got every time her eyes met his was the same feeling she had now with Curtis.

No, thank you.

Her mom had tried to tell her that was just the feeling a boy gave you. That she'd get used to it. Learn to like it, even.

In the end—and to Nya's relief—Joseph married someone else.

Nya pushed the mildly icky feelings to the same place she shoved the anxious churn about her student loans. Curtis was sweet and cute, and he clearly adored her.

All that really mattered right now was that she was safe, full, and happy for a glimmering moment.

They lay there on the grass, murmuring about the stars and enjoying the night sky for a few minutes longer before Nya sighed and sat up, then peeked at her phone. Ten-thirty already. More missed texts from Jade, demanding details about Curtis. And way past time to get some sleep.

Curtis sat up next to her on cue, still holding her hand.

"Thanks for tonight," she said, standing up before he could think about kissing her.

Nya had kissed boys before. Two, to be exact. Both of them friends of Jade, her freshman year. However, the feeling of danger that accompanied physical affection ran deep. Blood of the Lamb forbade any sort of intimacy before marriage—including kissing.

He smiled shyly. "Maybe this can be our thing. You know, a tradition?"

She flashed him a wide smile. "I'd really like that."

* * *

Like he had the night before, Curtis waited in the shadows at the edge of the mulberry tree while Nya picked her way along the walkway toward the porch.

The broken white lattice rattled softly in the breeze, like a mouth full of chattering teeth. The dark, sticky mulberry smears staining the concrete gave off a sickly sweet smell that now felt synonymous with the rental house itself.

Which square of walkway had Arlo crawled to, gasping for breath and so badly injured he needed an ambulance? Sid had left him for dead. If it hadn't been for the student passing by who called the police, he might have actually died.

Nya glanced back at Curtis, trying to make out his shape through the gnarled branches of the mulberry. It was almost impossible to tell where the tree ended and Curtis began through the tangle of black branches. She stopped walking and scanned the pockets of moonlight until she saw him shift on his feet, revealing a flash of his nose in profile.

She drew in a breath and kept moving toward the front door, wondering if the sick churning in her stomach would go away by the end of the semester, or if she'd have to brace herself every single night to walk through her front door. The thought was incredibly depressing. *Suck it up,* she chided herself, trying to remember the way she'd felt standing up to Sid last night. She just had to stand her ground. She had the upper hand now.

When she turned her key in the lock, the sound of muffled drum beats rose up to meet her. Her heartbeat sped up in time with the steady, quiet *bomps.* She cocked her head to the side. The rhythm sounded less erratic than it had before. And maybe she was imagining it, but the house didn't smell quite so skunky and musty, either. Did that mean he was sober right now? She hoped so.

The house was dark, the only faint light coming from beneath Sid's door. The basement door was shut tight tonight. This was good.

Nya padded down the hall and slipped inside her bedroom, shutting the door and locking it behind her. The drumbeats continued their steady pulse, hypnotic and unending. Either Sid hadn't heard her come into the house, or he didn't care.

Either way was fine by Nya.

She flipped on the light and scanned the bedroom, looking for any sign that Sid had been in here while she was at classes.

The colorful little *alebrije* horse still faced her, its pert blue head trained on the door.

One drawer on the dresser was open a crack: her underwear drawer. Nya frowned. Had she left it that way? She couldn't remember.

She opened the drawer all the way and studied the contents: mostly old, high-waisted beige with broken elastic that her mother had insisted on buying. Nya always suspected that it was her parents' insurance against their daughter sneaking around with boys in high school. As if she'd ever even held someone's hand back then. A few delicate, lacy wisps of fabric stood out from the sea of dingy beige: a multipack of Maidenforms she'd splurged on with Jade her sophomore year. In the dim light, the slips of lace looked like delicate butterflies stuck in shapeless lumps of bread dough.

There was no way Sid—or anybody else—would touch the ugly beige underwear. It was ridiculous to think of them as *panties*. She counted the Maidenforms, including the pair she'd tossed into her dirty clothes bag in the corner. *One, two, three, four, five.*

All accounted for.

The soft drumbeats continued as she pushed the dresser in front of the door, turned off the lights, and stripped down to her underwear and T-shirt. Without the A/C unit on, the room was dead silent—except for the sound of that damn drum.

She dug her toes into the shaggy carpet and listened, wondering how long it had been since anyone had vacuumed in here. She hadn't even seen a vacuum yet. Maybe she'd look tomorrow.

The house groaned, and a soft thump came from somewhere beyond the doorway.

Nya held her breath. Was Sid exiting his room?

She sighed and hit the button on the air conditioner. Even if Sid left her alone for the rest of the semester, she'd be jumping at the sound of every little bump and noise—which meant no sleep. A little white noise was the best option for her to get some rest. If Sid wanted to get in badly enough, he would. It was a terrifying thought, but so was staying up all night with her ears pricked for every footstep.

The A/C roared to life, drowning out the sound of the drumbeats and sending a whoosh of mercifully cool air into the stuffy bedroom.

Nya got into bed and pulled the scripture quilt tight around her body, pretending that the soft squares were pieces of brightly-colored T-shirts, lovingly saved since the time she was a little girl. Jen McDonald's mom had done that in the ninth grade. Jen told the class all about it after winter break. Nya had listened in awe. She didn't even own a T-shirt. What would it be like to have so many T-shirts you had enough for a whole quilt?

When Nya mentioned Jen's quilt to her mother after school that day, her mom asked lots of questions. A few weeks later, the soft, folded scripture quilt appeared on her bed out of nowhere. Not a Christmas present. Gifts were a distraction from the sacred meaning of the holiday, of course. Just a surprise. Nya thanked her mom again and again, but she couldn't stop pretending that the lettered quotes from Ecclesiastes and Romans were worn jersey-T-shirts emblazoned with logos like GAP and Old Navy.

Nya closed her eyes tight and focused on the loud hum and the rhythmic whoosh of the air through the crooked vents.

As she tried to fall asleep, she thought about the T-shirt quilt she'd make herself one day. It would be a riot of color, filled with cartoon characters and name brands. Each square chosen and loved to pieces over the years.

It was a silly thought. What kind of grown-up slept with a T-shirt quilt? But imagining sewing those colored squares, one by one, was just the thing to make her tight jaw fall slack and tip her into sleep.

24

Nya woke just once in the night. To her surprise, the air conditioner was still running.

When she checked the display on her phone, she realized why: It was only twelve-thirty.

A soft *thud* came from somewhere nearby. The hallway? The basement? It was impossible to tell.

She blinked the sleep from her eyes and peered into the darkness, trying not to let her heartbeat speed out of control and wake her up all the way. Every house had noises. Especially old, gross ones like this one. Anyway, if Sid *was* up and about, he wasn't breaking the ground rules she'd set for him. He was allowed to walk around the house whenever he liked, even if it was creepy and weird.

Just stay six feet back, she thought sleepily. *Like the pepper spray says.*

When she squinted, she could barely make out the shape of the dresser across the room. She'd pushed it tight against the door again, this time tipped at an angle so there was no way to nudge the barricade without toppling it.

The dresser was still pressed tight against the door.

Another soft *thump,* barely audible this time.

She reached beneath her pillow to touch the canister of pepper spray she'd tucked within close reach. Still there, too.

Scritch.

The sound changed, turning to a quiet, methodical scratching. This time, she was sure it was coming from beneath her. In the basement. Sid had probably waited until she fell asleep to sneak down there and finish whatever he'd been doing last night. Most likely sorting out which of his cousin's valuables he could get the most money for.

For some reason, this thought comforted Nya more than the idea of Sid pacing in the hallway. She didn't actually care that he was stealing his cousin Rick's stuff. He could sell off every single hoarded treasure down there as long as he stayed away from her.

The scratching sound continued, melding with the rattle of the air conditioner.

She got out of bed and hit the power button on the air conditioner twice, restarting its cycle. It seemed to run for about four hours before it went silent. The white noise would almost last until morning now.

* * *

Nya's eyelids fluttered open at the sound of a door slamming shut, then footsteps clomping on the porch.

It was morning, but early enough that her seven-a.m. alarm hadn't gone off yet. Pinholes of sunlight prickled through the tiny spaces in the air-conditioning unit, which sat silent and sagging in the window frame.

The footsteps hurried away. Was Sid actually leaving the house? She knew a handful of his dirty secrets, but none of the boring stuff. Like, whether he was a student, working a job, or one of those aimless graduates who hung around college towns long after they'd earned their degree. He had to be doing something other than selling off his cousin's stuff. Rent wasn't much, but it wasn't nothing, either.

Curiosity getting the better of her, Nya stood on the creaky mattress and peered out the narrow strip of glass visible between the top of the window frame and the A/C unit. There, picking his way across the mulberry-strewn sidewalk, was Sid.

He had actually gotten dressed today. She recognized the shirt he was wearing as the same one from his Facebook profile photo: a retro-looking collared shirt with a brown-and-white houndstooth pattern. He looked almost presentable, aside from the stupid flip-flops. Her eyes moved to the drum set he carried under one arm: a long, tall cylinder she'd glimpsed the first day she set eyes on him. The drum itself was painted with red-and-green geometric shapes in a pattern that looked like gaudy wrapping paper. Sid supported it with both hands protectively, like he was carrying a loud, ugly baby.

Sid looked both ways and hurried across the street, away from campus. Maybe he was headed to his drum circle.

Nya hesitated. Part of her wanted to take a few minutes to poke around the rental house without Sid's presence looming. But the idea of going down into the basement alone gave her the creeps. So, curiosity about where he was going got the better of her. She got back in bed, pulled the scripture quilt around herself, and typed the name *Sidney Holcomb* into Google.

Dozens of search results popped up. She scanned them, looking for anything related to the fight with Arlo or other criminal activity. To her disappointment, there were no arrest records under his name. When she found him in the Idaho Repository, there were only a few dusty traffic violations. Then again, there wouldn't be an arrest record if the police felt there wasn't enough evidence against Sid, like Curtis had said.

A search of the campus directory revealed that he wasn't a current student at BSU. Based on the way he was hustling down the street toward Julia Davis Park—a good twenty-minute walk—he probably didn't have a car.

Her stomach rumbled and she sat up in bed, anxious to take advantage of the moments alone in the house. For the first time since she'd arrived, she had the place all to herself. She could take her time eating breakfast and getting ready, without wondering when she'd feel those beady black eyes on the back of her neck.

Nya was about to close the phone when she saw a Facebook group in the search results: Boise Heartbeats Drum Circle. Sid's name appeared in the preview text under the link.

Nya clicked on it and scanned the photo, which showed the lit-up band shell at Julia Davis Park. A few people sat in a circle on stage, poised around colorful drums. None looked like Sid. She leaned in closer: There he was, at the edges of the darkness with that same red-and-green drum he'd been carrying under his arm this morning. His hair was shorter, and not nearly as greasy. He was wearing a V-neck T-shirt, and his skin was clear. No sign of the rash.

She navigated to the group's description.

Boise Heartbeats is a freeform group for soulful seekers. We welcome all to join us every Thursday and Saturday morning (seven a.m.) at the Gene Davis band stage, to greet the day with music and soulful seeking. Let's find joy and rhythm together and lift each other up! Good vibes only. Weather permitting.
Boise Heartbeats.

Nya rolled her eyes. If you replaced *joy and rhythm* with *God*—and deleted the part about "good vibes"—you'd have the welcome message for Blood of the Lamb, printed on the program each Sunday.

She took a screenshot of the information on the page, planning to make the most of the time he was out of the house every week.

* * *

Nya was relieved to find the line she'd drawn on the milk exactly where she'd left it.

There were a few smears of something brown on the card table, and a smattering of fresh crumbs on the countertop, but other than that the kitchen was still in decent shape. She took her time drinking her instant coffee and enjoying her bowl of cereal.

Her eyes kept going back to the basement door, closed at the end of the dark hallway. She'd considered taking photos of Rick's belongings down there, as extra proof of any missing items in the event. But the idea of walking down the creaky steps into the lead-filled basement was unappealing to say the least. What if Sid forgot something at home and suddenly returned to find her down there, trapped like a rat? Or what if the basement door closed and locked behind her? It was the type of thing that happened in every horror movie she'd seen—the ones Jade had introduced her to throughout college. You never went into the basement alone. And if you did, the door *always* locked behind you.

The mental images sent a fast shudder down her spine. As long as Sid kept his promise to stay away from her—and stay clean—it didn't really matter what he did with Rick's storage in the basement. She wasn't here to play detective. She was here to get through the semester alive.

Anyway, she needed to get to class soon.

As she tipped a handful of crumbs into the garbage can next to the counter, she saw the corner of something white at the bottom of the nearly empty sack.

Nya gingerly reached down to pick up the handful of dirty napkins piled on top of it. Beneath the napkins, she found several crumpled white envelopes.

More letters. Sid had tossed them right into the trash.

Glancing over her shoulder, she picked up the letters and flipped through them.

More random, unfamiliar names. And, at the bottom, another letter to Arlo marked *urgent*.

The cereal and milk she'd just eaten threatened to rise in her throat.

She stared at the name on the envelope, *Arlo C. Hunter*, imagining the astronomical numbers inside the letter growing higher and higher as the bill sat in collections. It would ruin his credit if he didn't start making payments soon. Surely he had family or friends who might be able to help. If he couldn't, the hospital might be willing to forgive part of the debt. She'd learned that tip freshman year, from her janitorial coworker, Angie, who had to go to the ER after she slipped on a patch of ice in the early morning and hit the back of her head hard on the cement.

Nya was the one who drove Angie to the hospital, white-knuckling the still-dark snowy streets in the Honda and demanding the girl keep talking, despite the paper towels wrapped nearly all the way around her head to contain the blood.

It was the first time Nya had actually been inside a hospital. At first, the waiting room filled with sick kids, a woman vomiting into a wastebasket, and a man with an enormous open gash on his thigh made her queasy. But as she sat with Angie in the corner, Angie's lolling head resting on her shoulder while they waited to be admitted, she saw something else.

The intake staff and the nurses bustling in and out were un-flappable. They gently guided the obstinate man with the leg wound into a wheelchair and through the double doors, ignoring the swear words he spat at them. They brought a fresh trash can for the woman who couldn't seem to stop vomiting. They tapped at their computers, admitting a nonstop trickle of more damaged bodies, and directing traffic in the waiting room. They did it all with a compassionate, practiced, no-nonsense patience.

Nya watched in awe until Angie was admitted. The antiseptic smell that made Angie wrinkle her nose made Nya relax a little. This was a place where you could get help if something really bad happened. This was a place where people who knew what they were doing took charge. There were no flowery oils or magic remedies or priests who told you to pray harder. Just beeping machines, sharp minds, science, and medicine.

Angie had to get a CT scan to rule out swelling and skull fractures. All in all, her total for the visit was more than two-thousand dollars—even with her parents' insurance. As soon as the bill arrived, she'd called the hospital and sent over her parents' financial statements.

The hospital had forgiven all but one-hundred dollars. There was an angel grant set aside for people who really needed it, they said.

Nya unzipped her backpack pocket, where she'd tucked the first letter to Arlo. As she slipped the second alongside it, she hesitated.

Do unto others as you would have them do unto you.

She hated that the voice sounded like her dad's as he read them Bible verse after Bible verse in the morning before school, but she believed the sentiment.

If she were in Arlo's shoes, what would she want someone to do for her?

The answer was pretty simple: Get those letters to their rightful owner. It was the least she could do. How was she going to find him, though? Putting them back in the mail on campus with "Not at this address" wouldn't help much if the post office didn't have a forwarding address. According to Curtis, he had gone completely off the radar. Not responding to text messages. Not returning to classes.

Was it possible there was more information inside the letter that she might be able to use to get in touch with him? Maybe an emergency contact or phone number along with his records? She could start Googling whatever info she uncovered, and maybe the breadcrumbs would lead to Arlo.

She took both letters out and sat down at the card table, drumming her fingers on the smooth plastic surface.

It was illegal to open someone else's mail. She knew that. It was also illegal to throw it away—which Sid had done. But surely opening the letters, with the goal of finding their rightful owner, was better than letting them languish at the bottom of a trash can?

Nya glanced at her phone. She still had a few minutes until she needed to leave for class.

Before she could talk herself out of it, she sliced through the end of the first letter with a butter knife.

25

Nya clutched the letter so tightly that her fingerprints left little divots in the paper while she read, scanning for any information she could use to find Arlo Hunter.

The first page was a letter from the collections department. Her stomach clenched as she read it. It was worse than she'd thought. Much worse.

Dear Mr. Hunter,

Our records indicate that you have an outstanding balance of $20,400.76 for the medical services received during your recent hospitalization at St. Alphonsus Hospital. Despite our previous attempts to contact you regarding this matter, we have not yet received payment for these services.

We understand that medical bills can be overwhelming, and we are here to assist you in any way we can. Please note that payment options are available to you, including payment plans and financial assistance programs. We urge you to contact our billing department at (888) 555-5678 to discuss these options and find a solution.

Please be advised that failure to pay this outstanding balance or contact our billing department to arrange payment may result in further collection efforts, including legal action. A timely response will help avoid any such measures.

Thank you for your attention to this matter. We appreciate your prompt payment and look forward to hearing from you soon.

Sincerely,
St. Alphonsus Hospital Billing Department

Holy shit. Twenty-thousand dollars. Legal action. She had to get Arlo these letters.

The second page was a form with patient information and a patient summary. This was what she needed.

She scanned the details, looking for anything she could use to find him on Google or the Idaho Repository. Date of birth, address—the rental house—and phone number. Curtis had told her that Arlo went off the radar, but it was still a solid starting place.

The phone number was a 986 area code. Where was that? She snapped a photo of the letter, intending to start searching for Arlo online when she finished classes for the day.

The hospital admission date was June first. The discharge date, June fifth. She shuddered. He'd had to stay in the hospital five entire days after what Sid had done to him. That explained the astronomical medical bill.

Something about that admission date—June first—stuck in her mind. It felt wrong. But why? What did the date he'd been admitted to the hospital matter?

She kept scanning through the long list of line-item expenses. Pathology, operating room services, imaging fees, CT scan, IV, each one a new blow.

Her eyes finally landed on the procedure summary.

Splenectomy performed June 1, 2019 under general anes-thesia by Dr. Jane McNamara. Laparoscopic surgery con-ducted through a 5-mm incision on patient's abdomen. Addi-tional incisions for surgical instruments. Surgical site closed using sutures and adhesive strips.

A splenectomy. He'd had his spleen removed. Professor Stern's lecture, the one she'd just listened to in her lab, flashed to the front of her memory. It wasn't the worst place he could have gotten injured. You could live without a spleen, but you could die from a rupture if you didn't get medical attention quickly. If those students hadn't found Arlo and called for help when they did, the injury could have easily been fatal.

She glanced at her phone. If she didn't leave the house now, she was going to be late for class. But surely between the phone number and date of birth, she could track Arlo down.

Her phone pinged in her backpack the second she shut the front door behind her and started toward campus.

It was Curtis.

On for tonight?

Her heart swelled. As awful as she'd felt two days ago, she never could have guessed that she'd be walking to class in the sunshine with a smile on her lips right now. Yet here she was. She had a friend—maybe even a boyfriend—and dinner. And she was going to help Arlo.

See you at the library, she typed back.

* * *

"The library will be closing in one hour," the robotic female voice announced.

Nya sighed and finished scanning her last reading.

Time to switch gears and find Arlo.

She spent the next thirty minutes Googling different combinations of Arlo's name, birthday, and phone number with little luck so far. She had found a few things, though.

For one thing, 986 was an area code from Bingham County in Idaho. That was a surprise. While most of the state, including Clearwater, used the 208 area code, some counties apparently had unique codes.

Otherwise, the phone number was a dead end. She'd even tried calling it, unsure exactly what she'd say if he answered— and got a disconnected message right away. If this had been his phone number, it wasn't anymore.

She found a record of Arlo in the Idaho Repository—the same place she'd found Sid. There wasn't much information there either. Just what she already knew: That he was from Bingham County. No driving violations. However, there was an intriguing entry stating, *Removal of Child.*

She tried clicking on the entry for more information, but because the entry involved a minor, it was sealed. When she Googled the phrase, the article that popped up first in search made her stomach clench when she read the preview text.

Removal of a child from the home for placement in foster care is child welfare's most severe intervention. This measure should be a last resort rather than the first. While often necessary, removal can have severe physical, legal, and emotional consequences. This traumatic experience can traumatize a child in lasting ways, even in instances of emotional or physical abuse. While many thousands of children enter foster care each year, most of these children are ultimately returned to the same home from which they were removed.

The words hit like a brick. Arlo had been removed from his home when he was little. This particular trauma had nothing to do with Sid. At least, she didn't think it did. It was still awful, though. No matter how much she wished her own childhood had been different, her parents had at least drawn the line at spanking. They'd never done anything awful enough to prompt people with badges to show up and lead her away from her own home. She could only imagine the kind of environment that would make Idaho CPS step in and remove a child.

Poor Arlo.

She sighed and checked the time, realizing she must have gotten so engrossed in the search that she'd missed the library's final closing announcement. It was nearly ten. Time to go.

She logged out of the computer and was just tucking Arlo's collection letter back into her backpack when she glanced up to see Curtis walking toward her. His eyes lit up, and he smiled when he saw her. *Hey,* he mouthed, lifting a hand.

Today, he was wearing worn jeans and a fitted blue T-shirt that made his eyes look pool-blue. He wasn't a muscular guy. If anything, he was skinny, but the T-shirt fit just right on his shoulders.

He really was cute, Nya observed with a smile. Jade would definitely approve. She loved the unassuming guys. The quiet, sweet ones. Anyone who smelled like "bro culture" was a hard pass for her.

Curtis held up a familiar brown bag. She was starting to think that maybe it was the same brown bag she'd seen the last two nights. It was so wrinkled that it had taken on almost a fabric-like texture, and she could see a spot of grease from the chicken they'd eaten last night.

She zipped her backpack and stood to meet him with a smile.

To her surprise, he scooped her into a hug.

A blush crept onto her cheeks. A couple of lingering students closing down the library gave her an annoyed look and went back to their last-minute studies. Nya wrapped her arms around Curtis and hugged him back. So what if people stared?

He didn't give her butterflies like she'd always hoped her first boyfriend would. But it was so nice to be held.

Her stomach gurgled. It was also nice to be fed.

He led her to the same spot they'd picnicked the night before and laid out a spread of cling-wrapped hoagies, mandarin orange cups, pasta salad, and chocolate chip cookies.

"Is this okay?" he asked when he saw the way Nya was staring at the food. "I know the lettuce on the hoagies is kind of … subpar."

She laughed and reached for one of the cookies. "Are you kidding? A few days ago I was worried I might starve … Now I'm worried I might have to get new clothes if I eat like this every night."

His forehead creased, like what she'd just said pained him. She'd meant it to come out lighthearted, but the look in his eyes told her she'd miscalculated.

Heat rose in her cheeks, and she hoped he couldn't tell she was beet-red under the soft spot lights illuminating the hilly slope. "I'm fine. Really. Everybody lives on ramen and cheap food in college, right?"

He shrugged. "Sort of. But most of them do it so they can splurge on drinks and pizza on the weekends. There's a difference between being a *poor college kid* and a *poor kid at college*."

Nya nodded. He understood. Of course he did. In so many ways, he understood her better than anyone ever had.

He looked away, a blush spreading across his cheeks, too. "If it wasn't for my roommate's grocery-store connection, I'd be in the same boat. I get it." He finally met her gaze. "I don't think we should be embarrassed about it, though. I ... I think you're incredible."

He reached for her hand, and the bite of cookie she'd swallowed flip-flopped in her stomach.

When she didn't pull away from his hand, he scooted closer, until his face was just inches away from hers.

Nya held her breath. Did she want him to kiss her?

She slapped the thought down hard. Of course she did. He was incredibly sweet. What more could she want?

"I really like you," he said softly.

She pushed away the violent butterflies in her stomach and nodded, heart beating hard as she wondered when he was going to close the gap between their lips and kiss her.

He leaned in, and Nya shut her eyes tight until she felt his lips on hers.

A little chapped. A little too eager. Otherwise, not bad.

She pressed her lips against his, trying to get lost in the moment. After a few seconds, she pulled back and smiled at him. Baby steps.

He grinned back at her with such undisguised joy that she leaned in to peck him on the lips one more time before she pulled away from him. "I like you too," she said, scooting back a little to reach for a hoagie. She held it up to him like a glass of champagne. "To poor kids."

His smile widened, making deep crow's feet appear next to his big blue eyes. He grabbed the second hoagie and touched it to hers. "To poor kids."

Nya happily unwrapped the sandwich and took a bite. He was right—the lettuce was dry and wilted, the texture of tissue paper. The rest of the sandwich was still plenty fresh, though. "Speaking of poor kids," she said as soon as she swallowed. "I—I opened Arlo's mail."

Curtis's smile disappeared and he winced as he swallowed.

"To find him," Nya clarified quickly. "I wasn't snooping. I know it's illegal to open somebody else's mail, but I feel so bad for him—and I hate the idea of collections sending him these awful bills that just keep getting bigger and bigger. This could wreck his credit forever. And maybe he doesn't know he could get the bill forgiven... " She knew she was rambling. And to her horror, tears pricked the corners of her eyes. She felt a kinship with Arlo. She really did want to help him. Before she could wipe them away, one escaped and rolled down her cheek, splashing onto the bread of the hoagie. "My old coworker got her hospital bills forgiven. I bet Arlo could do the same."

Curtis's expression softened. "Did you find him?" he asked gently, his gaze locked with hers.

"No," she admitted. "I thought I'd find him on Google ... but it was all dead ends. I tried the phone number on the bill, but it's disconnected."

He frowned. "Do you have the letters with you?"

Nya nodded and unzipped her backpack. "They're here."

He was silent while he scanned both letters. "Yeah, doesn't look like there's that much useful info in here." He tilted his head and shrugged. "I can give them to my buddy from class if you want. He seems to know Arlo a little. Maybe he can sleuth out a new phone number for him."

"Thanks," Nya said gratefully, even though she felt a little pinprick of disappointment. She'd been secretly hoping that when —or if—she found Arlo, she could talk to him about what had happened that day with Sid. She suspected there was even more to the story than what Curtis knew.

Still, the point was to find Arlo and get him his mail. That would have to be enough.

When they were finished eating, Curtis zipped the letters into his black Jansport and then lay back on the slope, patting the spot next to him on the grass.

Full and content, Nya curled up next to him and closed her eyes, wishing she could just fall asleep here.

While she rested her head on his chest, listening to his heartbeat, she imagined herself as Curtis's girlfriend. Pooling their money and getting an apartment together instead of trudging back to the horrible rental house in the dark. Introducing him to Jade on speakerphone. Maybe even inviting him to Indianapolis for Christmas when she'd finally secured her diploma at the end of the semester.

The fantasy had some holes in it. For one thing, she was pretty sure Jade would question the depth of her feelings for Curtis. Was she really falling for him, or had he simply appeared in her life when she desperately needed a shoulder to lean on—and a picnic to look forward to? Jade was Team Nya all day long, but she had a way of reading Nya—and everyone else—like a book.

Nya squeezed her eyes shut and dismissed the unsettling thoughts that were ruining her fantasy. Between studying and her evenings with Curtis, she'd barely talked to Jade lately. Anyway, the end of the semester was still months away. She had plenty of time to figure out her feelings for Curtis. As for her living situation, she'd keep taking things one day, and one picnic, at a time.

26

By the time midterms hit, Nya had settled into a routine that, if not completely comfortable, was at least survivable.

And after that first hellish week, *survivable* was a dream come true.

On most days, she managed to outright avoid Sid, leaving the house before he was even awake and getting home late enough that he'd shut himself into his bedroom for the night. A few times, she returned home to find the light on in the basement. She didn't confront him about what he was doing down there again, though. Whatever Sid wanted to do was his business, as long he kept that six-foot distance between them. For the past eight weeks, he'd kept up his end of the bargain. No more rattling doorknobs. No more late-night visits. Plus, the line on the milk carton was always exactly where she'd marked it.

There were still the occasional bumps in the night—moments where she woke up panicked and breathless, sure that he was right outside her bedroom door. Once, she was nearly certain he'd been in her room again by the musty, body-odor smell when she got home for the night and walked inside her bedroom. A pair of her underwear had mysteriously gone missing. One of the pretty ones, not the beige granny panties. It had happened after a trip to the laundromat, though, so there was every possibility it had gotten trapped in the washer. Nothing overt. Nothing she could prove.

There were just eight weeks left in the semester. Eight weeks until she'd earned her diploma. Eight weeks until she could leave the awful rental house with its broken-teeth lattice, bloody mulberry stains, and rattling air conditioner. It was all she could do not to make a paper chain and count down the days.

Curtis had asked her to be his girlfriend, and she'd said yes. It was one more thing she was keeping a secret from Jade. She told herself it was because she and Jade had barely had a chance to talk on the phone after that first whirlwind week. Between Nya's late-night picnics with Curtis and the time difference, they mostly kept in touch by text.

It was more than that, though. Curtis was a decent kisser, and the nightly picnics he provided after they closed down the library were usually the highlight of Nya's day. He found her every day without fail in the library, even weekends, and produced a surprisingly diverse spread of food from that same crumpled brown sack each time. It meant she'd been able to skip grocery shopping pretty much all semester, except to buy more Wheaties and milk. But the truth was, Nya suspected their relationship might only last until the end of the semester.

No matter how hard she tried to force it, the chemistry wasn't growing on her end. Not the way it clearly was for Curtis, anyway. When they were lying on the grass, holding hands and staring at the stars, she could convince herself that he was more than just a fling. Whenever he pulled her into a kiss, though, she could never quite lose herself in the moment. Once, when the kiss continued for longer than a few seconds, she'd opened her eyes a tiny bit to see him staring back at her with an intensity that made the food they'd just eaten roll in her stomach.

Nya still hadn't invited him inside the rental house she shared with Sid. Curtis hadn't invited her to his place, either. He was still couch-surfing in a one-room basement apartment with the benefactor of their nightly picnics. He'd hinted at the idea of renting an apartment together when the semester ended. Nya didn't have the heart to tell him that she'd already purchased her Greyhound ticket to Indianapolis for the last day of finals—using the money she'd saved on food.

She wasn't sure when she'd pull the plug. He'd always been sweet with her—if anything, he was overly attentive—but something about the intensity in those blue eyes made her nervous to find out what he was like when he got upset.

Thursdays and Saturdays were the best days. They were the only days Sid hustled out the door bright and early to spend a couple of hours at the drum circle in Julia Davis Park. She set her alarm earlier than usual those days so she could maximize every moment with him out of the house, enjoying her coffee and taking a long shower without his presence tainting it.

Nya had also started checking the mail compulsively, keeping watch for more letters addressed to Arlo. For all she knew, Sid had been throwing them away for months. Curtis said he'd given the letters to his buddy. The last time she'd asked about it, he said that his friend had managed to make contact with Arlo to deliver the letters. Nya hoped that was the reason there weren't any more collections letters in the mail. Maybe Arlo had gotten in touch with the hospital about his bill. Maybe they'd even forgiven the debt, and Arlo was finding his way in the world, just like she was. She hoped so. That thought made her happy.

One day, a letter addressed to Sidney Holcomb in chicken-scratch handwriting had appeared in the mailbox. The letter had a return address of Riggins, Idaho, and the name Louisa Holcomb. Nya resisted the urge to tear it open and snoop. Sid certainly deserved it. And she was already a felon in the mail-reading department. But her curiosity wasn't worth the confrontation it would inevitably cause with Sid when he realized what she'd done.

So she'd left the letter on the card table in the kitchen.

To her delight, she'd found the wadded-up envelope and letter in the trash the following day after Sid left for his morning drum circle. Like she'd suspected, the letter was from his mom. The short note he'd wadded up implied that there had been a check in the envelope—and that it was for tuition. The rest of the note was a run-on sentence of questions. How was BSU? How soon would he be coming home for a visit? Did he have a girlfriend? Had his cousin Rick been by the rental house lately?

Nya already knew Sid wasn't going to classes at BSU. The only time he ever left the house was to bang on that drum. Which meant that he was probably using the tuition money his mom was sending him to pay rent. Or drugs. Or both. Nya tucked the crinkled letter back into the trash. His mom sounded nice. Sweet, even. It was obvious she loved her son. Why couldn't shitty kids and shitty parents get matched up a little more evenly?

* * *

When Nya walked out of the student testing center on Friday afternoon, she felt like bursting into song. She wouldn't get her grades back until next week, but she'd done so well in all of her classes that even if she completely bombed her midterms—which she wouldn't—she'd still have a respectable grade.

Way to suck it up, buttercup, she thought to herself proudly. She felt a tickle in her throat and coughed into her sleeve. Her hand went to her throat, where her fingers prodded for the lymph nodes beneath her neck. They did feel a little swollen. Maybe she was getting a cold.

She smiled as she tried to imagine the bean-shaped structures where her antigen-presenting cells and lymphocytes were gathering en masse to mount a defense against whatever virus she was trying to fight off.

"Get 'em, girls," she murmured, suppressing another cough. She really didn't have time to get sick, but the knowledge she'd gained in her anatomy classes gave her a deep appreciation for the complicated dance her immune system was doing at this very moment.

Advanced Human Anatomy had become her favorite lecture and lab. Even without the expensive book, she'd managed to find a wealth of charts and even a free interactive Human Anatomy app that had allowed her to go above and beyond Professor Stern's stringent requirements for memorizing the intricacies of the human body's organs and tissues. Her mind buzzed happily with the new information she'd learned.

In eight short weeks, she would graduate with honors and a 3.9 grade-point average. If Nya kept up her grades and graduated as planned, she'd be a shoo-in new hire at Interim Health in Indy. The semester wasn't over yet. But the weeks were flying by, and to Nya's surprise, she was actually enjoying them a little now.

It was only five-o'clock as she exited the testing center, but the October air already had a cool edge to it. The trees on campus brimmed red and yellow with a riot of colorful leaves, blazing impossibly bright in the low-hanging sun.

Nya sat down on a bench under a fiery maple and closed her eyes, breathing in the smell of barbecue coming from the nearby Student Union Building. One of the clubs on campus had set up grills to tailgate for the evening's football game, and her stomach whined at the tantalizing smell of greasy burgers and hot dogs. Maybe she should treat herself. Just this once.

As if on cue, her phone chimed the sound she'd programmed to play anytime a text from Curtis came through: A wolf whistle.

Done with midterms? Got something special for dinner tonight to celebrate you.

Nya grinned. It was like he'd read her mind—or maybe her stomach.

She texted back right away. *Yes, please! Where should I meet you?* With the fall weather turning colder at night, Nya wasn't sure where they were going to share meals. The student food court and other buildings on campus closed at eight-thirty every night, and food wasn't allowed in the library.

Meet me in the GLB.

Nya frowned. Was that a building on campus? She'd never heard of it, but when she typed the letters into her phone she realized why. It was the grounds maintenance building at the edge of campus. It appeared to be a storage facility for landscaping equipment. No classrooms. Were they allowed in there?

Shrugging, she slung her backpack and started walking. She'd only taken a few steps when her phone wolf-whistled at her again.

LMK when you get here. South entrance, gray door.

Ten minutes later, she stood in front of a squat, nondescript building. An unassuming plate-metal sign beneath a pine tree read *Gearhardt Lederman Building.* She must have walked right past it every day on her way to classes but had never paid any attention to the bland gray warehouse. On one side of the building, a long outdoor canopy sheltered a half-dozen riding lawn mowers that were locked behind a chain link fence.

A short walkway led to what appeared to be a main entrance door. Beside it, a wide stretch of blacktop flanked a rollup bay door for the main warehouse. Nya cautiously approached the bay door. Where was Curtis? There wasn't a locked gate or a fence anywhere—except the chain link surrounding the riding lawn mowers—and this was a campus building. So she wasn't trespassing, but the building didn't exactly scream a warm welcome to visitors. Unlike the rest of campus, there were no helpful signs or maps stating "You are here" or "Leading innovation, transforming lives."

When she walked around the corner of the warehouse to reach the south wall, she saw the gray door Curtis had mentioned on the side of the building.

I think I'm here? she texted him.

The text had barely popped into the conversation thread when the gray door swung open with a loud *whoosh.*

Nya startled and took a step back, but it was just Curtis.

He poked his head out the door and grinned when he saw her. His curly hair was shorter than usual, and his face looked red and blotchy like he'd just barely finished shaving. He wore the same faded flannel shirt he'd been wearing the first day she met him, only this time it was tucked into his jeans. "Hey, babe."

She laughed. "Hey yourself." Her heart beat a little faster. Was he hoping they were going to take things to the next level in here? They hadn't had sex yet, and Nya still wasn't sure she wanted to go there with him.

Her stomach twisted with nerves, but she ignored the feeling. "What is this place? Are we allowed to be here?"

He reached for her hand and smiled. "We're here, aren't we?"

27

Nya reluctantly let Curtis pull her into the cool darkness beyond the doorway. It took a moment for her eyes to adjust to the dim light. The shapes in the dark, quiet warehouse revealed themselves as lawnmowers, trimmers, and stacked bags of fertilizer.

To the left was a room that looked to be filled with painting supplies. A single fluorescent light flickered above the exit sign, illuminating rows of ladders, long-handled paint rollers, and trays.

"My buddy used to work here on the landscaping crew," Curtis explained as he led her past a workshop on the right and down a narrow dark stairway. A panel of light switches sat at the top of the stairs, but he didn't bother flicking any of them on. "The building technically closes at five, but the doors don't auto-lock until six. Figured it would be like our own little hideout for a date tonight."

When he saw the look on her face, he added, "Don't worry. The doors still open from the inside."

Nya nodded. If the doors weren't locked yet, they weren't technically breaking and entering. Her stomach tightened anyway. Would she get in trouble if someone found them here? The kind of trouble that might jeopardize her scholarship or academic standing?

She shook the worries away. The warehouse was pretty iso-lated. And anyway, the girls who lived next door to Jade and Nya sophomore year had done much worse and gotten away with it. They'd been arrested following a prank at the baseball dugout on campus. They'd broken in and decorated everything in hot pink—and a whole lot of unwrapped pink sanitary pads. It had been part of some kind of rivalry between the men's and women's baseball teams. None of the girls had lost their position on the team or been officially reprimanded. If they'd gotten away with Maxi-pad vandalism without repercussions, surely eating a picnic in an un-locked campus building wouldn't be a big deal.

Her anxiety flared when Curtis flicked on the fluorescent light at the bottom of the dark stairway. The pale yellow bulb cast stark shadows on the worn concrete walls of the basement room. It was another storage area—although from the amount of dust on the floor, this part of the building looked like it wasn't used much.

In the center of the room was a foam statue of the campus mascot: A rearing horse, missing part of its head and one leg. It looked like it was wheeling back in the final throes of agony after whatever fate had just partially decapitated it. It must have been used for some kind of promotion or event on campus, but it didn't seem likely to make public appearances any time soon.

Nya clutched Curtis's hand tighter. Were they really going to do it in here? It was so creepy. "Where are we—"

"Ta da," he said, spinning her toward the far side of the room and motioning to the pale blue blanket spread across an empty section of the dirty concrete floor.

The ball of anxiety in her stomach loosened a little. The worn blue blanket had been smoothed out and set with two large, white bags of food. She blinked when she recognized the hot-pink logo. *Chicken Chick.*

"No way," she breathed. "You got us Chicken Chick?!" She knew Curtis couldn't afford this. The swanky sandwiches cost more than fifteen dollars each, fries not included.

Curtis's cheeks flushed. "You deserve it. I figured after everything you've been dealing with this semester, you deserved a little treat." He took her hand again and led her over to the dusty blanket.

She could smell the tantalizing aroma of warm fried chicken now, along with greasy fries. "You shouldn't have," she whispered. "This is too much." But even as she said the words, she was already tearing into the first white bag with the pink logo.

Inside were not one, but two crispy chicken sandwiches wrapped in hot-pink wax paper, dotted with grease and dripping with some kind of delicious-looking sauce. Her eyes widened when she saw the enormous order of waffle fries at the bottom of the bag. She glanced at Curtis in bewilderment and watched him pull a third chicken sandwich out of his own bag, followed by a sleeve of sweet potato fries and tater tots.

She couldn't help doing a quick mental estimation of what he'd spent on this meal. At least sixty dollars, without a tip. "You didn't need to get me two sandwiches," she protested, even though she felt sure that she could pack away both of the enormous sandwiches. "This is too much. Can you really afford—"

He shook his head and shrugged, then took a big bite of the sandwich he'd unwrapped, smiling when a dribble of sauce rolled down his chin. When he was finished chewing he said, "If you can't eat both of them, take one home for lunch tomorrow. I wanted to spoil my girl."

Her cheeks reddened when he called her *my girl*. It didn't sound right, but why wouldn't he call her that? She *was* his girlfriend. Nya dismissed the thought and popped a waffle fry into her mouth, letting the perfectly crispy garlic and rosemary take center stage in her brain.

"Holy shit, this is good," she murmured, looking around for a drink. The scratchy feeling in her throat was back with a vengeance. The beleaguered lymph nodes must be losing the fight.

She held her hand up to her mouth and coughed a couple of times before popping another waffle fry into her mouth and digging into the first chicken sandwich.

When she looked up, Curtis was staring at her. "Are you getting sick?" His voice was suddenly flat. The smile in his big blue eyes was gone, replaced by a confusing mix of anger and—terror? Why was he looking at her that way?

Nya stopped chewing. "N—no," she said. "I don't think so. Just a tickle in my throat. I swallowed wrong." It wasn't true, but he looked so horrified that there was no way in hell she was going to admit she'd been wondering the same thing.

He studied her carefully with narrowed eyes, clearly waiting for her to cough again.

The room was suddenly just a dank, dark maintenance basement again instead of a secret picnic. He'd never looked at her like that before. What was going on?

She swallowed painfully and suppressed another cough.

After a few long seconds, Curtis's face relaxed and he smiled like it had never happened. He fidgeted with the wrapper of his chicken sandwich, and his cheeks reddened again. "I just ..." he paused. "I just have a job interview on Monday. I don't want to miss it."

Nya nodded. That made sense ... sort of. He hadn't mentioned the interview before now. "That's great," she said, scooting back a little so she wouldn't breathe on him. "Where's the job?"

He smiled. "AMC. Big construction company. They've got job sites all over the country ... so ... you know, they could really place me anywhere." He shot her a hopeful look, and Nya tried to smile back. He hadn't outright mentioned moving in together after graduation, but she knew it was on his mind.

She knew by the way the chicken sandwich tasted like sawdust that she didn't really want that to happen.

He was still looking at her intently, waiting for her to respond. "What do you think?" he prodded.

At least he didn't seem fixated on her potential cold virus anymore.

The unmasked hope in his impossibly large, intense blue eyes and the way he was leaning toward her on the picnic blanket he'd laid out especially for her made her stomach hurt.

She couldn't break up with him tonight. Not when he'd probably just put himself into debt to surprise her with this picnic. Not when he'd been her saving grace in helping her survive the semester with Sid.

She'd break up with him at the end of the semester. People had flings all the time. This wasn't much different.

It didn't have to be a big deal. One more night wouldn't change anything.

Suck it up, buttercup, she told herself firmly. Then she set her sandwich down on its wrapper, leaned forward to wrap her arms around his waist, and drew him into a deep kiss. Because, why not? They were already here. Besides, it felt like giving the middle-finger to Blood of the Lamb.

He kissed her back, slowly at first, then more eagerly, lying back on the thin blue blanket and pulling her down with him.

The concrete bit into her elbows as she shifted onto her side. She was okay with a makeout session, but the way he kissed her back warned her to slow things down. This was the first time they'd really been alone together in private, and the idea that he probably wanted to take things farther than a makeout session tonight made the food she'd just eaten sit like a brick in her stomach.

He snaked one hand along the hem of her T-shirt, and she tried not to hold her breath or freeze up. *This isn't a big deal,* she told herself. *Sex isn't a sin. You're twenty-one years old.* Gathering her courage, she moved her hand to the spot where his shirt was riding up past his jeans.

His skin was warm and soft. It was strange exploring someone else's stomach, someone else's skin. She hadn't told Curtis that she was still a virgin, although she suspected he knew by how slowly he'd taken everything. As she felt along his hips, her fingers met the dips and bumps of old scars and pockmarks. Acne, or something worse? She winced, remembering what he'd told her about his dad. Her anatomy brain turned on as she explored the ridges of his rib cage running prominently along his side, imagining the network of cartilage, muscle, and bones beneath his skin.

Acromion, coracoid process, glenoid cavity, costal cartilage. She relaxed a little and let her hand explore farther along his chest, keeping her eyes shut tight.

More scar tissue here. Unlike the rest, this one was puffy. Barely healed. Keloid? A contracture?

To her surprise, he was suddenly the one to tense up under her touch. His hand took hers and moved it gently but firmly to the top of his shirt.

"Sorry," she whispered, just as the tickle in her throat rose up again.

She tried to clear her throat, but it only made the scratchy feeling worse. She sat up and tucked her mouth into the crook of her elbow, turning her head away from Curtis and coughing quietly.

"Maybe I am coming down with something," she began apologetically, but Curtis was already scrambling to his feet away from her.

He flashed her a grimace and fished around for something in his pocket that made a familiar rattling sound.

"I'm sorry—" she fumbled, trying not to cough again.

He ignored her and pulled an orange prescription bottle out of his jeans pocket, removed the lid, and spilled a large white pill onto his palm. Nya frowned. Did he always have that bottle with him? Was that the rattling sound she'd heard before?

Then he tipped his head back and swallowed the pill dry.

Nya stared at him, completely baffled. "Are you … okay?"

He took a few steps away from her and grabbed his backpack from the spot he'd left it on the floor. "You *are* getting sick."

Her cheeks flushed. Why was he making such a big deal about this? "I'm sorry," she repeated. "I thought it was just a tickle in my throat earlier, but maybe you're right—"

Something dark and unreadable flashed in his eyes. The intensity of it made her scoot back on the blanket away from him. What was going on?

"I'll see you later," he said tightly, then turned and raced up the stairs, leaving her alone under the buzzing fluorescent lights in the strange little basement with the remains of their picnic.

In the distance, a door slammed, and the building went silent.

NOELLE W. IHLI

28

Nya got to her feet and stood looking up at the dark stairwell, stunned.

He'd left her—and the bags of food and the dusty blue blanket on the floor—before she could even say goodbye. What the hell?

With shaky hands, she pulled her phone out of her backpack and typed and re-typed a text message to him, apologizing for the fourth time.

In the end, she shook her head and erased the text, sat back down on the blanket, and picked up the Chicken Chick sandwich she'd only partly finished.

There was no point letting the rest of the picnic go to waste, and she wasn't quite ready to go back to the rental yet. It was still early, and she was still starving. She'd text Curtis in the morning when he'd had a chance to calm down over whatever had set him off so much.

She finished her sandwich, then polished off her own waffle fries and the sweet potato fries that Curtis had left lying on a napkin by his side of the blanket. While she ate, she sent a text to Jade.

Call me soon? It's been forever since we talked. I miss you. 45 days till Christmas.

The phone rang seconds after she sent the text.

"Girl, it's Friday night. Why aren't you on a hot date right now?" Jade demanded. "Are you still seeing Picnic Boy? Where the hell is he at?"

Nya laughed. She'd told Jade Curtis's name, but the nickname "Picnic Boy" had stuck. "Why aren't *you* on a hot date right now?"

Jade sighed. "My hot date was drinks with the other RNs after work, but they all have kids and went home after *one* glass of wine. So now I'm watching trash TV with *Abuela*. She fell asleep an hour ago."

Nya grinned. "That sounds like an amazing Friday night to me."

Jade tutted. "Okay, *loca*. But what about Picnic Boy?"

Nya looked around at the bunker-like basement and imagined the look on Jade's face if she could see her through the phone. She shrugged. "We were going to hang out, but I think I'm coming down with something. He brought me some food, though. From Chicken Chick." It was a simplified version of the evening to say the least, but Nya still wasn't ready to tell her the whole story. It belonged with the rest of the information she'd intentionally held back from Jade.

Jade gasped. "That rich-kid bistro place off campus? *Bebé,* that boy *loves* you."

Nya shrugged, remembering the way Curtis had looked at her when she coughed. "I don't know about that ..."

"He *definitely* loves you," Jade crowed. "You should bring him home for Christmas."

Home. The unexpected rush of hope and longing that accompanied the word made it hard to swallow. In some ways, Nya wasn't sure she'd ever really had a home. Shelter, sure. A bed, yes. But somewhere she belonged? Somewhere she got nostalgic for when she was away? Never.

That was what was waiting for her with Jade and the Estradas in Indy.

"I—I don't know," she admitted. "Curtis is … nice, but—"

"But what?" Jade demanded. The TV went quiet in the background, followed by the sound of couch cushions squeaking.

Nya frowned. How could she explain the relationship without getting into the full story of what happened with Sid—and the fact that she was basically using Curtis so she didn't have to buy groceries? "I just think Picnic Boy might be … more of a temporary thing. Not … anything serious. I was actually thinking about breaking up with him," she admitted.

Jade let out a sigh. "Bummer. But …" She laughed. "If I'm being totally honest, I kind of want you all to myself for a while in Indy. Forget all these nursing bitches with kids and their one glass of wine."

Nya grinned and dusted off the seat of her pants, grimy from the blanket and her brief romp with Curtis. The grounds maintenance building was too quiet—and creepy—to hang out here by herself. She'd go to bed early and hit the library first thing in the morning. She'd deal with Curtis—and the breakup—later. "I can't wait. Forty-five days."

"Forty-five days," Jade repeated. *"Te quiero,* bebé*!"*

When Jade hung up, Nya opened one of the crumpled bags with the pink Chicken Chick logo to collect her wrappers. Should she bring the blanket home with her? Did it belong to Curtis? After a moment's hesitation, she folded it up and tucked it under her arm.

When she opened the side door to the maintenance building, it was just past sunset. An automatic light on the side of the building had flickered on, illuminating a trash can.

She was about to push the bag through the opening of the trash can when she saw a narrow, white piece of paper sticking out of the flap.

The paper fluttered in the wind. It was a receipt for Chicken Chick. A piece of tape on one edge had attached it to the garbage can flap.

Curiosity getting the better of her, she peeled off the tape and scanned the receipt. How much had Curtis paid for all this meal?

Her eyes went to the number at the bottom—$63.50.

She swallowed. Ouch. It was worse than she'd thought.

She was about to toss it back into the trash can when she saw the words at the top of the receipt.

Order for: Rashelle.

Who was Rashelle? Nya frowned, letting her eyes trail down the rest of the line items. Two deluxe chicken sandwiches. An extra-large order of waffle fries. Everything that had been in her bag. But there were also two cherry milkshakes listed.

A disturbing thought made her reach an arm into the trash can and pull out the Chicken Chick bag she'd just tossed inside.

There it was, on the front of the Chicken Chick bag. A fuzzy, torn spot right above the logo. Something had been taped there, then ripped off.

Nya pursed her lips. No, not something. A receipt.

Her mind flashed back to the only time she'd stepped foot in the swanky restaurant. A shelf of pick-up orders stood next to the soda fountain. Rows of pink-and-white bags with receipts and names taped to the front.

The staff didn't really scrutinize the revolving cast of students coming and going to grab their orders from the wall.

Not unless someone complained that their order was missing.

She felt slightly ill. Curtis hadn't splurged on this order.

Rashelle had, whoever she was.

Curtis had stolen it.

29

Nya wrapped the threadbare, dusty blanket around herself while she walked home in the dark. The air had a bite to it, but it wasn't the only reason she was shivering.

Curtis stole that food.

The words ran through her mind like bad, repetitive lyrics accompanying the erratic drumbeat of her footsteps.

All around her, off-campus house windows were lit up. It was a Friday night, after all. Some revealed cozy living rooms adorned with fairy lights that someone had lovingly strung. Others showed glimpses of kitchens bustling with games of flip-cup. An Uber driver carrying an impossible number of pizzas hurried to one doorstep and was met by cheers when he set down the food on the porch. Snatches of laughter and music carried through the night, following her while she walked toward the older neighborhoods, where the houses were quieter and most of the windows were shut tight with curtains.

It was impossible not to feel alone.

Just an hour ago, she'd been bursting with optimism over her midterms, the surprise dinner Curtis had arranged, and the fact that she'd made it halfway through the semester.

Now, Nya swallowed a painful lump in her throat. It felt raw and scratchy, as much from whatever virus she was fighting off as the fact that she was trying to hold back tears.

She wouldn't cry, though.

She was so close to successfully finishing the semester. A stolen bag of Chicken Chick food, a breakup with someone she didn't like that much anyway, and an oncoming cold didn't change that.

The idea of breaking up with Curtis was starting to feel more pressing. Yeah, she'd have to go back to granola bars and a growling stomach. But the reasons she couldn't in good conscience keep dating him were growing.

She wasn't angry at him about the stolen food. If anything, she understood on a deep level what it was to deal with the indignity of giving up the basics—let alone the extras—again and again. It was demoralizing. He'd just wanted to give her something nice. Something besides day-old food from the grocery store.

He'd lied to her, though. And the more she thought about his reaction to her getting sick, the more she knew deep in her gut that she couldn't drag this relationship out until the end of the semester. Stolen food aside, the intense disgust that flickered in his eyes when she'd coughed had scared her a little. Who reacted like that to a *cough*?

She wrapped the blanket tighter around her shoulders while she walked. A small part of her still argued back. Was it that big a deal to keep seeing him for a few more weeks? Couldn't she just pretend she didn't know about the stolen food? Maybe his intense, strange reaction to her getting sick could be explained by germophobia or that job interview he'd mentioned.

But deep down, Nya knew that the main reason she was still dating him after two months was the loneliness that hollowed out her chest each time she passed a blazing window and students laughing. And the inevitable growl in her stomach that would return once the leftover chicken sandwich in her backpack was gone. How could she get upset with him for lying to her about the food—when she was essentially lying about how she really felt about him?

She had to break up with him. Tomorrow, she promised herself.

Nya crossed the street toward the rental house, but she hesitated before moving any closer. There was a car out front, directly adjacent to the walkway leading to the porch, and the lights in the living room were on. Did Sid have company? The dread that always accompanied her return back to the rental house sloshed in her stomach.

Her phone pinged, and she pulled it out of her pocket, glad to delay going inside the house.

The text was from Jade, with a meme of a skeleton overlaid with the words "Patiently waiting for Christmas like ..."

The tears Nya had been holding back suddenly brimmed over and spilled down her cheeks.

"Same," she texted back along with a long string of heart emojis.

She *wasn't* alone in the world.

She had a home—and it wasn't the ugly, dilapidated monstrosity looming in front of her right now. Her home—and her heart—were with Jade and the Estradas.

And she'd be there soon.

"Forty-five days," she whispered to herself, unwrapping the blanket from around her shoulders and picking her way along the walkway to the front door of the Gore Shack. The mulberry tree had finally stopped throwing the disgusting, juicy berries down onto the concrete. All that remained were the dark, desiccated husks of the old fruit and a mess of smears that would probably stain the sidewalk until next year's crop of fruit fell down.

By then, Nya would be long gone.

She reached the door and put in her key, careful not to let her arm touch the enormous tangle of cobwebs hanging low from the dim porch light.

She hesitated. There were voices coming from inside the house.

30

As far as Nya knew, Sid had never invited anyone over. The house wasn't exactly an inviting place. Although now that the kitchen was presentable, maybe he'd changed his mind. She leaned on the door to listen more closely.

A sudden yank from the other side of the door made her lose her balance and tumble over the threshold as the door swung open, bathing the porch in warm orange light.

Nya stumbled into the entryway with a yelp. She managed to catch herself with her hands on the dirty linoleum next to Sid's gross flip-flops, then whipped her head up, blinking.

Sid hovered above her, side by side with a man she'd never seen before. He looked to be in his mid-fifties. Skinny, with a thick head of carrot hair and a strange little goatee. When he frowned down at Nya—the shape of his mouth identical to the scowl Sid wore—she finally saw the resemblance between the two men.

This must be the cousin—and landlord. Rick.

Sid reluctantly held out a hand to Nya. His face was calm, but his eyes were wild with panic and a simmering rage. She ignored him and scrambled to her feet without taking his hand. The last thing she wanted to do was touch his skin. She didn't even want to walk around the house in socks for fear of contracting the mysterious rash on his neck and body. If anything, it had gotten worse over the past few weeks. He was wearing his usual gray sweatpants that looked even dingier paired with a popped-collar polo shirt that mostly obscured the blistering skin on his body. Still, hints of the angry, mucousy red bubbles peeked out over the collar of his shirt, refusing to be hidden completely.

It wasn't just his skin anymore, either. His eyes had turned yellowish where they were supposed to be white, sinking into his skull like the air had been let out of them. His breathing had a raspy, labored sound to it now, too. Like he'd just run up a long flight of stairs even when he was standing still.

He really needed to go to the doctor.

"This is Rick," Sid said with a tight-lipped grimace, indicating the skinny man with red hair. Sid kept his beady, sunken eyes locked on Nya's while he talked. *Don't say a fucking word,* his gaze insisted.

Rick didn't offer his hand to Nya. His lips twisted slightly in disgust when he met her gaze, like she was the one who had a wicked full-body rash. Then he glanced at Sid and cleared his throat. "I was just on my way out."

"Oh, okay." Nya's face burned red. She got the distinct feeling the two men had been talking about her—and that it wasn't a flattering conversation. What had Sid said to their landlord? Was he trying to paint her as a bad tenant so Rick wouldn't trust her if she turned him in over the stolen storage items? Had Rick been in the basement to check on his stuff? Even if he had, with the amount of clutter down there, it would be pretty difficult to identify anything missing unless someone really combed through everything and took inventory.

"Sid told me he didn't take a deposit for the sublease," Rick said suddenly, turning to scrutinize Nya, then flicking his eyes back to Sid. He had a strangely formal, clipped way of talking. Like his tight grimace didn't give him the leeway to fully form the words coming out of his mouth. "But he let me know that you're behind on rent."

Nya's mouth flew open. *Pay me in cash,* Sid had told her when she'd asked about the rent when she moved in.

Her blood boiled.

He was clearly pocketing the rent money she'd carefully counted and placed in an envelope with his name on it, then left on the empty kitchen table. She'd done it twice now—including two days ago—and each time the envelope had been gone by the time she'd returned home from studying.

Rick kept going. "I know this isn't the Ritz Carlton, but this isn't a homeless shelter either—"

"I paid him cash in an envelope," Nya blurted out, the shame of what he'd just accused her of smacking her like ice water even though it wasn't true. "Both months. I left it on the table with his name on it." She gestured to the kitchen, where a half-empty pizza box lay open on the card table. A mostly empty cup of ranch lay tipped on its side, dripping down onto the floor.

Rick studied Nya, then shifted his eyes to Sid, who was trying to hide the fact that he was itching the skin beneath his T-shirt. "Why would you pay him cash? The rental agreement specifically states that you need to send *me* a check every month."

Nya blinked. She was sure that the agreement Sid had given her said absolutely nothing about Rick. She'd read it twice, to make sure she wouldn't have to pay anything other than what she was budgeting for rent.

"No, I swear—"

Rick and Sid exchanged a look that made the feeling of shame sloshing in Nya's stomach roil again. Was Sid running a rental scam on top of everything else?

Sid cleared his throat and shrugged. "I haven't seen any envelopes," he insisted.

To her shock, he held her gaze when he said it, like he actually believed what he was saying. Why wouldn't he have said something before now, though?

Along with that sheen of panic, his eyes were still filled with unmasked hatred.

His sunken, yellow eyes warned her to keep her mouth shut —or else.

She fished her phone out of her pocket, ready to pull up the informal rental agreement Sid had emailed her—and the video Arlo had taken. Rick would have to believe her then.

Sid took a subtle step toward her, drawing himself up to his full height. His ghoulish appearance made him look even more terrifying.

He was clearly warning her.

You break your end of the bargain, I break mine.

She wanted to scream at him that he'd already broken his end of the bargain by stealing her rent money, but she bit her tongue. The actual deal was that if he left her alone, she wouldn't nark on him about the basement. These new developments technically weren't part of their agreement.

How was she going to make up those two months of rent if Sid didn't give it back, though? Tears burned behind her eyes. The situation was infuriating—and humiliating—but was it worth jeopardizing her safety tonight by calling Sid out in front of his cousin?

No. She wouldn't let him get away with the stolen rent, of course. As soon as Rick left, she'd demand he "find it" and clear everything up. She could tell by the look in Sid's eyes that if she tried to push things any further right now, she'd be skating on thin ice.

Rick cleared his throat, breaking the silent stalemate. "Also, since you're only renting for the semester, I'm not going to be a stickler about it, but please try to respect the space while you're here. The kitchen is disgusting."

Nya bit her cheek. Apparently Sid had pinned the messy kitchen on her, too.

Piece of shit.

The kitchen wasn't exactly sparkling, but it looked like a dream compared to the state it had been when she arrived. She remembered what Curtis had told her about Arlo getting kicked out of the rental house after the fight. Sid had thrown his old roommate under the bus back then, too. Apparently, it was what he did best.

The tickle rose in her throat again, but this time she didn't bother to hold down the cough.

Rick wrinkled his nose and hurried out the door when she let loose, not bothering to cover her mouth. "Sid will inspect the place when you move out," he muttered as he slipped out the door and into the night. "I'll be expecting a check for the rent owed."

Nya couldn't help rolling her eyes. "Great," she called after Rick. "I'll try to clean up after myself a little more." She turned and gave Sid a pointed look.

Sid had the gall to flip her off just as Rick slammed the door shut.

She stared at him. "Fuck you."

He glowered back. "Fuck me? Fuck *you.* You come riding in here on your high horse, acting like I'm a bad guy while you're so sweet and innocent? And then you try to blackmail me over some total bullshit? While you're not even paying rent? I can't wait until you're out of here."

Nya balled her hands into fists, seeing red. "I *have* been paying rent," she seethed.

He had the gall to look shocked. "I never saw any envelopes."

Panic fluttered against her ribs. He was lying to her face. "Then look again," she demanded.

He stared at her, pure disgust in his eyes. He shrugged. "Fine, your funeral. If you don't pay rent, Rick will hunt you down. He's not a nice guy. Just stay the hell out of my business. You're the craziest bitch I ever met."

Just walk away, she told herself. *Don't engage. It's not worth it.* But at this point, she was too angry to back down. "I'm crazy? And your *business*?" she spat. "Is that what you call what you're doing, pretending to go to classes while you get high? The only time you even leave the house is for that stupid drum circle. This house is *disgusting. You* are disgusting. What the hell is that rash, anyway? It's getting so much worse. You look like shit."

His eyes widened with rage, and he took a step toward her.

She held her ground, too angry to back down. Between her pounding head and scratchy throat and what happened with Curtis tonight, she was already in a terrible mood. Sid had pushed her too hard, though.

When he spoke again, his voice was low and dangerous. "I haven't come near you in weeks. You're the one banging around with that stupid air conditioner and moving furniture around. You sound like a goddamn elephant tromping all over. And what I do with my time is none of your fucking business." He pulled his stringy hair over his shoulders, so it covered the red blisters on his neck. "I told you, it's eczema or something," he muttered through tight lips. "But it wasn't that bad until you showed up," he added accusingly—as if she were the one who had given him the rash.

She nearly laughed. This conversation was pointless. Nya shook her head in disgust and backed down the hall. "Find the rent I paid you. If you don't, I still have the video."

He took a step to follow her, and a prickle of fear cut through the anger. She needed to get away from him before things escalated any further. And she needed to think about what to do next.

Without looking at him again, she fled to her room and slammed the door shut.

As she sank to the floor, hating the feel of the grimy carpet beneath her, the phone in her pocket buzzed.

She saw the name on the screen before she read the text.

Curtis.

Her stomach tightened, then twisted.

Sorry about tonight. But you ARE getting sick. You should have told me. I really can't get sick. So I don't think we should see each other until you're better.

Nya gritted her teeth and dashed off a response before thinking it over.

I actually don't think we should see each other at all anymore. Sorry. Thanks for everything.

Head and heart pounding, she watched the screen for a response.

She waited one minute, then five.

When she was about to plug in the phone and go to bed, Curtis's response finally came through: *Wow.*

She stared at it, waiting for more, but that was apparently the only response he had to give. *Wow.* She could imagine him saying the word the same way Sid had said "bitch" just a few minutes earlier.

Sighing, she finally stood up and threw on a tank top. She hadn't planned to break up with Curtis over text. It was definitely a shitty thing to do.

Maybe tomorrow she'd apologize to him for the snarky tone. Thank him for everything he'd done for her this semester and wish him well.

She didn't regret breaking up with him, though. If anything, she felt relieved.

"Forty-five more days," she whispered to the little *alebrije* horse atop the dresser as she pushed the clunky piece of furniture in front of the bedroom door and locked it. "Keep me safe," she whispered like she always did.

Then she turned on the air conditioner to drown out the sounds of the monster outside the door, trying not to think about what would happen if he didn't "find" the rent she'd paid him.

Forty-five more days.

31

When Nya's eyes popped open early on Saturday morning, something felt off.

Yes, she was sick. Yes, she was exhausted despite the anxious thudding of her heart. But that wasn't it.

It was something else. What, though?

Her head pounded in time with the drumbeats thundering down the hall. Sid must be up early getting ready for his drum circle.

Nya shuddered when she thought about what had happened last night with Rick. She kept waking up during the night, imagining Sid suddenly appearing next to her bed. That mental image, plus the worsening sore throat, had her tossing and turning all night long. This morning, she felt like shit.

Her bedroom door was still shut tight, though. The little wooden horse stood at its post, watching for any sign of trouble.

She shivered and pulled the scripture quilt over her head and tried to swallow. Her throat felt like a pincushion. Her skin was feverish one second and ice-cold the next. It didn't help that the air conditioner had turned the room into an icebox overnight. That would also explain why she hadn't heard any of the rental's usual bumps and thumps.

She blinked, suddenly confused. Why was the air conditioner still on? It always clicked off during the night.

She was sure she hadn't reset the button. Yet it was still
blasting cold air into the room.

She coughed again, wishing she had someone who could
bring her some medicine.

Nya couldn't go to the store like this. Which meant she was
going to have to count on her lymph nodes to suck it up and kick
this virus to the curb so she could go back to classes on Monday.

On shaky feet, she stood and wobbled to the air conditioner.

When she turned the unit off, the drumbeats got louder. Nya
winced and looked at her phone: There was a new text from Jade
—and Curtis, too.

She forced herself to ignore them both for now, shifting her
focus to the time. It was only six-thirty a.m. Sid would be leaving
for Julia Davis Park and the drum circle soon. At least then, she'd
have the house to herself for a few hours and could get some more
sleep.

With midterms over, she was effectively in the eye of the
storm when it came to her class workload. On Monday, she'd dive
back in to prepare for finals and graduation. But this weekend, she
could finally get a little rest. No library study sessions. No readings. Her body couldn't have chosen a better time to get sick, if
there was one.

When the front door slammed shut a few minutes later and
the sound of Sid's footsteps carried along the walkway until they
disappeared altogether, her body finally released the tension she'd
been carrying all night.

Not wanting to waste another moment of precious time with
Sid out of the house, she closed her eyes and drifted back to sleep
without bothering to read her texts.

* * *

Nya awoke with a start. Her throat wasn't quite as sore, but her nose was stuffed up, and her head still hurt.

She groaned and rolled over.

What time was it? A strange, repetitive scraping sound was just audible beneath her head. It sounded like it was coming from the basement. Sid must have gotten home from his drum circle. She shuddered when she imagined him beneath her head, greedily scanning Rick's storage for what he could steal most easily.

She rolled her eyes, feeling angry all over again.

Sid was probably planning to blame her for anything that turned up missing, just like he'd done with Arlo.

Forty-four days.

Her stomach growled insistently, and she thought of the left-over chicken sandwich waiting for her in the fridge. It was only a little after eleven, but her stomach was already begging for lunch.

Careful not to make too much noise, she padded to the bedroom door and scooted the dresser aside. Then she tiptoed down the hall and opened the refrigerator.

She frowned.

The sandwich was still in there, but she was sure that the foil wrapper had been tight and uniform when she'd tucked it on the shelf the night before. Had Sid opened it?

Her stomach flipped queasily. She unwrapped the sandwich and inspected it, relieved to see that he hadn't eaten any of it. Still, the idea that he'd touched it—especially with his awful rash —was off-putting, to say the least.

She wrinkled her nose and considered tossing the chicken sandwich into the trash, but it was too delicious. Not to mention it was the only fresh food she had in the house until she went to the store. She'd been so reliant on Curtis for her nightly picnics that she'd hardly been grocery shopping since that very first week.

Sighing, she popped the sandwich into the microwave. E-coli and Salmonella could survive the radio waves, but they would kill bacteria, fungi, and viruses. She remembered learning that some hospitals actually used microwaves to disinfect certain tools.

If Sid had left any cooties on the sandwich, they'd be nuked. The thought made her feel just a little better about eating the sandwich.

When the microwave dinged, she took her plate and hurried back down the hall to her room. The last thing she needed was to run into Sid when he came up from the basement.

Just as she stepped into the hallway, the sound of a key in the front door made her freeze in her tracks.

She turned her head just in time to see Sid slam the door behind himself, that garish red-and-green drum tucked under his arm.

He gave her a murderous look. Nya turned on her heel to hurry the rest of the way to her room without even acknowledging him.

As she rushed down the hall and slipped into her bedroom, she saw that the basement door was shut tight.

She stared at it. If Sid had just gotten home, what were the noises she'd heard a few minutes ago?

She tried to remember the exact scraping sound she'd heard a few minutes earlier. Was it possible there was an animal living under the porch? It was more than possible. In fact, it would surprise her if a skunk, raccoon, or even a badger *wasn't* living under the porch behind the broken-teeth lattice. Or maybe Rick had come by the house again. She wasn't sure how long he was in town. Maybe that's what she'd heard earlier.

Nya shrugged, then settled down to read her texts while she devoured the chicken sandwich. It wasn't quite as tasty as it had been the night before, but that was at least partly due to the fact that she could barely taste anything with how stuffed up her nose was.

Jade's text was a long story about one of the residents who had proposed to another, and that the two ninety-year-olds were now busy planning a wedding. Nya smiled. She could just imagine Jade offering to decorate the whole residential care facility with streamers and balloons for the wedding.

Curtis's texts were a different story. They had come through late last night, a couple of hours after she'd sent the breakup text.

Painfully swallowing her last bite of chicken sandwich, she read the messages he'd sent, one after the other like a stream of consciousness.

Are you fucking with me?

You're seriously breaking things off?

Over text?

WHY?

Jesus.

She shook her head in disbelief as the tone abruptly changed from angry to pleading.

Can we just talk?

I'm sorry I left you like that last night.

I'm immune compromised. A cold is an emergency for me.

I'm afraid to fall asleep. My throat hurts.

Fuck, I just coughed twice. I'm definitely sick.

Please don't end things.

Nya?

Hello?

Call me????

A pang of guilt cut through her annoyance as she read his string of messages. She hadn't realized he was immune compromised. Why hadn't he said something about it before? That explained his weird reaction—and the pill he'd had handy. If he had a severely compromised immune system, he might carry a stash of antibiotics with him. The phrase "pill in pocket" drifted to the front of her brain. She'd heard it in some lecture.

He'd sent the last text at around one a.m. She grimaced as she looked at the time now: It was noon. He must think she was full-on ignoring him. The twinge of guilt grew. Was he okay? She'd feel awful if he got seriously ill because of her.

Her finger hovered over the keyboard on her phone, but the pounding in her head was back in full force. It was worse than it had been earlier.

Her brain suddenly felt fuzzy. All she wanted to do was sleep. She'd text him back when she woke up again, but she wasn't changing her mind. They were not getting back together.

Her eyelids felt so heavy. She knew she should push the dresser back in front of the locked door, but she could barely manage to pull the quilt over her body, her arms felt so leaden. This must be one doozy of a cold. The idea of getting up and walking across the room suddenly felt impossible.

The little horse had toppled over at some point. From where she lay on the bed, she could just see its three matchstick legs sticking up.

Nya giggled to herself. The *alebrije* was taking a nap, too.

It would keep her safe while she slept, even if it was lying on its side.

Everything would be fine.

Daylight streamed through the tiny cracks in the air-conditioning vent.

It was the last thing she saw before she closed her eyes, and it comforted her.

Everyone knew that bad things only happened in the dark.

32

The sound came again: A soft, metallic *clink* on the far side of the bedroom.

Nya tried to open her eyes, but they were too heavy.

She tried to roll over in bed, but her muscles refused to obey. Even her tongue felt like it had been glued to the roof of her mouth.

Clink, clink.

Adrenaline prickled through her veins. Her heart hammered in her chest, an impossibly fast tempo while the rest of her stayed sluggish and slow.

Why couldn't she wake up? Why couldn't she move? What time was it?

She managed to force her eyelids open, but it made no difference. She couldn't see anything. The bedroom was pitch dark.

Clink, clink.

Oh, god. She knew the sound now. It was her bedroom doorknob, jiggling back and forth.

He was trying to get into her room.

Again.

The realization moved through her murky brain like a slippery fish. Tiny white dots began to cloud her field of vision, thick as snow, no matter how much she blinked.

Had he drugged her this time?

The panic pulsed harder, pushing her to get out of bed. To run. To scream. To do *something*. But all she could do was lie there, leaden legs tangled uselessly in the sheets.

Was the dresser still pushed against the door?

No. She knew it wasn't.

Was this how she was going to die?

You should've gotten out while you had the chance, bebé, Jade's voice whispered through her thoughts, sad and solemn. *Nobody can help you now.*

Nya's heart squeezed in her chest. "Help!" The word, meant to come out as a scream, dribbled out of her mouth in a quiet splutter.

Click.

She heard the bedroom doorknob turn.

Then the door opened with a *whoosh*.

No, no, no. Oh god, no.

Oblivion was pulling her back under, no matter how hard she tried to fight it.

Her panicked thoughts skittered just out of reach.

The last thing she heard before the darkness closed in was the sound of his footsteps, moving toward her bed.

* * *

When Nya jolted awake for the second time, her mind wasn't quite as foggy. However, the fog had been replaced by a spinning tilt-a-whirl. The dark shapes in the room whipped around in her field of vision, shifting shades of black and gray, faster and faster no matter how much she tried to get them to stop. It took her a moment to realize that the room itself wasn't moving. Her eyes were lolling back and forth, like they were sloshing in her head. She couldn't seem to stop them.

For a moment, the dizzy out-of-control spinning got so bad she thought she might vomit on the bed.

Despite the frenetic motion from her rolling eyes, she couldn't move. Couldn't even fling an arm over the side of the bed to reach for her phone. Even her breathing felt slow and heavy. Her throat was on fire, but she could barely swallow. She worried that if she fell back asleep that the rise and fall of her chest might stop altogether, and she would die.

A sound from the bathroom a few feet away drew her attention. A soft footstep on the linoleum.

The air conditioner was off now, she realized. The room was dead silent—except for the footsteps.

She remembered the jiggling doorknob she'd heard when she woke up earlier. Had that been hours ago, or minutes? Was the door open? Was Sid inside the room right now?

"Help," she tried to scream, but the word only came out as a weak, pathetic croak.

She squeezed her eyes shut with all her strength, and the spinning feeling mercifully subsided.

That was when she heard the breathing.

33

Nya held her breath.

Not because she wanted to, but because she couldn't do anything else.

The haze lapped at the edges of her consciousness like the tide, threatening to draw her back into blackness.

You're going to die, bebé, Jade's voice echoed in her mind.

The footsteps tapped quietly on the bathroom linoleum until they were lost in the carpet.

The breathing got louder, like the person had just run a marathon. Or like they were excited. A raspy, wheedling in-out that got closer with each passing second.

Tiny white pinpricks swam in front of her eyes.

"No," she tried to say again.

The word dissolved into a thin line of drool on her chin. She was sure now that she wasn't just deathly ill.

She'd definitely been drugged.

The realization should have hit with a slap. Instead, it floated through her mind aimlessly, bouncing around like a balloon.

The breathing was so close now, but she still couldn't see anyone. She lay on her side, facing away from the bathroom door. He must be right behind her.

Time seemed to stretch, each moment an agonizing eternity. With each disembodied, raggedy inhale and exhale, her pulse beat harder in her ears.

The room began to spin again.

The breathing got louder.

Nya fought the spinning, the fog, acutely aware that she was completely powerless. If Sid wanted to hurt her, he could. There was nothing she could do about it.

No, no, no. The word ripped through her mind again and again, as loud as the room was silent.

She was certain he was standing right behind her now, just inches from her bed. She wanted to roll over and face him. Fight him. But all she could do was lie there, heart pounding. Her skin prickled with goosebumps as fear begged her to run.

Something—his leg?—nudged the bed ever so slightly.

Then she felt his breath, hot and shallow, on the nape of her neck.

He cleared his throat in a sticky-sounding growl.

With every ounce of strength she could summon, she tried to inch her fingers closer to the edge of the pillow, fingertips straining toward the pepper spray tucked just beneath it. Her phone was lying just out of reach on the floor, but it felt impossibly far away.

His hands were in her hair now, coiling the tangled strands together. The motion brought back a sudden, visceral memory of the many times her mom had made the same motion, brushing all the hair back flat against her head to create a tight bun for church.

For the first time in years, she wished more than anything that her mother was here.

She was alone and helpless. Utterly, completely defenseless and alone.

Panic threatened to consume her, but she forced it back. She couldn't fall apart.

His grip on her hair tightened, drawing Nya's head back on the pillow a few inches.

Her stomach churned when she felt his other hand stroke her forehead. One finger trailed down her cheek to her lips.

He made that disgusting sound in his throat again.

"Stop." This time, the word came out of her mouth fully formed, trailing off in a fit of coughing.

He yanked her hair back in response, sharp enough to hurt.

Tears leaked from her eyes, but she couldn't brush them away.

She didn't try to scream again when he sat down on the bed beside her, his weight making her body roll against him and farther away from the pepper spray.

He leaned over her, and she could feel that hot, raspy breath on her neck again.

Something brushed against her bare skin in tandem with the warm breaths on her neck.

Fabric. He was wearing some kind of mask.

Strangely, the thought comforted her. He wanted a way out if she recognized him. If she managed to break free from the grasp of whatever he'd drugged her with.

Was this what it felt like to trip on mushrooms? Was she high on whatever Sid had been hoarding in that gross plastic bag in the refrigerator?

He trailed one hand along the hem of her tank top.

More tears welled in her eyes. The terror of not knowing what he was about to do next was excruciating. She'd managed to inch her fingers back beneath the pillow. Had he noticed? If she reached just a little bit farther, she'd be able to grab the pepper spray. As long as it hadn't shifted, anyway.

From somewhere in the distance, that maddening clicking sound in the wall came to her. What the hell was that? She'd heard it so many times, it had almost become part of the background noise in the house. Almost. Part of her knew it wasn't.

The adrenaline pumping through her body made her mind work faster, cutting through the stranglehold of the haze from drugs.

His hand lingered on the elastic of her underwear, drawing a little, lazy circle over the exposed patch of skin where her tank top ended.

No. The feeling of his hands on her bare skin was too much. The surge of adrenaline was strong enough that she was able to push her hand farther under the pillow just far enough that her fingers brushed the smooth surface of the little canister.

Six feet.

Her trembling hand wrapped around the familiar shape in an awkward grasp.

It wasn't as good as a phone, but she wasn't sure she could make a call successfully right now, anyway.

Jade wasn't going to save her. Neither was Curtis. But she could save herself.

Praying she'd be able to point the nozzle in the right direction, she mustered all her strength and flung her arm backward, pressing down on the button as hard as she could.

An acrid, stinging cloud filled the air.

The weight on the bed recoiled immediately. He stood up and made a strangled, angry gurgling sound.

"Cunt," he screamed, his muffled voice filled with rage.

The sound of footsteps thudded across the room. Then there was a series of sharp bangs. What was that?

She listened hard for the sound of the doorknob jingling, but it didn't come.

She blinked, tried to see, but the pepper spray and the dark room had turned her already-foggy vision into a total void. There were more footsteps, more banging. It sounded like the heavy mirrored doors clattering together as they slid on their tracks. Like someone was pulling them open hastily. That didn't make sense, though. Was he hiding in the closet?

More footsteps, moving farther away. A soft thud.

Then silence.

Nya's eyes stung, and her throat burned more fiercely than ever as the pepper spray particles filled the room. Without the air conditioner circulating air, the stinging mist drifted slowly down on top of her.

A violent cough burst through her throat until it swelled so much that it felt like it might close off her airway completely.

It was already so hard to breathe with her nose so stuffed up and her lungs made of lead.

She strained to listen, terrified she'd hear that horrible breathing sound again.

But the room was still silent. He was gone.

She hoped she'd hit him square in the eyes with the pepper spray, and that he was fighting for breath as much as she was right now.

Except he wasn't trapped in a drug-induced haze.

The white dots reappeared in her field of vision, threatening to rip her away from consciousness.

Maybe you'll still die after all, the voice in her head said sadly.

34

Nya's eyes felt like salted slugs. Equally gritty and slimy at the same time.

Even the pale tendrils of sunlight winking through the vents in the silent window A/C unit hurt to look at.

Everything hurt. Her throat was raw. Her face was puffy and painful. Her whole body felt like it had gone through the wringer.

She was alive, though. She was still alive, tangled in her scripture quilt, with John 3:16 halfway across her face. She knew it by heart even with the fuzzy too-close words swimming in front of her bleary eyes. *For God so loved the world, that he gave his only begotten Son.*

The memories of what had happened in the dark last night came roaring back when she tried to sit up then fell back down against the bed. Her limbs were jelly.

The drugged haze.

The footsteps in the blackness.

His breath—and hands—and face against her neck.

The pepper spray she'd managed to grab hold of.

What would he have done to her if she hadn't managed to discharge the stinging spray and send the fiery mist raining down around them?

She needed water badly, but was terrified she'd pass out if she tried to stand.

She blinked away the crust in her blurry eyes and stared at the door.

It was shut tight.

She could tell by the position of the knob that it was still locked.

How the hell had he gotten inside? She didn't care right now. Last night had gone beyond creepy. She needed to call the police.

She thought of the look of hate burning in Sid's eyes during Rick's visit.

She thought of the way he'd gripped her hair tight. If she hadn't gotten a hold of that pepper spray in time …

Revulsion and fear raced through her, making the pounding in her head worse. She suddenly wished she could call Curtis. Beg him to forgive her. To come over and keep her safe until the police arrived.

She couldn't suck it up anymore. Couldn't handle the high stakes. She felt like she was teetering on the edge of a tightrope above a pool of sharks.

One misstep, and she'd fall.

How had she let things get this bad?

Nya flopped over and reached for her phone with trembling hands, scraping the carpet for the charger's short cord.

Nothing.

The phone wasn't there. Even the charger was gone.

She gasped, then coughed. Her throat burned painfully. She was sure she'd plugged the phone in last night. And she never moved the charging cord.

Sid must have taken them last night.

So she wouldn't be able to call for help.

Dread prickled through her frozen limbs. What would happen if she left the room to look for her phone? The thought filled her with despair. She wasn't sure she could even walk. Her head was still spinning, and she felt so weak.

She'd have to crawl.

She imagined a raging Sid, nursing his pepper-sprayed eyes in his bedroom across the hall.

If he'd taken her phone, he wasn't finished with her yet.

The nightmare had paused, not concluded, despite daylight turning the room a soft gray.

And the escape she thought she'd pulled off had only just begun.

35

Nya clutched the scripture quilt hard. *Don't panic.*

Panic froze you. Adrenaline fueled you. She pictured her adrenal glands working furiously while she slid out of bed and crawled a few feet.

Her arms wobbled dangerously as she moved.

She was so weak.

Breathing hard, she looked up at the little painted horse still lying on its side at the edge of the dresser, looking as pathetic as she felt.

Think, she told herself, forcing the thoughts through the murk. *Think. Try to make it out the front door or stay inside the room?*

Could she call for help through the crack between the air conditioner and the window? Surely someone would hear her.

Would they come running to help before Sid got to her, though?

She looked at the air-conditioning unit wedged tightly into the window, wishing she could move it. But there was no way. She'd tried adjusting its position once—to make it sit less crookedly in the window. Even then, it hadn't budged. Not only did it weigh a ton, but it was wedged so tightly into the window frame that the wood was splitting at the corner seams.

She stared at the bedroom door, listening hard.

Was Sid right outside in the hall, or in his bedroom?

Another coughing fit struck, and she buried her face in the quilt. If she wasn't so weak—and sick—she felt pretty sure she could outrun him. Sid wasn't exactly the paragon of health with that horrible rash and his diet of old food, beer, and drugs, but even then, he was still a man.

Men have an average of 36% more muscle mass than women.

The trivia floated to the front of Nya's brain, in Professor Stern's voice.

As disgusting as Sid was, he was stronger than she was.

The only reason she'd been able to get him away from her last night had been the pepper spray.

The pepper spray. Where was it now?

A distant memory of the canister rolling from her fingers while she gasped for air peeked through the fuzz in her head. It should still be on the bed.

But of course, it wasn't.

She pushed herself up to a sitting position and carefully looked through the quilt and the scratchy sheets. There were oily dots everywhere from the dried pepper spray residue, but the hot-pink canister was nowhere to be found.

Another wave of coughing burned through her throat. She had to get a drink of water, even if it meant making noise. Her head was pounding hard and the dizziness was back with a vengeance. Every part of her body begged for the release of sleep.

She couldn't let that happen, though. She wouldn't fall asleep again in this house if she could help it.

As quietly as she could, she crawled to the bathroom, dragged herself to standing, and turned the faucet on just a trickle, cringing at the metallic squeak and the soft burble of the water running down the drain.

She cupped the water in both hands and drank, pausing between mouthfuls to stare at the door and listen. With each passing second, she expected him to start rattling the doorknob—and then do what he'd done twice. Finagle his way inside, somehow.

Nya scooped up a final mouthful of water and turned off the tap. The water helped, and she felt just a little better.

But as she crawled back across the carpet, toward the bed, her eyes landed on the mirrored closet doors.

One of the heavy doors was open just a few inches.

The memory of what she'd heard last night, during the chaos of the pepper spray, zoomed to the front of her mind: The distinctive clatter of those closet doors. She'd wondered if Sid was hiding in there.

The mirrored doors usually slid smoothly and quietly on their tracks when you pulled them straight across. Although if they were anything like the old sliding doors in her closet back in Clearwater, they made a lot of noise if you used a rough touch.

Just like the noises she'd heard last night.

Nya tried to replay the sequence of sounds in her mind. Footsteps. Bangs. More footsteps. More bangs. A thud. Distant footsteps, then silence.

She was certain, despite the chaos, that she would have heard the bedroom door lock with a *clink.* Followed by the door opening and shutting.

Those were the sounds she'd been listening for, waiting for, so she knew he was finally out of her room.

They'd never come.

36

Help me, she demanded of her brain as she slowly sat down on the edge of the bed, staring at her own reflection in those mirrored doors.

Her eyes were wide and terrified. Her face was pale and sickly.

Her hair hung in tangles down her back. She looked defeated. Weak.

Not like a girl who was about to fight.

Without a weapon.

Without a phone.

Without a friend.

Nobody had any idea she might be in danger, since she'd cut off her only lifeline to Curtis.

Thick regret pooled in her stomach, and she was suddenly sure she was about to vomit.

She should have told Jade what was going on before now. She should have apologized to Curtis instead of giving him the cold shoulder and breaking up with him by text like a jerk.

The girl in the mirror blinked back tears, but it was no use holding them back. They rolled down her cheeks in hot rivulets. What the hell was she supposed to do now? Whether Sid was inside her closet right now or just outside the door, he had the upper hand. She could barely walk, let alone defend herself.

Suck it up, buttercup.

The words came back to her with a bite of sarcasm.

She'd done a flawless job of doing exactly that: sucking it up.

All the warning signs. All the fear. All the instincts that roared at her to get out, no matter what the cost.

She'd imagined herself as a vacuum cleaner, keeping everything locked away until this nightmare was over and she could toss everything she'd dealt with in the trash and leave it behind.

Really though, she was an appendix. The ultimate organ of "sucking it up."

The appendix tucked away bacteria and germs like a champ —until it had squirreled away too much crap. Then it blew up like the Death Star, creating a life-threatening emergency as it spewed toxins and bacteria into the very body it had been trying so hard to protect.

The crap had been piling up at the rental house for a while now.

And things were about to blow.

Her next moves would determine whether everything she'd "sucked up" over the past two months would come back to destroy her in one fell swoop.

Nya balled her hands into fists at her side and stared in mute terror at the two-inch, dark gap in the closet door. Was Sid in there right now?

She wanted to believe that he had just bumped into the closet while he stumbled out of the room in the dark. He wouldn't have been able to see very well in the pepper spray cloud. Maybe she passed out before she heard him exit through the door, but that wouldn't explain how he'd been getting into her room without her knowing it—with the door locked.

It was certainly big enough. The closet wasn't especially deep, but it ran nearly the length of the entire wall. It was definitely big enough for a person to hide inside. If that was the case, Sid had certainly done it before. She had barely any clothing in there.

Nya slowly swung her legs over the bed. The girl in the mirrored closet doors did the same, glimmering like a mirage in front of her bleary eyes. Between the cold and whatever Sid had drugged her with, she still felt shaky and weak. The adrenaline making her heart pump faster was helping her think more clearly, but her body was still excruciatingly clumsy and slow.

Unfortunately, the clearer her thoughts, the more she knew she needed to run.

Slowly, so slowly, Nya slid off the bed and crawled toward the closet.

She held her breath, inching forward on all fours. If he was in there, she would crawl down the hall as quietly as she could and escape the house. Her worn-out lungs protested at the lack of oxygen, tickling like they were packed with goose down.

She listened for the sound of breathing. Any sign of movement. Anything that might give him away, while trying hard not to give herself away.

Silence.

The tickling feeling in her lungs was getting worse, like the down feathers fluttering against her throat had also caught fire. She had to cough.

Was he in the closet?

No, her instincts confirmed. When she'd last seen Sid, he looked—and sounded—awful. Whatever was causing his rash seemed to be affecting much more than his skin. From all appearances, he was very unwell. She felt sure she'd hear some hint of that heavy breathing coming from inside the closet.

She had to know for sure, though. Steeling her nerves, she slid open the mirrored doors and peered inside.

Thank god. The closet was empty.

She released the breath she'd been holding in a whoosh that sounded a little like a sob.

Bang.

The sudden noise made Nya jump, then swivel her head toward the bedroom door.

Above the sound of her own heartbeat pounding in her head, she could hear a strange moaning sound coming from across the hall.

The fear pulsing through her body shifted course.

Sid definitely wasn't in the closet.

He was in his own bedroom. Awake.

And any minute, he'd open his bedroom door and come for her.

She grabbed a wire hanger that had fallen to the floor at the front of the closet. It wasn't the weapon she wanted, but at least it was something.

A coughing attack racked her body, making her head pound harder. She covered her mouth with one hand, desperate not to make any noise.

Thump.

Sid's door rattled on its hinges.

Then came the unmistakable sound of his doorknob twisting.

What the hell was she supposed to do now? If she crawled into the hall, she'd only run into him. And the idea that she'd escape him in her current state was laughable.

Tears poured down her face, running through the fingers covering her mouth.

She darted her eyes around the room wildly, landing on the mirrored closet doors just a few feet away.

It was the closest refuge.

Body shaking hard, she crawled toward the closet, still clutching the hanger.

Hide, NOW, her most primal instincts insisted. Because there was nowhere to run.

The heavy closet doors made a soft rumbling sound as they glided along the tracks, clattering quietly against each other as they went, recreating the same sound she remembered hearing during the night.

"Fuck," she whispered, body shivering violently as she leaned farther into the closet.

The closet smelled different from the bedroom.

Danker. Earthier.

The smell warned her to back away, to get out. It cut through her swollen, stuffy nose, promising danger. But she was already trapped.

The least she could do was press herself into the darkest corner of the room.

It was what a cornered wild animal would do. And that's what she felt like right now.

Careful not to bump the mirrored doors, Nya backed herself into the very back of the closet and waited, terrified, to hear the sound of Sid's door open.

He'd find her in here.

Of course he would.

Yet some small part of her brain still hoped that maybe he was stupid enough—or drug-addled enough—not to look for her in here.

To think she'd escaped the room somehow.

He'll find you, the logical part of her brain despaired.

Then he'll finish what he started.

Tears trickled down Nya's cheeks. The only reason she'd stayed in this godforsaken, awful house was to survive her final semester of college. To grab her degree by the skin of her teeth and get the hell out of Dodge.

Now she wasn't going to leave, ever.

Not alive, anyway.

37

Nya stared, wide-eyed, at the dingy cream paint on the closet walls, listening for the moment Sid rattled the knob on her bedroom door.

What was he waiting for?

From across the hall, there was another flurry of movement and a string of unintelligible words.

Her eyes ran over the lumpy paint inside the closet. It was so thick that it cast shadows against the wall where the dim shaft of light coming between the mirrored doors hit it.

And that was when she saw it.

A flaw in the paint.

Nya squinted, unsure what she was seeing at first.

What the hell was that?

A narrow, straight line came into focus among the thick paint at the very back of the closet. A fissure of black snaking through the haphazard whorls of paint, running up the wall just inches from her face. The line veered abruptly to make a right angle, then again to form a square the size of a large pizza box.

She never would have noticed it, if she hadn't been staring right at it.

A small handle the same color as the wall jutted out from the bottom of the square.

Nya gaped, barely able to breathe.

She shifted to kneeling and tugged on the door handle, opening it just a crack.

The unmistakable smell of the basement and a rush of cold wafted toward her.

Somehow, this panel door led down to the basement.

Was this how Sid had been getting into her room at night?

Bile rose in her throat.

The idea was too sinister, too horrifying. But it made a sort of twisted sense.

This was why locks couldn't stop him.

He had his own door.

She couldn't help but imagine Sid's sallow, red-raw face and stringy hair emerging through this hole in her wall, in the middle of the night. How many times had he done it?

Thump.

Nya bit back a scream and eased the panel door shut, panic making her breaths come fast and shallow.

As she started backing out of the closet and the shadows shifted, her eyes landed on a perfect footprint in a slice of light, just beneath the panel door.

The print was huge, its treads etched in the soft, silty dust at the very edge of the closet.

That's not right, were the words that inexplicably flashed through Nya's brain.

The thought slipped away as quickly as it had appeared.

Because the thump she'd just heard hadn't come from Sid's bedroom.

That noise had come from directly beneath her.

Sid was in the basement again.

38

Nya froze, confusion and terror fighting for center stage in her mind.

How had he gotten down into the basement so quickly—and so quietly? She felt sure she would've heard his bedroom door open, followed by the sound of his footsteps.

Did that mean Sid had a secret passage to the basement in his closet, too?

Her mind swam with dark possibilities.

There was another set of faint thumps beneath her. Footsteps. Her heart constricted. How long until he forced his way into her room?

Nya crawled out of the closet, toward her bedroom door, keeping the hanger between her fingers. With each step, she listened hard, trying to gauge where he was in the basement. The thumps and scrapes were more erratic now. Getting fainter.

She had to take her chance to escape now, while Sid was in the basement. Open the bedroom door and crawl as fast as she could toward the front door.

If he heard her trying to leave the bedroom, it was all over. She had to move fast. Faster than her shaking body could go.

She crawled to the bedroom door, then used the old wooden dresser to pull herself to standing.

Her legs were wobbly, but they held.

The human body was capable of some incredible feats, especially when fueled by adrenaline. All she had to do was run thirty feet.

Her life depended on it.

But her brain and body still felt so slow. So clumsy.

She unlocked her bedroom door.

Where was he right now? Was he about to emerge through the panel door in her closet?

Her legs shook dangerously as she gripped the doorknob.

Shit, shit, shit.

She had just turned the knob when a new sound, louder than the others, made her freeze.

It was Sid's voice again.

The blood drained from her face.

"Nya!" This time, he was screaming her name.

Terror and despair crashed together like waves in a riptide, pulling at her feet and eager to suck her underwater.

It couldn't be.

His voice wasn't coming from the basement.

Or the closet.

It was loud enough—and clear enough—that she was positive it was coming from just across the hall.

39

Nya wavered, trying to understand what was happening.

How had Sid gotten back into his room so fast? And why? What was his plan?

Was there someone else in the basement? Rick?

Sid let out a moan that verged on a scream.

It sounded like he was dying. Actually dying.

She wanted to plug her ears to the sound. It was so unexpectedly pathetic and wrenching that every instinct pushed her to help him.

She pushed through the fear making her heart beat out of control. Nothing made sense.

Nya opened the bedroom door a crack and peered out.

The hallway was dark. Sid's bedroom door was closed.

She took a tentative step into the hall.

Her legs felt wildly unsteady, but they held her up.

"*Fuck!*" Sid made another horrifying sound from inside his room, like an animal with its leg in a trap. Something solid hit the wall from the inside of his room. "Nya!"

His words were loud, high-pitched, and full of anguish.

Had he hurt himself?

She swiped hot tears that rolled down her cheeks before she could blink them away. His cries were so pitiful that they stopped her in her tracks, just outside her bedroom door.

No. Run, her brain roared.

She gritted her teeth and stumbled down the hall.

As she passed his bedroom door, the screams from Sid's bedroom suddenly went quiet.

Nya inched forward, her pace agonizingly slow. The entryway and front door were maybe forty feet away, but it felt like a football field.

Just a little farther, and she'd be free of the Gore Shack.

As she reached the end of the hall, a hard knock came at the front door.

Then another.

Nya's terror suddenly bloomed into hope.

Someone was knocking on the front door. Surely, they would help her.

"Nya?" called a familiar voice.

It was Curtis.

Tears sprang to her eyes. She didn't know how he'd sensed she needed help. All she knew was that she'd never been more grateful for anything in her entire life.

40

"Nya?" Curtis's distant, muffled voice called out again. He knocked loudly.

She had just taken another step toward the front door, her hamstrings and quadriceps propelling her wobbly legs forward, when her brain screeched out a warning.

Sid's doorknob was rattling behind her.

There was a banging sound as his bedroom door flung wide open and hit the wall hard.

Nya's head swiveled back to look down the hallway.

What she saw stopped her in her tracks.

All she could do was stare at Sid.

41

To her disbelief, Nya found herself wobbling a couple of steps back toward Sid.

She could barely believe her eyes.

If Sid had looked awful and unwell before, it was nothing compared to what Nya saw now.

The hanger fell out of her hand.

Sid was lying on the shag carpet, stretched between his bedroom and the hall. His body contorted on the ground in a writhing heap.

One hand was stretched in front of him. Shaking and floppy. It looked like he'd used every last bit of energy he had left to fling open his bedroom door.

His body was trembling so hard she wasn't sure if he was having a seizure at first. His mottled red face tipped toward her, eyes wide and vacant. Beads of sweat dripped from his forehead, creating a sheen over the rash that had finally reached the lower part of his face.

Most of his skin was a fiery mess from the blisters that bloomed like poisonous flowers. The unbroken skin beneath his eyes and along his cheeks and forehead looked pallid and clammy. Each breath he took rattled through his lungs, shallow and labored.

A new thread of fear unspooled in the back of Nya's mind, warning her to be careful with her next steps. Not to get any closer. But the thread whirled alongside so many others, it was impossible to follow.

What the hell was happening?

The smell of sickness and sweat drifted through the air, warning her to stay back. Everything about Sid's appearance made her want to run. Get away from him. She couldn't move, though.

"Nya," he croaked. His voice was both pitiful and accusing, like his dire condition was her fault, somehow.

She stared at him in mute horror, still unable to move or speak.

He convulsed again, curling onto his side and coughing. He was wearing the same shirt he'd had on the last time she'd seen him. It was soaked through with sweat and stains.

This wasn't the monster she'd been imagining when she stared at that panel door hidden in her closet.

Sid looked like he could barely stand, let alone scramble back and forth through a hidden passage.

"Give it back." He gasped the word and rolled onto his back. "Please."

She gaped at him, sinking a little deeper into the quicksand of confusion and fear. There was something very wrong with this dynamic, but she was less sure than ever of what to make of the horrifying scene unfolding around her. She needed to open the front door and let Curtis inside, but she couldn't tear herself away.

He shuddered again and made a gurgling noise in the back of his throat.

This wasn't a ruse.

From the looks of it, Sid actually might be dying.

He clearly needed an ambulance. If he didn't get medical attention right away, he was the one who'd be leaving the rental house on a stretcher. Not Nya.

"Give it back," Sid roared again, sounding like a keening animal.

Confusion edged out the fear. She took another shaky step away from him, toward the front door. Toward Curtis.

"My phone," he growled. The words came out with a thin line of saliva that dribbled over the edge of his chapped, raw lips.

His phone? If he wasn't in the middle of a medical emergency, she'd laugh. Fire back that he'd tried to steal *her* phone. *And* charger. *And* pepper spray.

He probably had no idea what he was saying. If his physical condition was any kind of mirror of his mental state, he was pretty far gone. It was possible he'd already forgotten what he'd done last night. He must have lost his own phone somewhere in the basement, after she'd pepper sprayed him.

It was the only explanation that made sense.

That same niggling thread of fear in the back of her mind pulled taut, warning her that there was something she was missing. Some bit of critical information floating somewhere in the ether.

She tried to grasp it, follow it, but it spun away just out of reach.

Sid's sunken, black eyes blinked rapidly, fixed on hers. They were filled with every bit as much hate as they'd held when he glowered at her during Rick's visit, but there was something else there now, too.

He looked terrified. And … pleading?

Was he actually afraid of *her*? It made zero sense.

The front doorknob rattled hard, finally jolting her out of her stupor. "I don't have your phone, Sid," she managed, her voice shaking but firm. "But I'm going to get you some help."

He gave her one last withering look. Then he sank to the floor and lay still.

She kept her eyes trained on the shuddering rise and fall of his chest for a moment longer. He was breathing, but unconscious. Still alive, but not for long.

There was another loud volley of bangs at the door.

Curtis would be able to help.

Nya spun around and stumbled toward the front door as fast as her shaky legs would move. In the span of just a few seconds, she'd gone from terrified that Sid was about to end her life, to terrified she was about to watch *him* die on the floor at her feet.

42

When Nya flung open the front door and Curtis rushed into the living room, she expected the relief to hit her hard.

Help was here.

Curtis would call the police and an ambulance.

This nightmare would be over soon.

But instead, the relief she'd hoped for lapped at the corners of her brain reluctantly, inching forward then drawing back into fear. Something still wasn't right.

For one thing, Curtis looked awful. He'd definitely gotten her flu bug. Not nearly as bad as Sid. And not that she had any room to judge anybody else considering her own swollen eyes, bedhead, and runny nose. But Curtis really wasn't okay. He was bundled up, even though the October day was sunny and warm for a coat. He was wearing a dingy-looking cloth medical mask that obscured most of his face. He was clearly sick—because of her.

Curtis closed the distance between them and pulled her into a tight hug. "What the hell is going on?" He stroked her tangled hair. "When you didn't text me back, I got so worried something was wrong—" he said in a raspy whisper.

Nya tried to speak, but the words were caught beneath the lump in her throat. So for a moment, she let herself fold into his embrace, trying to feel the comfort he offered. If anything though, the warning bells in her brain chimed louder. Her legs threatened to give out beneath her. She could feel his heart beating fast even beneath his heavy coat.

"You have to call the police," Nya interrupted, pulling away from him and craning her neck to see down the hall. Despite her panic, she couldn't help examining Curtis's eyes, peering over the stained white fabric of the mask. Those wide blue eyes, always a little too big for his skinny face, were little more than slits this morning. The skin around his eyelids was puffy and swollen, and the whites of his eyes were bloodshot and red-rimmed. It looked like he'd been crying all night.

She rushed on, trying to help Curtis understand the urgency of the situation. "I think he drugged me last night. He took my phone. And he was down in the basement. But now he's making these horrible sounds. Please, can you call the police? An ambulance?" She was leaving out so many details. She'd explain everything later, and then she'd apologize for breaking up with him over text. But right now, she needed him to call for help.

To her horror, Curtis didn't pull out his phone.

Instead, he planted his feet in a wide stance, crouching a little, like Sid might suddenly pop out from the pattern on the linoleum in the entryway. His eyes rested on the dark hallway that led to the bedrooms. "Where is he?"

The living room was now eerily quiet without the sound of Sid's moans and cursing.

"He—he's passed out in the hall. But he's still breathing. Do you have your phone? He needs help."

Curtis's expression—what she could see from his red-rimmed eyes anyway—shifted from disbelief to something else. His brows furrowed, like he was disappointed to hear that Sid was still breathing.

That couldn't be right. But there was no mistaking the look in his eyes.

Confusion and horror pulsed in Nya's chest, still screaming a warning that this nightmare wasn't over yet.

Curtis ignored her and took a step into the living room. At first, she thought he was going to check on Sid. Instead, he closed the distance between himself and Nya once more, drawing her back into another tight embrace.

"I don't want to get you sick," she protested, trying to pull away. "I'm fine. Sid's the one who needs help."

"I'm already sick," he replied firmly, pulling her closer against his skinny frame. "I've been thinking about you all night long. I couldn't sleep. I've been crying my eyes out. I'm so sorry, Nya. So sorry. Can you forgive me?"

He was right about the flu bug. If she'd already gotten him sick, there was no point in avoiding him. But this wasn't the time for hugs or rehashing the breakup. She was so full of dread and anxiety her body was thrumming. There was a man dying a few feet away. A fact that Curtis seemed completely indifferent to.

"Stop," she protested when he reached for her again. "Where's your phone?"

He stroked her messy hair, his gaze never wavering from hers. "I love you, Nya."

The words hit like a sucker punch.

She couldn't help recoiling, taking another step out of his embrace, toward the hallway. "No," was all she could manage. Regardless of how glad she was to see a familiar face, he wasn't reacting to this emergency with even a shred of urgency.

His swollen eyes narrowed to mere slits, and he stared at her in disbelief.

The tension in the room shifted when Sid moaned from the hallway.

He was still alive.

Sid made a retching noise like he was about to vomit, and Nya rushed toward him, expecting Curtis to follow.

To her surprise, Curtis stepped forward and caught her arm, digging his fingers hard into her skin to keep her from moving away. "No," he growled, his voice raspy. "Leave him."

"Ouch, stop. What are you doing? We have to help him," she cried, whirling around to face Curtis. "Let me go."

Curtis didn't let go, but he ducked his chin into the crook of his elbow and coughed into the rumpled coat he was wearing. It made a hoarse, painful sound. His grip on her arm loosened just a little, and she pulled away from him.

"Why aren't you calling for help?" she asked. There wasn't time to dick around. "I don't know what's wrong with Sid, but it's bad ... I think he might actually be dying."

The sound of Sid's moans had gotten even louder.

When Curtis stopped coughing and looked at her, it was impossible to misread his expression despite the mask. He was fiercely angry.

He shook his head. "No," he rasped again. His voice was so quiet she could barely hear him over the awful sounds Sid was making.

Nya stared at him and shook her head, scanning his baggy jeans for the telltale outline of his cell phone. He wasn't holding it in either hand.

"What's wrong with you? We have to help him," Nya repeated.

There was a thumping sound from the hall, then a gurgling noise. Then a heavy shuffling noise, like the sound the dresser had made when she pushed it across the carpet a few minutes ago.

Sid retched again, the sound closer this time. There was another thump. Nya watched in horror as the shadows in the hallway shifted. He was dragging himself along the carpet, toward them.

"Who's there?" he called. "This girl ..." He gasped for breath, and the thumps came faster. "She's trying to kill me. Please, h—help me," he begged.

Curtis grabbed Nya's arm again.

No, she wanted to scream. *I'm not afraid of Sid anymore. He needs help. Where is your phone?*

The words wouldn't come, though. Because she was still stuck on what Sid had just screamed: *She's trying to kill me.*

The idea that Sid was trying to pin this situation on her somehow—like the messy kitchen, like the stolen rent money—made her so angry she nearly let Curtis yank her out the door.

Fuck Sid.

But regardless of how much she hated him, she wasn't going to let him die. Not on her watch. She wasn't like him.

She yanked her arm away, trying to get back to Sid. To ask him what he'd done with *her* phone so she could call for help.

Curtis grabbed her arm again, so hard Nya nearly fell over. "Tell me what happened last night," he said sternly. "How did he get into your room?"

Nya pulled away. Last night—and this morning—had been harrowing, but all that felt distant compared to the emergency unfolding right now. She was alive. That was what mattered. "Give me your phone," she demanded again in a high voice, ignoring his question. "I have to call for help, tell them we need an ambulance, too." Hot, frustrated tears slipped down her cheeks. Her legs were shaking so hard she was going to have to drop to her knees soon. She was nearly hysterical now.

"I don't give a fuck about Sid Vicious. All I care about is you," Curtis said, his voice steely.

In a different setting, she might have found his words—and his rage—comforting. Sweet, even.

But right now, all she felt was horror.

"I don't know how he got into my room," Nya lied. It was abundantly clear how much Curtis hated Sid. He wasn't even willing to call an ambulance. The idea of telling him about the panel door felt like pouring gasoline on a fire.

Nya took a shaky step toward the front door. If he wouldn't call the police, she'd flag down somebody outside. Nothing was stopping her from leaving the rental house anymore. Certainly not Sid.

Then, without another word, Curtis leapt toward her, grabbed her arm, and pulled her back toward him.

"Stop it. Let me go—" Nya cried, resisting.

But, even sick, he was too strong.

She fought him for a few steps until her legs buckled beneath her, finally forcing him to let go as she sank to the ground at his feet.

He immediately knelt beside her. "Oh my god, I'm sorry, Nya. I didn't mean—"

It was at that moment that Sid's greasy head appeared around the corner of the hallway.

Curtis scrambled to his feet and stared.

The way Sid dragged his shaking body, pulled up on his elbows, looked like something out of a horror movie. There was a sheen of mustard-yellow vomit on his chin. It looked like it took every ounce of energy he had to drag himself along the floor like that.

He tried to get his knees underneath him, like he might be able to stand. But before he could even get to a crawling position, his body seized up and he slammed hard against the wall.

Nya watched in horror as Sid's head hit with a muted smack. His body crumpled at a painful-looking angle, convulsing. Then he lay unmoving on his back. His eyes blinked rapidly, like they were still spinning in his head. His body shuddered violently, and then the room went completely silent.

"Oh my god," Nya whispered. "Is he dead?"

She crawled toward Sid, trying to see whether he'd finally stopped breathing.

The idea of giving him CPR or mouth-to-mouth was unthinkable. Those grimy, chapped lips and that inflamed broken skin were warnings to stay very far away. But if she had to, she would.

Still, there was a small part of her that was terrified he might suddenly shoot out a hand and grab her if she got too close.

From behind her, Curtis made an impatient sound in his throat.

Nya kept her eyes fixed on Sid's chest. *There.* His ribcage shuddered as it rose and fell. A high-pitched wheezing sound started up once again.

He was still breathing.

For now.

Nya whirled around to face Curtis. His eyes were fixed on the motionless Sid. His expression shifted beneath the cloth mask, impossible to read. He tore his eyes away from Sid's body and looked at Nya.

Her sense of time felt completely broken. How long had it been since Curtis got here? There was no way to tell without her phone. If Curtis had called the police as soon as he arrived like she'd asked, there would have been sirens flashing outside by now. Police officers knocking on the door. Instead, there was only the stale stillness of the Gore Shack.

"Please, Curtis," Nya whispered. "Please, call."

Curtis muttered something. Then he strode toward Sid's body, crouched beside him, and cocked his head to get a better look. Sid's chest still rose and fell in shuddering stops and starts.

Curtis sighed again, like whatever he was about to say pained him. When he said the words though, his voice was flat beneath the rasp. It was clear he was anything but troubled.

"I'm not calling the police."

43

Nya stared at Curtis as if he'd just told her that water wasn't wet.

When someone was hurt, you called the police.

When someone was dying, you called the police.

When your home had turned into a horror film, you called the police.

Curtis wouldn't, though. When he spoke, his voice was full of disgust—not panic or fear. "Why the hell should we help him? Think about what he's been doing to you over the past two months. Think about what he did to his old roommate. Just look at him. He's fucking disgusting."

He pointed a finger down at Sid's pathetic figure on the carpet beside his feet. "You said he was on drugs, right? I bet he never stopped using them. Just look at that rash. Jesus. He'd be better off dead."

Nya shook her head back and forth in disbelief, shivering even though the air in the room was stale and getting warmer by the minute. The smells of vomit and body odor were getting stronger, too. Her head was pounding so fiercely she was afraid she might pass out again if she didn't get some water soon.

The terror in her chest was expanding. Things were spiraling from bad to worse.

Curtis seemed to take her silence as an indication that she was willing to be convinced. "It's not like you did this to him. He did it to himself. It's just karma."

A phrase from one of Professor Stern's lectures came floating back to her. *There is a complex but reliable law of cause and effect in biology. The body is a scoreboard of genetics and choices that can lead to disease, injury, and dysfunction.*

Basically what Curtis had just said: The shit you did usually caught up with you. *Karma.*

Still, what Curtis was saying was clearly crazy. Completely crazy. No matter how awful Sid was, they couldn't just let him die.

Curtis pulled Nya away from Sid and knelt beside her on the carpet. She winced when she saw his blue eyes. They looked almost … excited.

The tendrils of fear squeezed her stomach tighter. For the first time, she realized she was afraid of Curtis, not Sid.

"The world is a worse place with him in it," Curtis insisted, his voice losing some of the rasp. "Right?"

Nya shook her head, tears pooling in her eyes. Curtis wasn't wrong. Everything that had happened in the little rental house— *the Gore Shack*—played through Nya's mind, the film moving faster and faster. Each slide was more awful than the last. Sid breaking into her bedroom. Sid taking her food and stealing her rent money. Sid stealing from his cousin for drug money. Sid lying to his parents about the tuition money they sent him. Sid putting his old roommate in the hospital. Sid trying to attack her last night while she slept—maybe even trying to kill her. That unassuming, horrifying panel door in her closet.

Curtis didn't even know about that part yet.

She tried to think of even one moment when Sid had been kind instead of just awful.

She couldn't think of any.

Not a single moment. He was a trash human, as Jade would say.

But even trash humans deserved medical care when they were sick.

It was the whole point of everything she'd be promising in the Hippocratic Oath as a nurse. Everything she'd been working toward for the past three years.

I will apply, for the benefit of the sick, all measures that are required, avoiding those twin traps of overtreatment and therapeutic nihilism.

What Curtis was suggesting was pretty much the definition of therapeutic nihilism. A passive pessimism that whispered, *Don't bother with this one. Let nature take its course.*

Curtis spoke, as if reading her mind. "Forget about him. You don't owe him anything. Not a single fucking thing."

Nya shook her head again angrily. All she wanted to do was forget about Sid and the horrors inside the rental house. Her head hurt so badly. Her eyes hurt. Her body hurt. The black box in her brain screamed at her to get out of the house, like it had done from the very beginning. But no. Not yet.

"Why do you hate him so much? *I'm* the one he's been torturing. And I don't want him to die," Nya whispered, eyes fixed on Sid, following the erratic rise and fall of his chest. From everything she'd learned about what the human body looked like when it was fighting for its life, he didn't have long to live.

By the time an ambulance arrived, it might already be too late.

"You say you love me?" Nya challenged Curtis when he didn't respond. "Then call for help."

He gave her a look like she'd just spit at him.

Sid made a gurgling noise. His arms twitched at his sides. The labored breathing stopped.

He was suddenly very, very still.

Curtis saw it too.

He leaned closer to Sid. Waiting to see whether Sid kept breathing this time—or if that shuddering gasp had been his last.

Curtis didn't look concerned. Just intent.

Nya's stomach churned. The thought suddenly struck her that this whole situation was eerily similar to what had happened to Arlo back in June. Only this time, it was Sid who was at the mercy of a stranger's cell phone call.

Once again, she began edging toward the entryway. Curtis was watching Sid so intently, he didn't even seem to notice. But before she'd made it to the entryway, she heard chaos behind her.

Curtis was standing right next to Sid now. He leaped back when Sid thrashed onto his side, gasping and shaking. His wild eyes landed on Curtis as he finally managed to sit up.

"Help me," Sid moaned again, reaching a hand toward Curtis.

Nya's heart wrenched. How could Curtis just stand there, staring at him like that?

Then Sid went rigid. For a second, Nya thought he'd seized again. Or had passed out. But that wasn't it. His jaundice-yellow, bottle-black eyes were impossibly wide in that sunken, pale face. He stared at Curtis like he was looking at a ghost. "Holy shit," he whispered. Then repeated himself louder. "Holy fucking shit."

Curtis backed away, toward Nya.

Sid leaned against the hallway wall for support, slumping down like a sack of potatoes. Sweat soaked through his shirt and glistened on his forehead in beads, but his eyes stayed fixed on Curtis's retreating form.

Before his head lolled back and he crumpled against the wall, he said just one word, forcing it out loud and clear through his chapped lips so there was no mistaking it.

"Arlo."

44

Arlo.

Sid spat the word so forcefully that Nya was positive she hadn't misheard him.

It was abundantly clear that Curtis had heard Sid, too.

The warning bells in Nya's brain chimed louder, faster, harder.

Only now, they sounded a little like the chime of a correct answer on a gameshow.

Because finally, everything made sense.

Curtis *was* Arlo.

45

The scene in the bleak living room suddenly felt like it had been paused.

A freeze-frame of peeling linoleum, dirty brown shag carpet, and three people whose faces were twisted up for very different reasons.

One of them was dying.

One of them was terrified.

And one of them thought he'd fooled them both.

While the world around her moved in slow motion, Nya's brain whirred faster, connecting the dots of everything she'd learned about "Curtis" and Sid over the past two months. It was like a camera had suddenly panned out on a zoomed-in scene. Everything she'd thought was real was actually carefully scripted scenes on a movie set, complete with scaffolding, fabric backdrops, and fake walls.

Shit, shit, shit.

She thought about the first day she'd met Curtis—not Curtis, *Arlo*—in line behind her at the bookstore. How he'd made that comment about her Def Leppard T-shirt. Had he already known who she was at that moment? Was that why he approached her?

Yes, she knew in her gut.

Then he'd just happened to be at the library later that night. There was little question he'd been following her. And she'd made it so easy on him. She'd been so eager for a friend. So eager to confide in him about her awful roommate—who had been *his* awful roommate, too.

How many evenings had they spent together since then? Those picnics he'd brought her. The way he'd helped her come up with a plan to blackmail Sid into staying away from her.

She slowly turned to look at the boy with the choppy, curly hair and the puffy eyes. The one who had just told her he loved her. Was any of that true? Had he developed real feelings for her, or was this all part of his plan to get back at Sid? How many other lies had he told her? Had he ever liked her?

Or was he just obsessed with his old roommate?

His old roommate Sid, who had beat him up then put him in the hospital. Hurt him so badly he'd ruptured his spleen.

His old roommate who was now lying on the floor at his feet. Dying.

Nya's heart beat faster. Had Curtis done something to Sid? She suddenly felt certain that he had. She had no idea how he'd done it. But there was something self-satisfied about the passive expression on his face. And Sid had been getting progressively sicker for weeks.

She pictured the video Arlo had sent her after their first picnic. The shaky, *Blair Witch*-style video that she'd watched on her phone multiple times to reassure herself she still had some kind of leverage on Sid.

She remembered what "Curtis" had told her.

While Arlo was in the hospital, Sid told his cousin that he'd caught Arlo stealing stuff from the basement. The landlord believed Sid. So on top of everything, Arlo got kicked out of the rental. He had nowhere to go after he got discharged from the hospital. Big old pile of medical bills. Had to drop all his classes.

Arlo C. Hunter.

She'd bet anything the C. stood for Curtis.

"Nya, what are you thinking," Arlo asked. He knelt beside her and lay a hand on her arm in a gesture that might have been comforting if she weren't a hostage. He wasn't going to call for help, and he wasn't going to let Nya call for help.

Because he wanted Sid dead. And now Nya knew why.

She shook her head, trying not to let panic take over. She could still feel his eyes on her, waiting for her to say something, but she couldn't even look at him. She could barely breathe.

She felt certain she was still missing something. But what?

Her eyes went to Sid, lying motionless on the floor except for the labored rise of his chest. What would he tell her about Arlo if he could speak?

What else was Arlo lying about?

Look at his face, Jade's voice whispered through her brain. But no, it wasn't Jade's voice at all, Nya realized. It was her own voice. Her own gut.

Look closer. You'll see it.

Every part of Sid looked terrible. His greasy hair. His raw, rash-covered body. His sweaty clothing. His chin and neck glistening with a slick of vomit.

Every part of him, except his eyes and nose.

The skin there was pale and pristine.

"Nya," Arlo prompted her again, a new edge to his voice. His grip on her arm tightened.

When she finally looked back at him, he was staring at her intently with those red-rimmed blue eyes boring into hers.

That was when the final, horrifying piece of the puzzle clicked into place.

Those red-rimmed eyes were much too raw and inflamed to be the result of a cold, even a bad cold.

She had no doubt that his nose looked much the same beneath the cloth mask. Pepper spray inflamed the mucous membranes. Nya hadn't even been sprayed directly, and her own eyes and nose were a mess just from breathing in the mist.

With a direct hit to the face, your face would be a hot mess.

It would look like Arlo's.

Which meant that Sid hadn't been pepper sprayed last night. Arlo had.

46

"What are you thinking, Nya?" Arlo repeated in a low voice, moving his hand up and down her arm. The rough calluses of his hand were chafing at her skin, but she barely felt it.

He'd been in her room last night.

He'd assaulted her.

Then he'd come running to "help" her this morning, somehow knowing just when she needed him.

Nya pictured the outline of that hidden panel in her closet.

She thought of all the strange sounds she'd heard at night. Thumps and bumps.

She remembered how many times she'd been certain someone was in her room, even though she was also certain she'd locked the bedroom door.

That faint footprint she'd seen in the dust of her closet zoomed to the front of her memory.

The only shoes Sid ever wore were those ugly black flip-flops. There was no tread on the soles.

She glanced down at Arlo's dirty blue sneakers, feeling sick.

He was the one who had made that footprint. She was suddenly sure of it.

Which meant that Arlo was the one who had been coming into her room at night—through her closet.

Nya closed her eyes, terrified Arlo might be able to read her mind if she held eye contact. That he might be able to tell that the blinders had come off.

"Nya?" Arlo prompted again, his voice as tight as his fingers on her arm. "I need you to tell me what you're thinking."

She blinked, letting the tears that had been welling in her bleary eyes fall. She knew she needed to focus on dealing with the question Arlo was asking her first. *What are you thinking, Nya?*

She was thinking that everything was getting clearer now.

That it was Arlo—not Sid—who had been rattling her doorknob. Making thumps and bumps in the night that he could blame on her scary roommate.

Of course, Arlo was really asking how much she knew. How many of those puzzle pieces she'd managed to put together. Whether she was still on his side. Whether she knew that he was the one who had drugged her last night.

She had to respond to him. Had to find a way out of this mess. Had to help Sid somehow. But the horrifying realizations elbowing their way through her brain were all she could focus on.

Had he done what he'd done last night because he'd been angry she'd broken up with him—and reckless because he was already sick?

Bile rose in her roiling stomach as she remembered the leftover chicken sandwich she'd put in the fridge. Maybe that's how he'd done it. He knew she'd eat it. She'd made things so easy for him.

She'd fallen for everything he'd orchestrated, head over heels, hook, line, and sinker.

There were just two questions begging for answers right now. And Nya had a feeling that the answers would mean the difference between whether or not she or Sid got out of here alive.

What had Arlo done to Sid?

And what did he want from her now?

There was no use pretending that she hadn't heard what Sid had just said: *Arlo.* The shock on her face had given that much away. So she couldn't outright lie to him. He'd see through it.

She had to acknowledge the fact that Curtis was actually Arlo. But the alarm bells in her head and the voice screaming at her to run—as if she could—were warning her to keep back everything else she could manage. Including the knowledge that Arlo was the one who'd been coming into her room at night. Not Sid.

She knew in her bones that was the only way she was getting out of here alive. The only way Sid had any hope of getting to a hospital.

"You're Arlo," she finally told him, keeping her voice steady and compassionate, her eyes locked on his.

47

Arlo's eyes widened, then narrowed suspiciously. He shifted on the floor beside her, so he could face her.

Reassure him, her gut prompted. *Use the truth to hide the lie. Tell him you still want to be with him.*

She wrangled the pieces of the lie together, trying to remember the information he'd supposedly gotten secondhand from his "buddy." Big pile of bills. Nowhere to go ... except the rental house he'd been staying in right before Sid sent him to the hospital. He must have been so desperate when he was discharged. Desperate enough to come back here, to the Gore Shack. To the storage basement beneath her room.

Because he had nowhere else to go.

"I'm not upset you didn't tell me who you really were," she told him with as much sincerity as she could muster. "But I'm so sorry for what happened to you. For what Sid did to you. I can forgive him for what he did to me ... but not to you. I'm so sorry, Arlo."

His expression relaxed just a little. So did his grip on her arm.

She kept going. "And … you're right," she added. "The world would be better off without Sid. I understand what you mean now."

She scooted a few inches closer to Arlo, revulsion crawling across her skin. "Did you mean what you said earlier when you told me you loved me?"

He slowly nodded, finally letting go of her to cross his arms warily in front of his chest.

She forced her jaw to unclench and offered him a shy smile. "I … love you too. I'm sorry I pushed you away earlier. I panicked. Sid really scared me last night. I thought I was going to die … and then this morning when he was like this." She gestured to Sid's twisted, motionless form behind them in the hallway. "Thank you for coming to help me. It was like … you knew how much I needed you."

Just like that, his shoulders slumped with relief and he pulled her against his chest, leaning into the crook of his coat to cough one more time before wrapping her in his arms.

She held her breath against the horrible, mildew smell of his clothing. This coat must have been crammed into a corner of the basement for months.

His raw, raspy voice was thick with emotion as his spindly fingers gripped her arms and pulled her to him in a tight embrace. "Oh god, Nya. I love you so much. I'm sorry I didn't tell you who I really was. I didn't know how you'd react. All I want is to be with you."

It was everything she could do not to wrench herself away from his grip and scramble toward the door.

He'd only catch her.

So instead, she relaxed against him, beyond grateful that he was still wearing that mask. The idea of kissing him was too much.

The answers to her questions were getting clearer by the moment.

His feelings for her *were* real. Twisted and warped, but real.

He really believed that if they let Sid die like this, they could sail off into the sunset together somehow. Did he think he'd move in with her *here*? That he'd crawl out of the basement like some tunnel-dwelling monster and share her bed? That she'd never be the wiser to everything he'd orchestrated?

After what he'd done to her?

After whatever he'd done to Sid?

If Arlo was telling the truth about what Sid had done to him, she understood why he was so angry. It was pretty awful, and the hospital bills seemed to confirm the story. But this was pretty awful, too.

"Let's get out of here," she told him, grabbing his hand and squeezing it as she moved toward the door. The smile on her face was starting to tremble, cramp a little, threatening to crumble into the terrified grimace she really wanted to make. Once they were out of the house, she'd scream for help. Tell the first person she saw to call the police and an ambulance. Tell them everything that had happened right beneath her nose in the rental house.

To her horror, Arlo didn't move toward the door.

He shook his head and kept hold of her hand, then gestured to the card table in the kitchen. "I don't want to risk leaving him alone," he said simply. "Once we know he's dead, we can leave. Maybe grab something to eat. Call the police when we get home."

When we get home. He said it like it was his house.

And in a way, he was right. He'd been a tenant too, this whole time. She just hadn't known it.

48

Nya recalculated the distance between herself and the front door. Now that he'd relaxed a little, she felt confident she could break away from him. But how many steps could she run before she stumbled—or he grabbed her?

No. She thought about his viselike grip on her arm earlier. Those long arms would pull her right back inside the house before she made it to the linoleum of the entryway.

Even ill, Arlo was stronger than her. Besides, if she bolted, he'd know for sure that she was playing him. Lying to him.

What he'd do then, with that betrayal, was anyone's guess. She couldn't trust him. That was the only thing she knew for sure.

She had to get out of the house and get help for Sid—and herself. She had to get away from Arlo. How, though?

Help me find a way, she begged the voice in her brain, even as she let him help her up off the floor and be guided to the rickety card table to sit in one of the metal folding chairs. He sat her down in the chair farthest into the kitchen, just out of view of Sid. He seated himself closest to the carpet. Between Nya and the front door. Where he had a clear view of Sid.

To see him take his last breath, Nya knew.

She did the only thing she could think of. Dig for information. If she knew what he'd done to Sid, maybe she'd have a better idea of how long he had to live.

"What do you think is wrong with him?" she asked him, trying to sound curious instead of horrified. She cocked her head to the side, doing her best to broadcast a thoughtful expression.

When Arlo didn't respond, she added, "Just thinking ahead. If the police question us separately, I want us to be on the same page."

He studied her, then nodded slowly. "Yeah. Good call. Just tell them he was taking drugs. Who knows what might have gotten cut into his stash. Maybe tell them he was on meth," he added, warming to this idea.

Nya forced herself to nod. "Yeah. Meth. That'd explain the rash and the seizures," she said, going along with it. He wasn't wrong. The police probably wouldn't bat an eye at that explanation. She'd wondered about it herself, but she'd learned enough about the way common illegal drugs interacted with brain and body biology during a unit on the central nervous system to know that he wasn't using meth. Sid's other symptoms—like the yellowing eyes and sweat—didn't feel right. He had none of the telltale twitchy energy or wrecked teeth, either.

She was sure Arlo had done something to Sid. She couldn't ask him that directly though, since it would give away that she knew he'd been living in the house. And he clearly wasn't going to offer that information unprompted.

She watched the cloth surface of his face mask lift slightly at the cheeks, like he was smiling beneath it.

Think, she told herself. *Do something.* Without being able to see Sid, she had no idea whether he was even still breathing. She had to act, and fast.

Then an idea came to her.

A way out.

It wasn't pleasant. In fact, the idea of it made her skin crawl.

It would work, though—if she could just get Arlo to stay here with Sid.

She scooted a little closer to him after he coughed. "I can't leave the house looking like this ..." She gestured at her ratty pajamas and unbrushed hair. She hadn't bothered to put on a bra, yet. "I haven't even brushed my teeth today. People will notice. Someone might think it's strange that I left the house in such a hurry on a Sunday."

He tore his eyes away from Sid and studied her. A crease appeared between his brows, and she knew he was considering it. If she left the house like this, she'd draw a lot of stares. He might earn a few sideways glances for wearing that mask—a clear signal he was sick—but not the kind of stares she'd get if she wandered down the street looking like she'd just rolled off a hay cart.

He shifted his eyes back to Sid. "You look fine. You always look beautiful," he croaked, but she could hear the hesitation in his voice.

"I could just take a quick shower and get dressed? Ten minutes. I'm not sure I can stand longer than that on my own anyway. But I look seriously disgusting. And it's getting so hot in here—and stinky. I'll turn on the A/C. It'll slow down decomposition." The words made bile rise in her throat.

He shifted his chair so he could see the full view of the hallway. His eyes traveled between the two bedroom doors and the basement door. She had no doubt he was calculating the risks of letting her out of his sight right now.

But he'd be able to see her enter her bedroom. And he already knew that the air-conditioner blocked the window fully.

She wouldn't be able to escape that way. Not without causing a huge commotion.

There was only one way out of that bedroom.

And as far as she could tell, he thought she had no idea it existed.

She hid the shiver that ran down her spine when she thought about how close she'd been to blurting out what she'd discovered when he showed up earlier. *Sid's been getting into my room through the closet.*

There hadn't been time to tell him, though.

She imagined Arlo scuttling into the basement through her closet after she pepper sprayed him, eyes red and swollen. Nearly blind. Her phone and charger—and the pepper spray—tucked safely in his pocket.

He must have come running when he heard the telltale clatter of those mirrored doors in her closet, not wanting her to find that panel door.

But she had.

He seemed to have no idea that she'd tucked herself deep in the back of the closet to hide. Deep enough that she'd come face to face with the trap door he'd been using to get into her room.

It made sense now why she'd heard the noises in the basement at the same time she could hear Sid moaning across the hall. Arlo was scrambling out of the basement while Sid was flailing around on the floor of his bedroom.

"Are you okay to shower on your own?" Arlo asked, breaking into her thoughts.

Nya forced a smile, even though her skin crawled. "I'm feeling better," she lied.

She couldn't let him see her stumble, or he wouldn't let her go.

Thankfully, he seemed pretty immersed in watching Sid. "Fine, but be quick," Arlo said finally. "We gotta leave as soon as he's dead. Cops will be able to tell when he died—a window of time, anyway. We should stay out of the house for a while after that."

She nodded as she pulled herself to standing on unsteady legs, trying to look like she was still on board with all of this insanity. "Yeah, you're right." Technically, he was. Death times were generally accurate within about forty-five minutes, at the most. "I'll hurry. Just give me ten minutes, okay?" She managed a smile. "I love you, Arlo."

His swollen blue eyes softened as he tore his gaze away from Sid again. He seemed pleased she was calling him by his real name now.

She kept the smile plastered on her face until her back was turned and she was facing the hall. Facing Sid's body, lying at the edge of the hallway.

She was going to have to step over his body to get to her room.

Sid's arm lay on the carpet, fingers stretched toward the kitchen. Still begging for help. With the sleeves of his dingy sweatshirt drawn back, she could see the angry red boils and welts in perfect clarity. Some of them wept a yellow liquid.

Her stomach heaved and she braced one hand against the wall for support.

He lay at an awkward angle, legs partly tucked beneath him like he'd crumpled into a sloppy yoga pose. One cheek lay against the carpet. His greasy hair covered his face, but she could see a goose egg forming where he'd hit his head hard on the wall. A puddle of greasy vomit—mostly yellow bile—had splattered the thick white paint on the nearest wall.

His chest was still rising and falling, but so shallowly she knew it was only a matter of time before it stopped altogether.

Suck it up, buttercup, she told herself firmly. *Just a few more steps.*

Then she gritted her teeth and stepped over his body, feeling Arlo's eyes on her.

She suspected he wasn't going to like it if she shut her bedroom door.

She had to, though. That was the only way this was going to work.

Before she grabbed the doorknob, she turned to look at Arlo.

He held her gaze for a split second before his eyes shifted to Sid's body on the floor.

The way Arlo sat, hunched and waiting on the chair, leaning forward with his arms on his knees, made her think of something she'd seen on *The Discovery Channel* once. A special on the Serengeti, where a patient vulture waited for a water buffalo to die. The buffalo had gotten stuck in the mud. The rest of the herd had moved on. As the big animal grew weaker under the beating sun, the vulture waited in the shade of a nearby tree, eyes laser focused, waiting for the buffalo's last breath.

It was all Nya could do not to shudder. "I'll be right back," she told Arlo, not waiting for an answer before closing the bedroom door behind her.

She waited, listening, chest heaving. Her legs shook dangerously. Would he follow and demand she open the door?

The seconds ticked by. The chair scraped against the linoleum in the kitchen as he shifted his weight, but there was no squeak from the floorboards or thump of footsteps. He'd let her go—for now. He was busy watching his prey.

Nya let out the breath she'd been holding then carefully, quietly turned the lock on the bedroom door.

The locked door wouldn't stop him if he came after her. He knew the house better than she did—including all its entrances.

But maybe, just maybe, it would buy her a few precious seconds.

49

The first thing she did was stumble across the room to turn on the air conditioner. Then the shower and the bathroom fan, grateful for the racket all of them made. She didn't bother closing the bathroom door. If he made it into the room, she needed to be long gone.

The A/C poured cold, fresh air into the room that didn't smell like vomit.

Good. This was good. There were a few layers of white noise in the bedroom now.

Her heart beat harder in her chest as she thought about what she was about to try.

She frowned, second guessing herself. Was this plan brilliant? Or was it stupid? If Arlo realized what was happening, he would see her as a traitor and a threat. Nya didn't want to know what he'd do then. If he was capable of assaulting her in her bedroom while she slept, he was capable of worse if he decided she'd betrayed him.

Was this the right move?

Yes, her gut whispered, cutting through the indecision that threatened to root her to the floor while the bathroom began to fill with steam.

Just take deep breaths and keep moving. Send the oxygen and adrenaline to all your red blood cells.

As quietly as she could, she walked across the room and plucked up the little *alebrije* horse where it lay broken on the carpet next to the dresser, its three remaining legs jutting out defiantly.

Then she tucked it into the deep pocket of her pajama pants and faced the closet.

To her relief, the heavy, mirrored closet doors were still wide open. Just the way she'd left them after the horrifying discovery she'd made earlier that morning. She wouldn't have to waste any time carefully pulling them open along the tracks and risking the accompanying noise.

Nya steeled herself and stepped inside the closet. If she stopped to think too much about what she was about to do, she'd lose her nerve.

But the clock was ticking.

She had less than ten minutes before Arlo got suspicious. Surely it would prick his suspicion when the shower just kept running.

And Sid might have even less time than that.

Her mind felt like it was moving faster now. Whatever Arlo had drugged her with—Sid's mushrooms? Some kind of other drug?—was finally releasing its stranglehold. Her head still hurt like hell, her limbs still felt like Jell-O, and her eyes were a bleary mess, but at least she could think more clearly now.

Moving as carefully as she could so she wouldn't bump against the closet walls or trip on the raised metal door track on the floor, Nya crept to the far back wall where the black cracks outlining a barely visible silhouette of the panel door waited for her.

Then she grabbed that nearly invisible white handle and pulled.

There had to be another way out of the house, once she reached the basement. That was the only explanation for how Arlo had shown up at the front door so quickly when she called earlier.

He'd been in the basement, right beneath her feet, mere minutes before she heard Sid scream for help.

She was sure of it.

Then, moments later, he'd been banging away on the front door.

She pictured the broken lattice running along the ramshackle porch. She'd assumed an animal might be living under that porch. That a raccoon or an opossum had made the gaping holes. Maybe it had, once upon a time, but she was pretty sure that animals weren't the only ones using it to crawl under the porch and access the basement.

She only hoped she could find her way out in time.

To her horror and delight, the panel door in the closet opened without a sound.

The smell of dust and a trace of mold—the same smell as the basement and Arlo's clothing—came stronger, wafting into the closet in a stream of air that was cooler than the air in the stale closet.

Her hands shook as she lowered the panel door until an open square of darkness yawned wide in front of her, at chest level. It was plenty big enough for a person to slide through, but there was no telling what waited for her beyond it.

Breathing fast, she leaned as far into the hole as she could, blinking in the dark and willing her eyes to adjust.

Her hands found the ladder rung before her eyes did.

The wood was rough and angular. Less like the store-bought ladder her dad used to clean the gutters each fall when the big elm in the front yard shed its leaves. More like the homemade ladder on the treehouse that Mr. Estrada had built for Jade's younger sister the summer before they moved to Indianapolis.

She tentatively pressed her hands onto the nearest rung. Would it hold her weight? Or would it shift beneath her, creating a clatter that would alert Arlo—or send her tumbling headfirst into the basement?

She drew her hand back, trying in vain to keep it from shaking.

If this ladder held Arlo, it would hold her, too.

50

And it did.

With each shaking step Nya took, the dim rectangle of light at the top of the panel door got farther away. And with each step, Nya descended farther into the darkness of the basement.

The wood creaked softly each time she put her full weight on another rung, but not loudly enough to alert Arlo. Not loudly enough that it would have alerted Nya any of the times Arlo had ascended these same rungs to enter her room at night. Especially not underneath the loud, erratic hum of the air conditioner. How many times had he been in her room to watch her while she slept?

Her heart thumped harder. She only knew about the times she'd woken up. He'd probably been in her room plenty of other times. Watching. Staring. Spinning his sick fantasies of revenge on Sid. Night by night, becoming more obsessed by the idea that Nya was going to be part of the spoils in his plans, too.

Another realization clicked into place as she reached for the next rung in the dark.

The very first time she'd watched the video "Curtis" sent her, she'd known right away that the person holding the phone was filming from inside the Gore Shack. It would have been impossible to get that angle, unless you were standing in the front yard directly under the mulberry tree. And in broad daylight, Sid would have seen Arlo filming him.

That video had been taken from *inside* the bedroom, through the tiny slit of window not completely filled by the air-conditioning unit. A tiny slice of the bulky gray A/C unit had even flashed onto the screen right before the video ended.

That video had been taken after Arlo's hospital stay. After he'd been evicted.

That was why the hospital bill had seemed wrong the very first time she saw it.

Arlo's hospital stay had been from June first to June fifth. But the metadata on the video revealed that it had been filmed— from inside the house—on June tenth. Five days *after* Arlo had been discharged from the hospital.

She gripped the sides of the rough wood ladder and blinked rapidly, trying to get her bearings and focus on the task at hand. It was much darker than she'd expected. She'd only been in the basement the one time—when she'd confronted Sid. It had been dark then, but she'd seen a couple of narrow rectangular windows along the walls. *Non-egress,* Sid had said when he talked about Rick's attempts at renovation. They weren't the way out of the basement. Not only were the windows too high for her to reach without dragging over some of the junk in the basement, but they were clearly too narrow for a person to fit through.

She lowered another foot down, careful not to let the ladder tip. This time, her left foot met cement. The basement floor.

Only this wasn't the basement she remembered.

For a moment, she held onto the sides of the ladder, trying to orient herself. Trying to make the dark shapes around her come into sharper focus. She reached a hand out in front of her, suddenly realizing that what she'd assumed was a thick blanket of darkness was actually a wall.

When she turned to the right, she could see a sliver of dim light running parallel along the floor. Another wall of sorts.

This was a tiny, enclosed room.

The air in here was cool and musty, like the rest of the basement. But there was also the subtle smell of food, sweat, and body odor. Old, rank smells. Smells that suggested a human had been spending a lot of time in this space.

Every part of her screamed at her to get out as fast as she could walk—or crawl. However, the knowledge that Arlo was going to come looking for her any second sent ice water through her veins, slowing her down. This must be the same kind of fear a prey animal felt when it was being stalked. That age-old pull between fight, flight, and freeze.

And, of course, fawn. It was the trauma-response nobody talked about. She'd learned about it in the same neurobiology class where she'd studied the effects of different substances on brain function.

Fawning was what she'd done a few minutes ago, when she told Arlo she loved him. Fawning was where you made yourself small and vulnerable and unthreatening, in hopes that the predator who wanted to swallow you whole would let you live a little longer.

But being a fawn wasn't going to help her anymore. She couldn't be a fawn now, batting her lashes at him or hunkering down to hide.

She had to get the fuck out of here and *run*. She had to be a gazelle.

Forcing down the revulsion churning in her stomach, Nya inched forward, looking for yet another secret panel in the dark walls of this tiny, strange room. The cement at the bottom of the ladder seemed to be the only clear spot in the tiny enclosed space. The rest of the floor space was covered in piles of clothing and other unidentifiable objects.

She felt her way forward with her feet, hoping she wasn't about to step on something that would make a clatter. Piles of debris. Crinkling wrappers. A long, soft, lumpy object that might be a sleeping area.

Nya ran her fingers along the far wall, where the slit of dim light shone through. It had a strange, smooth, chalky texture. A sheet of drywall, maybe. When she pressed her hand lightly against it, it didn't budge even a little. But when she pressed her eyes to the crack of light, she caught her first glimpse of the rest of the basement.

In front of her was a tight cluster of exposed beams, like jail cell bars, that ran vertically in her field of vision. Beyond that, she could just make out the nearest piles of items that Rick had left in storage. Some stacked bins. A lamp. A set of skis.

The skis. Those stood out. She remembered seeing them in the corner of her eye—while she leaned against the stairs—when she was looking down at Sid that night she'd confronted him in the basement.

She forced herself to let out the breath she'd been holding so long her pounding head felt like a drum. At least she knew where she was now. This tiny, hidden room was a makeshift home beneath the stairs.

How to get out, though?

Nya ran her hands along the surface of the drywall, back and forth and up and down, feeling for any aberration in the chalky surface. When she was halfway down the sheet of drywall, her fingers hit something smooth and metal, running vertically in line with the crack. Hinges.

She felt to the right and found a portion of the drywall that had been cut away into a shallow notch and threaded with a looped rope that acted as a handle.

Another little door.

She wasn't sure what she'd expected to find down here. Definitely not a makeshift tiny house, though. The idea that Arlo had built this foxhole down here—complete with a clever, working doorway—was equal parts terrifying and fascinating. She remembered what he'd told her about his college major: construction management. The summers he'd worked on job sites with his awful father. All of that must have been true.

She thought of the scar tissue she'd felt on his body that night in the grounds maintenance building. The one bit of information she'd uncovered in the Idaho repository—*child removed from home.* Had his dad done that to him?

She winced, a drizzle of sympathy trying to mix with the fear like oil and water. There was little question that Arlo had lived a miserable existence, but there was no time to dwell on that now.

When Nya applied pressure to the rope, a squat, waist-height door—like the one she'd seen in a playhouse at the Blood of the Lamb church nursery—opened inward a few inches, scraping softly across the concrete floor.

More dim light filled the tiny room, bringing the lumps and piles into focus.

She couldn't help spending a few precious seconds gaping at what she saw, unable to tear her eyes away.

It was surprisingly tidy in here. Short stacks of neat clothing along one wall. The long, lumpy cushion she'd stepped on earlier—that she could now see was actually some sort of mattress formed out of layered coats. One of them was leather and looked similar to the coat Sid had sold in the video.

A vintage-looking Mickey Mouse stuffed animal lay at the head of the makeshift bed, its black eyes glimmering faintly in the dark. A pillow, maybe.

Did all of this stuff belong to Rick? Had Arlo stolen it? The irony might have struck her as slightly funny if she wasn't terrified she'd hear his footsteps at any moment while she was still scrambling to find a way out of the basement.

She scanned past a gallon jug of water and precarious piles of food and wrappers on the floor by the Mickey Mouse pillow, preparing to duck out of the little doorway and into the basement.

But as she crouched, something about the neatly stacked food caught her eye.

A small stack of cling-wrapped sandwiches.

She knew without looking that they were peanut butter and jelly. The same ones "Curtis" had brought to their picnics so often.

My roommate works at Albertson's. He brings home some of the stuff they're going to toss in the dumpster. Another lie. Her stomach turned. He definitely hadn't gotten this food from his roommate. His only roommates were Sid … and Nya.

Still, the wrappers on the food did display the Albertson's logo.

Had he stolen it, like the Chicken Chick meals?

Her stomach flipped. *No.* The dates on all of the wrappers were several days' expired. The store couldn't sell that food anymore. Which meant he'd likely gotten them out of the dumpster.

Her stomach churned even though, to be fair, none of the food had ever been rotten. It had all been surprisingly delicious. She knew now that if anything, Curtis had an extra incentive to be careful about germs because of his spleen removal. All the food was sealed and wrapped. And Nya wasn't beneath the idea of dumpster-diving to satisfy a hungry belly.

A fresh wave of sympathy swelled in her chest, colliding with the white-hot horror in a way that hurt her heart.

Then her eyes focused on the pile next to the food.

She recognized the pattern on the lacy fabric immediately, even in the dark.

It was her missing pair of underwear, wrapped in the dangling cord of her phone and its charger, like it was being strangled. She reached down and snatched it up.

It was, of course, dead. And there wasn't time to sit around charging it.

Next to the underwear was a thin wad of bills tucked into an open envelope. The same envelope she'd left on the kitchen table with Sid's name written on it.

Her rent money.

The sympathy she'd felt seconds earlier vanished, replaced once again by horror and anger. No wonder Sid had been so belligerent about the rent money.

He'd actually never gotten it. Arlo had taken it.

As Nya scanned the floor, searching in vain for the pepper spray, her eyes landed on what Arlo had spent that rent money on.

Not food. Not anything that would make the cramped living space under the stairs more comfortable.

There, next to the coat-makeshift mattress, was a tiny video monitor, the cord snaking through a rough-cut hole in the drywall.

A white thread of text displayed on the screen. Unable to stop herself, she leaned closer to read it. "No motion detected."

She nudged the video monitor with her foot ever so slightly, and the screen flickered to life, casting an eerie glow over the floor.

Her heart pounded so hard she was sure, for a moment, that she was going to pass out.

It was a live feed of her own bedroom. NYA, read the white text on the screen now. A second smaller square in the corner—another live feed—was labeled SID.

Nya's hands shook hard. She shoved them into the pocket of her pajama pants and touched the three prickly legs of the little wooden horse, pressing them deep into her palms until it hurt.

The wide-angle camera lens showed nearly every detail of her bedroom. The closed bedroom door. The angled dresser she'd left beside it. The open closet door where, just moments ago, she had entered and felt her way down the ladder. Her half-open bathroom door.

The fidelity on the video was so good that she could even see wafts of steam coming through the open bathroom door, from the hot shower.

Not only had Arlo been living beneath her. Pretending to be her friend. Trying to be her boyfriend. But he'd been watching her every move.

How many nights had she walked out of the bathroom after a shower with her towel wrapped around her, then walked around the room naked for a few minutes while she enjoyed the feel of the cool air from the A/C unit on her freshly showered pink skin before slipping into her pajamas.

How many times had she—

Nya shook her head, shutting down the stream of terrifying thoughts. There would be time for that later. Time to feel every nuance of fear and revulsion of knowing that Arlo had been watching her most private moments any time he chose.

No wonder he always seemed to know just what to say to her.

No wonder he knew how hungry she was. How desperate she was to get to that used book sale.

Her mind raced. Why hadn't she noticed the camera? How long had he been watching her and Sid?

There was little doubt in her mind he'd been doing it all along. There were too many coincidences. Too many conversation topics that at one time had made him seem like a kindred spirit … and now made him the ultimate stalker.

The feeling of violation intensified, threatening to pull her under. Where was the camera hidden? She felt sure she would have noticed something amiss. Some piece of technology. From the angle of the lens, it was low to the ground, along the wall.

Her mind raced. There was nothing on that wall.

Nothing except an electrical socket.

She suddenly remembered the soft clicking sound she'd heard in the room so many times. The one she'd thought must be an electrical circuit or any number of noises old houses made.

Instead, it had been a camera.

Bile rose in her throat as she imagined him unscrewing the wall plate and mounting the tiny lens inside, then scurrying down to his hidey hole to watch her.

"Fuck you," she whispered, taking a step backward toward the hinged door in the drywall.

She'd already spent too much time in here. She had to find a way out of the basement.

However, as she ducked to pull the rope handle of the door wider, one more horrifying discovery drew her gaze.

She nearly scanned right past it, intent on getting the hell out of the house once and for all.

It was a little mug and a spoon tucked against the wall. The one real wall against the back of the stairs, where the thick swaths of paint curled in their haphazard whorls.

The mug and the spoon were nothing shocking. Not at first. But all of a sudden, the final puzzle piece clicked into place.

She knew what Arlo had done to Sid.

51

The mug was white with forest-green block letters proclaiming "I Love Shelley." The shape of the state of Idaho, cocked like a gun, shot a pine-tree bullet beneath the text.

She remembered what Arlo had told her. *I'm from out East. Shelley.*

She'd bet anything that Shelley was in Bingham County, Idaho. Which was the location of the Idaho Repository listing for Arlo: *child removed from home.* If only she'd Googled just a little further that night.

The spoon had been placed in the mug, as if it contained just-stirred coffee or tea, but the thick paint above the wall told a different story.

A few inches above the rim of the mug, the irregular whorls and thick swashes of paint on the wall had been chipped away. Jagged edges remained where the spoon had scraped away at it, forming a fist-sized crater. The scene looked like a lackluster attempt at a jailbreak.

Bits and pieces of crumbled paint lay near the mug itself. She had no doubt that if she peered inside, she'd see more.

The basement is filled with lead, Sid had said.

He'd almost certainly told Arlo the same thing when he moved in. Not because the lead could hurt him, locked inside the paint, but because he wanted Arlo to stay out of the basement.

Arlo definitely hadn't listened, but he'd remembered the information about the lead paint.

And ever since he'd moved into his little hidey hole beneath the stairs, he'd been chipping away at that paint, extracting the poison.

Nya thought of Sid's awful, worsening rash. Those yellow, sickly eyes. His erratic behavior. The way he'd ultimately collapsed in the hall, seizing and vomiting.

It was acute lead poisoning.

Tearing her eyes away from the nightmare scene, Nya crouched and tugged on the rope in the door. The panel of drywall resisted a little, then slid smoothly across the cement and opened fully with a soft swishing noise.

As she stumbled through the doorway and into the dark basement, she couldn't help taking one last look at the tiny monitor showing her bedroom.

Her mouth went dry.

The screen had gone dark again, showing "No motion detected."

It wouldn't stay dark for long, though. Because above her, she could hear the scratch of a chair pulling away from the kitchen table on the linoleum.

Followed by the faint sound of her own name. "Nya?"

Then footsteps moving down the hall toward her bedroom.

52

Nya bit down hard on her cheek to stop the scream from tearing through her throat.

Her eyes cut to the top of the stairs.

She could hear Arlo's voice more clearly now, calling her name. "Nya? Nya, are you okay in there?"

Her breath came faster as she stared at the tall, dark rectangle of the closed basement door. He was just on the other side. He still thought she was in her bedroom. He wouldn't think that for long, though.

How long until his concern turned to rage?

How long until he rammed his shoulder into her bedroom door—and realized where she'd gone?

Seconds at worst. Minutes at best.

She had to find another way out of the basement before that happened.

Would he come tearing down the basement stairs, or would he skitter down the hidden ladder like he had so many times?

It was impossible to guess.

While he kept screaming her name, she at least knew where he was in the house. But that might change any second.

He banged louder on the door. "NYA!"

She ignored him, frantically scanning the basement walls for a way out.

The tiny, non-egress windows were, like she remembered, way too small for a human body to fit through. And besides, they were too far up the wall to reach without a lot of effort trying to pile up objects.

BANG.

No more knocking politely. He was ramming his body against the door.

BANG.

Hot tears filled her eyes.

"NYA!" Hardly any concern in his voice now. More frustration. More anger. He was going to get inside that room and find out why she wasn't answering him. She imagined his red-rimmed eyes fixed on her doorway.

It hadn't been very long. Maybe five minutes.

Did that mean that Sid had already died? That Arlo had gotten his final moment of revenge, and now he was ready to tie up the loose ends and get out of the house with his little bonus prize —Nya?

He was going to be very, very upset when he realized that wasn't happening.

One more *BANG.*

SLAM.

Then a brief silence.

He'd rammed her bedroom door open.

More footsteps.

Nya forced her wobbly legs to move faster, picking her way through the haphazard piles of Rick's belongings, scanning the wall for any sign of how Arlo had been getting in and out of the basement to the outside world.

Where was the way out? The dimly lit basement, combined with the strange shadows from the piles of storage items made it nearly impossible to make sense of the shapes she was seeing in the whorls of paint on the walls.

Then she heard the scream she'd been bracing for. The one that told her that time was up and Arlo knew she'd betrayed him.

"Nya! Nya, what the fuck. What the FUCK?"

His voice, unhinged and hoarse, sounded less human than animal. He'd realized she wasn't in the bathroom.

He'd realized she lied to him.

Everything went quiet again. She could imagine the wheels in his brain spinning, his voice cursing her name in a rage-filled hiss. The same rage that had made him drug and assault her, after she broke up with him. After she got him sick.

If you hurt Arlo, he got revenge.

And she'd just hurt him, big time.

She forced herself to keep moving, keep scanning the walls, keep looking for yet one more secret door that would let her out of the house and away from the monster upstairs.

A floorboard creaked above her head.

Adrenaline screamed through her veins, hot and desperate, begging her to think faster, move faster, find what she was so desperately searching for.

Was he creeping toward the door at the end of the hallway right now? Or was he easing himself down into the ladder and into his hidden room?

Where would he appear from?

Either way, she was a rat in a trap down here unless she could find a way out.

She gasped and kept moving, kept searching.

Either way, in just a few seconds, he would be in the basement.

53

There, behind a stack of Rubbermaid bins.

She would have missed it, if it weren't for a thin spray of crumbling white flecks on the cement floor that looked like grated parmesan.

Paint flakes.

When she looked closer at the wall, she could see the disruption in the thick whorls of paint. A smaller version of the patch Arlo had hacked at inside his hidden room beneath the stairs.

The chipped-away paint was directly next to a large, square air return grate. It was the kind of thing you'd look right past in a basement like this. Just part of the HVAC system.

Only something told her that if she pulled on that grate, she wouldn't find a vent on the other side.

And she was right.

Nya tucked the dead phone into her back pocket, then grabbed hold of the vent with both hands and pulled hard.

The vent came out of the wall with barely any resistance, without a sound, revealing a perfect square of darkness and the dank smell of earth. It was beyond her how many secrets the Gore Shack held all this time.

A few feet away, tantalizingly close, was the lattice covering the underside of the porch. The warm October sun beat down, drying the brown grass. The swaying branches of the mulberry tree, now bright yellow with dying leaves, were just visible.

Faintly, from somewhere in the distance, came a peal of laughter from the outside world.

There were people somewhere nearby. Walking to grab some lunch. Heading to see friends, to cap off the weekend with some beers.

If she screamed, they might hear her.

But would they find her before Arlo did?

JUST GET OUT, her mind screamed. *NOW.*

Trying not to think about spiders and earthworms and opossums in the dank, narrow space beneath the porch, she planted both hands on the hard-packed dirt at waist level, just beyond the hole in the wall.

The earth felt cool on her hands. For a moment, she had the irrational urge to lay her cheek against it. Her head was pounding so hard again, hot and feverish.

Keep going. Gritting her teeth, Nya pushed up on her palms and hoisted one leg into the dirt passageway, already rehearsing what she'd say to the first person she found on the street.

Call 9-1-1. An ambulance. Someone might be dead. In that house, right there. The Gore Shack, with the mulberry tree.

There would be time later to explain about the horrifying events that had unfolded over the past two months. About the hidden room and the cameras. About the lead paint that Arlo had carefully scraped into a mug and slipped into Sid's food. About what he'd done to her last night.

Nya got her second knee into the hole, ready to push off into the darkness. She coiled her body into the awkward angle required to propel herself through the narrow space underneath the porch, toward the sunlight prickling through the broken lattice.

That was when she felt hands grab hold of her bare foot. The grip was so tight on the delicate bones near the ankle that she cried out.

NOELLE W. IHLI

54

He yanked her back hard.

It was all she could do to put out her hands, bracing to land on the concrete floor.

"You lied to me," Arlo raged.

The words rang through her ears at the same moment she hit the ground hard. A faint crunching sound and a searing burst of pain accompanied the blow. Was that her tailbone or her phone?

"Curtis—Arlo—" she gasped, rolling away from the searing pain in her tailbone. The *alebrije's* remaining legs dug into the soft skin near her hipbone with a new, sharp pain, driving home what she already knew: There was nowhere left to turn.

"Shut up," he hissed. "After everything I did for you over the past couple of months, this is how you act?"

She wanted to kick him. To scream that he was the one who had been lying to *her* for months. From the very beginning. That everything he'd done was more horrifying than what she thought Sid was doing.

That would only make things worse, though.

Not that anything could make things better.

She was still stuck in this godforsaken rental house, flat on her back. And now she'd never leave.

Maybe she could keep him talking for a few minutes, draw it out. But then what?

If she screamed, at least he'd end her life quickly.

Maybe that was the best she could hope for.

"Why did you have to ruin everything?" he spat, and Nya heard real pain in his voice. In his own twisted way, he really had been convinced that this horror story could have a happy ending. That Nya wouldn't find out just how much he'd "done for her" over the past few months.

Her tailbone, definitely broken, throbbed painfully. Could she even run if she had the chance? She stared back at him, wide-eyed and mute.

She saw the moment his expression changed from hurt to resolve.

He couldn't let her leave this house. Not now. Not ever.

They both knew that.

He's going to kill you now, she thought calmly. *Maybe then he'll hide your body in that little room by the stairs. How long will it be before Jade gets worried enough to call the police?*

They'll probably blame it all on poor, dead Sid.

The irony of it brought hot tears to her eyes—along with a strange, wild bubble of laughter in her throat. She started to swallow it back, then changed her mind and let it out in a hiccuping, unsettling sound that made Arlo cock his head in surprise and take a small step backward.

His eyes narrowed above that dingy cloth mask he was still wearing.

"What the fuck are you laughing at—"

Her eyes went to his foot, which he'd brought to rest maybe ten inches away from hers.

Now, chula! screamed the voice that sounded like Jade.

Without hesitating, Nya swept her foot across the cement, ignoring the blinding pain as the motion ground her broken tailbone against the cement floor.

Arlo cursed as he tripped, catching himself on the stack of Rubbermaid bins.

"You bitch—" he screamed, the last part of the word squeaking out in a surprised, high-pitched yelp as the stack of bins shifted, sending him sprawling in the same direction he'd begun to fall.

His hand moved instinctively to the left side of his body, just beneath his ribs.

Protecting the tender place where his spleen used to be. Where the scar tissue was still new, still fragile.

Nya's eyes locked on that spot as he crumpled to the ground, already clawing to regain his footing. She already knew that spot by heart. Not just from Advanced Human Anatomy, but from the tissue she'd felt beneath his rib cage that fateful night in the maintenance building when she kissed him.

Her fingers found the *alebrije* in her pocket, prickling against its remaining legs.

They were maybe three inches long.

Maybe long enough.

Maybe not.

55

Arlo was too fast.

By the time she'd flung herself at him, the *alebrije* clutched tight in her hand with those sharp little legs sticking out, he'd already found his footing.

He twisted her hand backward, pulling her against him tight.

Not realizing that was exactly where she wanted to be.

She hesitated only a split second, the words *do no harm* screaming through her brain.

But this wasn't like the medical scenarios she'd learned about in any of her classes.

There would be harm taking place in this basement today. The only question was who would be leaving alive.

Twisting her body, Nya created just enough space to draw back her arm and thrust it under his ribcage, as hard as she could.

Every part of her recoiled when she felt the tender skin at the scar tissue give way to the *alebrije's* sharp legs.

Every part of her, except her hands.

One hand gripping his back, she pulled herself closer to him even as he struggled to back away.

The other hand drove the horse's legs deeper through the subcutaneous fat, into the muscle, into the lining of the abdominal cavity.

As deep as she could go, reaching for the splenic artery.

The dense network of blood vessels no longer had a spleen to supply with oxygen. But they were still there, pulsing.

Arlo screamed in pain, but Nya didn't stop.

Not until her hand was slippery with blood. Not until he let go, clutching his side and writhing on the basement floor.

Then, without a backward glance, she scrambled through the hole in the wall, across the dirt that whispered with scuttling legs and prickling weeds, and into the October sunlight.

56

Arlo's screams followed her.

But Arlo himself stayed right where she'd left him.

Nya still didn't look back. Staying low to the earth to avoid hitting her head on the spidery, dirty porch planks above her head, she crawled across the hard-packed ground. Her breath came in shallow gasps. It smelled awful under here. Not like death. Like something familiar but rotten.

Like urine, she realized suddenly. This was Arlo's bathroom.

She scrambled across a worn dirt path that stood out from the rest of the uneven earth, vaguely realizing that Arlo must have smoothed this pathway a little more each time he left the basement through the faux vent.

She was still holding the bloody *alebrije* in one hand, refusing to let it go even as those sharp matchstick legs dug into her palm with every step she crawled.

A faint snapping sound accompanied a sharp pain in her palm, and she knew that the little horse's third leg had broken off.

It must have been only a few seconds before she pushed through the hole in the dirty lattice surrounding the porch. But it felt like forever.

Arlo's screams had stopped. Did that mean he was dead? That there were now two dead bodies behind her in the awful rental house?

Thick swaths of bright-red blood, now covered in a layer of dust, ran up to her elbow on the arm that held the wooden horse.

A violent shudder rolled through her body so hard she had a difficult time scrambling through the broken lattice. At any second, she expected to feel Arlo's hands on her bare feet, dragging her back into the basement before she could finally, finally escape the house.

The sun on her face was blindingly beautiful.

She wanted to collapse on the lawn. To yank open the door of her beat-up Honda still parked on the street, the one she hadn't even bothered to lock because it was so shitty and still out of gas to boot, and drive away. To fall into a deep, safe sleep. To let her brain go dark on the horrifying memories while the police and the hospital took charge of the crisis.

But nobody knew there was a crisis in the little rental house.

Not until she told someone.

"Help," Nya screamed, the sound coming out as a pitiful croak.

The street in front of the house was empty, aside from a few parked cars.

She ran forward a few steps through the shade of the mulberry, the dead lawn crunching under her feet.

There.

There, at the end of the street, were three girls standing on the sidewalk. They'd just exited the crosswalk and were moving toward campus.

She nearly laughed. It was impossible to tell for sure, but they looked like the same three girls she'd nearly run down that first chaotic day she arrived at the rental house, when she drove to Walmart in a panic.

"Hey," she called, forcing the word to boom through her painful throat. "Help! Please!"

One of the girls, a redhead wearing a tight green crop top, cocked her head and turned around.

She frowned when her eyes landed on Nya.

Her mouth moved, and the other two girls turned around.

Nya waved her arm, the blood-and-dust-covered fingers still clutching the wooden horse.

For a moment, the three girls—clean, shiny, carefree on a Sunday—hesitated like they might be better off turning around and walking away fast.

"Please," Nya begged.

One of the girls punched something into her phone and held it to her ear.

Then all three girls rushed toward Nya.

She closed her eyes and dropped to her knees, wondering if this was the very same spot where Arlo had collapsed the day Sid put him in the hospital.

EPILOGUE

"She wants to know if it's too spicy for you," Jade translated, nodding at the *pozóle* and glancing between Nya and Grandma Tita.

The soft rumble of conversation around the big kitchen table quieted. "If it's too spicy, you don't have to eat it," Mrs. Estrada said before Nya could respond.

Jade's sister Emilia giggled. "It's extra spicy this time," she chimed in. "Mom told Abuela to tone it down for the *gueros*, but she said it wouldn't be *auténtico*."

Mrs. Estrada laughed and shook her head, holding her hands palm up as if to say, *Me? Never.*

Nya took another big spoonful of the spicy red liquid thick with hominy and shredded pork. She blinked back tears. "So spicy it's making me cry," she whispered. "I love it."

Grandma Tita's weathered face broke into a grin before Jade finished translating.

Nya smiled back, not bothering to wipe away the tears streaming down her face. The soup was delicious, but the fierce burning of the spices on her tongue wasn't too much. It made her feel alive. Something she'd never been more grateful for.

Outside, the Indiana winter had arrived with a vengeance. Sleet slapped against the kitchen window panes in wet *thwacks*, and there was an ice storm warning for the weekend. But inside Grandma Tita's cozy rambler, the world was warm, safe, and full of life—and spice.

Strings of *papel picado* hung from the walls, their delicate cut-out designs showcasing intricate scenes of el Niño Jesús and the Madonna. The twinkling lights on the Christmas tree reflected off worn metallic ornaments and tinsel, casting a warm glow and deep shadows over everything.

An entire wall of colorful *alebrijes,* shaped like all sorts of animals, watched from the shelf that separated the living room from the kitchen. There was every animal Nya could imagine— except horses. A fierce jaguar, its coat painted in deep blues, fiery oranges, and lush greens. A delicate purple-and-gold bird, wings spread wide in flight. A long, lean rabbit painted in different shades of rosy pink. Each wooden animal cast a watchful eye over the family from its place on the shelf.

Grandma Tita, who was still the matriarch of the family even if her memory was deteriorating fast, sat at the head of the dining table, her silver hair adorned with a festive red bow. She'd been telling stories all day. About her childhood. About Mexico in the 1940s. About Jade's mother as a little girl.

Tita had to be reminded of Nya's name constantly, since she'd arrived four weeks ago on the Greyhound bus. Nya didn't mind, though. She was the only one who didn't look at her with that distinctive tinge of sadness and curiosity. The only one who didn't say "How are you doing, Nya?" in that knowing way, every time she had to answer another call from the police, or do a Zoom interview with another detective.

* * *

Nya hadn't set foot in the rental house again.

The victim's advocate she'd been assigned in the aftermath had been kind enough to retrieve her minimal belongings from the bedroom. The scripture quilt. Her few toiletries and items of clothing. All of it fit in the duffel bag, still stained purple from the mulberries.

The little *alebrije* horse had to stay in Boise, in a blood-stained evidence bag, until the investigation and trial were over.

Nya, on the other hand, had gotten on a bus to Indianapolis as soon as the police told her she wasn't being prosecuted in Arlo's assault. He'd survived, somehow. So had Sid. Just barely. He was expected to make a full recovery, from what she heard.

The evidence in the basement left little doubt that Arlo wouldn't need to search for a new place to live anytime soon. He'd be staying in the Boise Correctional Facility without bail until his trial. His lawyers had announced that he would be pleading insanity, claiming the lead had gotten into his system, too.

Nya's abrupt move across the country to Indy meant dropping all of her classes with two months left in the semester and delaying graduation until spring. It just wasn't possible to complete her capstone anatomy labs online. However, the victim's advocate and the dean had assured her that finishing her remaining credits at IUPUI wouldn't be a problem. Professor Stern had even agreed to write a recommendation letter. It would mean out-of-state tuition. And a few thousand dollars on top of her mountain of student debt. But none of that felt too devastating anymore.

Nya had talked to her parents on the phone just once, from the Boise police station. The conversation had been brief and strained. They were shocked by what had happened, just like everyone else. But when her mom told her she'd pray for her at the end of the phone call, it felt less like a reprimand than an offering.

Maybe that wounded relationship would close over with scar tissue someday, too.

Next year, Nya and Jade were going to get an apartment together. But for now, the warm cocoon of Grandma Tita's house was just what Nya needed to heal.

It was the opposite of the Gore Shack in so many ways.

Spotlessly clean. Full of laughter, love, and chatter. The smell of something delicious constantly wafting from the kitchen.

And no basement. Not even a crawl space.

NOTE FROM THE AUTHOR

If you enjoyed this book, a positive review would mean the world to me. Like other small-press authors, I rely heavily on word-of-mouth recommendations to reach new readers.

I can promise you that I read every single review. Because each one is a new window into this story. And because if you loved this book, *you're* the one I wrote it for—which is why I'm placing this note *before* the acknowledgments.

Thank you for reading!

* * *

One last thing: One last thing: If you want to know what happened during that epic fight between Sid and Arlo, just scan the QR code below. It'll take you to a free short story called "Bottom Feeder."

ACKNOWLEDGMENTS

I'm so thankful to everyone who offered their talents in honing and polishing this book. Your kindness and generosity mean so much to me.

Special thanks to Steph Nelson, Anna Gamel, Faith Gardner, Lisa Hunter, and Brett Stanfill for your feedback, brainstorming sessions, and support. I couldn't do this without you.

In the same spirit, a huge thank you to the bookstagrammers, bloggers, booktokkers, and readers who have picked up my books. I'm so grateful for your reviews, messages, and enthusiasm.

Thank you to my editor, Patti Geesey: You're a true gem, and I deeply appreciate your attention to detail and care with my books.

Last but not least, thank you to Nate. You'll always be my favorite reader (and human).

ABOUT THE AUTHOR

Noelle lives in Idaho with her husband, two sons, and two cats. When she's not plotting her next thriller, she's scaring herself with true-crime documentaries or going for a trail ride in the foothills (with her trusty pepper spray).

Room for Rent is Noelle's fourth thriller-suspense novel. You can find her on Instagram @noelleihliauthor

*Read on for a thrilling excerpt
from Noelle W. Ihli's novel* Run on Red

RUN ON RED

A THRILLER

NOELLE W. IHLI

1

"They're still tailgating us," I murmured, squinting into the lone pair of headlights shining through the back windshield. The sequins on my halter top caught on the lap belt, snicking like ticker tape as I shifted in the passenger seat.

"Maybe it's the Green River Killer," Laura said evenly, keeping her eyes on the road.

I snorted but kept watching as the headlights crept closer. "They caught the Green River Killer. I thought you read that blog I sent."

"It was twenty pages long. Anyway, why do I need a crime blog when I have Olivia Heath in my car?" she asked. As she slowed down to take the next hairpin turn, the watery yellow headlights behind us turned a pale orange where they mingled with our brake lights.

I ignored her and kept staring at the headlights that had been tailgating us relentlessly for miles on the dark rural highway.

Everything is fine, I chided myself. There were "No Passing" signs posted every other switchback on the narrow road, and our ancient Volvo was going ten miles under the speed limit as we chugged uphill. Of course they were tailgating us.

When I blinked, two mirror-image red spots flashed behind my eyelids. It was impossible to see the drivers—and I was getting carsick. I glared into the headlights a little longer and committed the license plate to memory: 2C GR275.

"Liv? Earth to Liv. They're probably late to the bonfire. Same as us." Laura was the Scully to my Mulder: ever the optimist, ever reasonable. Ever the one who talked me down from my imaginary ledges. But the question always tapped at the back of my mind: What if there really *was* a ledge?

"The license plate *does* say GR," I grumbled, but turned around, smoothing down my wonky sequins and drawing in a slow breath to calm my sloshing stomach.

"GR?" Laura prodded, glancing at me as we came out of the curve.

"Green River," I clarified with an exaggerated sigh. "Or Gary Ridgway, same guy. Go easy on the turns." I rested one hand out the uneven window ledge, so the cool night air hit my face in a slap that smelled like sage.

The Volvo's passenger-side window had collapsed inside the doorframe a few weeks earlier. Laura's sister Tish had talked about taping up a sheet of plastic in the hole, but since the car didn't have air conditioning, the window just stayed open. I rubbed at a smattering of goosebumps on my bare arms. I should have brought a jacket. The hills were at least twenty degrees cooler than the city, but I'd been too rushed—and too sweaty—after work to care.

The bonfire at the reservoir had started more than an hour ago, and as far as I could tell we were the only car on the road—aside from the tailgaters. Laura had waited until my shift ended at the Pie Hole to make the tedious, winding drive through the hills.

The interior of the Volvo grew brighter as the headlights edged closer. Laura glanced in the rearview mirror. When I craned my neck to do the same, she sent me a warning glare. "Stay facing forward. The only thing you need to worry about is not getting barf on Tish's car." She flicked the fuzzy dice hanging from the mirror. "I can't believe she bailed on us again tonight."

"I'm fine," I insisted, even as my stomach lurched dangerously. I inhaled slowly through my nose to stave off the nausea. "But—"

"Breathe, Liv," she soothed. "They just want to pass us. I'll find somewhere to pull over."

"There's nowhere to pull over," I mumbled, wishing I'd gone to the library with Tish instead of "putting myself out there" tonight. "And this is definitely a no-passing zone." The isolated two-lane rural highway made me nervous, even in the daytime.

"Look, right there." Laura signaled and angled the Volvo toward a shallow gravel pullout carved into the hillside to our right.

The headlights stayed behind us, moving toward the same shoulder at a crawl.

"Why aren't they passing?" I demanded, even while I scolded myself for overreacting. I didn't trust my anxious brain to correctly identify a real threat. It had steered me wrong way too many times.

As soon as the words left my lips, a vehicle with one headlight out—only the second car we'd seen since leaving city limits—whipped into view. It passed us from behind, going way too fast and nearly clipping the driver's side mirror of the Volvo. Once its brake lights disappeared around the next bend, the tailgaters eased back onto the road and zipped past us as well.

Within a few seconds, the hills were dark and quiet again, except for the Volvo's idling mutter.

"See? They were just letting that idiot pass," Laura insisted triumphantly, flashing me a grin before hitting the gas and easing back onto the road. "No serial killers."

When I didn't respond, her eyes flicked toward me. "Have you heard anything from Tish?"

Shaking off the useless adrenaline rush, I sighed and reached down the front of my high-waisted denim cut-offs to open the slim traveler's pouch where I'd tucked my cell phone. Laura snickered at the sound of the zipper.

I ignored her and flipped open the phone. "You know she hasn't texted. You just wanted to see me open the magic fanny pack." I snapped the elastic of the traveler's pouch, tucked just beneath the top button of my shorts, for emphasis. "My pockets can hold half a Saltine, at most. Where the hell am I supposed to put my cell phone when I go out?"

"And your rape whistle, and your pepper spray," Laura chirped.

I rolled my eyes and laughed. "You really should read the blog."

My phone screen showed one service bar. I didn't have any new messages, but I took the opportunity to text Tish the car's license plate: 2C GR275. *Just in case.*

She wouldn't see it until she got home from the library later tonight. And even then, she wouldn't think anything of the text unless the apartment was still empty in the morning. Tish—like Laura—had come to expect the occasional license plate number—or blurry photo of some rando at the gas station who looked like a police sketch I'd seen on Twitter.

Laura shifted in the driver's seat to face me. "You know, we can turn around if you want," she offered gently, the bright white of her teeth slowly disappearing with her smile. "If you're not feeling up for the bonfire—"

"I'm good," I insisted more gruffly than I intended, avoiding her eyes. I could deal with jokes about my red-alert texts and travel pouch and rape whistle. But any hint of sympathy for the underbelly of my social anxiety … not so much.

I zipped my cell phone back into the slim travel pouch, refusing to imagine the last bar of cell service flickering out as we drove deeper into the hills. Then I reached over and turned the volume knob on the ancient boombox propped between us, where the glove box in the old Volvo used to live. It was an indestructible monstrosity, like the Volvo itself. I absolutely loved it.

"I did not wear scratchy sequins to turn around and go home," I sang off-key over Britney Spears. Laura had spent hours making this party mix, first downloading the songs, then burning them to a CD, then recording the CD onto a tape that would play in the ridiculous boombox.

Laura's smile brightened. "Atta girl."

2

The music pumping through the old boombox lasted until we approached the final turnoff onto the long dirt road that led to the reservoir.

The tape turned over with a loud click right as the Volvo clunked over a shallow pothole. When Britney's voice reemerged, it was slow and distorted, like the song had been dunked in syrup.

"Brit? Stay with us," Laura coaxed as the song subsided to a tinny whine. The boombox made a sudden, harsh buzzing noise, coughed out a burst of static, then went completely silent.

"I guess not." She laughed and wiggled the volume knob one more time.

I smiled and rested my arm on the edge of the open window, dipping my hand down, then up, then down in the breeze. *The bonfire will be fun,* I reassured myself. *You always have fun once you get there. Just stay with Laura.*

The nervous fizz deep in my stomach remained wary. I leaned out the open window a little and followed the smoky trail of the Milky Way until it disappeared behind the hillside looming to our right. The sounds of night creatures worrying among themselves took center stage in the quiet night as the Volvo slowly chugged up the incline.

A muted scratching coming from the dash suddenly broke through the geriatric drone of the engine. The seatbelt caught as I shifted in my seat, leaving a drooping curl of fabric across my chest. There it was again: a soft skittering. "Do you hear that? I swear there's something inside the dash."

Laura let go of the wheel with one hand to rap on the plastic of the dash. The sound stopped. "I think there might be something living in that hole, gnawing on the wires," she said, then shrugged as if she'd just made a comment about the weather. "Sometimes I hear that same scurrying sound while I drive. Tish said she does too. It's probably a mouse."

I looked at her in disbelief. "If I see a damn *mouse* come out of your dashboard, I am hurling myself out of the Volvo." I shuddered. "I still can't believe Tish spent money on this thing. It's amazing that it runs."

Laura shrugged again, unfazed. "She got it cheap from Tony's friend. It was like, five hundred bucks." Then she added, "The guy actually said he'd give it to her for two hundred if she threw in a blow job."

"Okay, pull the car over." I mimed gagging and grabbed the door handle.

"Olivia!" Laura shrieked and hit the brakes.

I laughed. "I'm kidding. Mostly. He actually *said* that to Tish?"

She rolled her eyes dramatically. "Yep."

"While Tish and Tony were together?"

"Uh huh."

"Gross." I sat forward in my seat, studying the sloping hills looming in the distance. If I remembered right, we were about twenty minutes away from the reservoir once we turned onto this dirt road.

"How is Tish doing, anyway?" I asked after a minute. "If I didn't see her cereal bowl in the sink, I wouldn't even know she'd been sleeping at the apartment lately."

Laura sighed. "She's okay—I think? I've hardly seen her lately either. Ever since the breakup, she's been weird."

I nodded, still half-listening for the mouse scurrying around in the dash, but Tish's drama was a welcome distraction. Tish and I were friends—but we'd never been especially close. Not like me and Laura, who had been inseparable since the seventh grade. "I thought she was definitely coming tonight," I pressed. "She even RSVPed on Facebook. Why did she stay home?"

Laura slowed the car down to skirt another pothole in the dirt road. "No idea. She texted a few minutes before you got home from work, saying she was staying at the library late." She shrugged again. "I think she just doesn't want to risk running into Tony at the bonfire."

I nodded slowly. "Do you think he'll be there? It's not really a Delta vibe."

"A Delta vibe?" Laura giggled. "You mean like, an AXE Body Spray commercial?"

I burst out laughing. "Pretty much."

Laura raised her eyebrow and smiled. "Are *you* hoping Tony will be there?"

Heat rose in my cheeks. "No way. Tish was *engaged* to him, dummy."

I'd seen plenty of photos of Tish's boyfriend—briefly fiancé—on Facebook, but I'd only really met him a couple of times. Once across the room at a party, and once on the apartment couch in passing. We didn't actually know each other. Not really.

I pictured the smiling, sun-kissed boy I'd seen on Tish's Facebook profile, wearing a Band of Horses T-shirt. He was incredibly good-looking.

Laura sighed and brushed her bangs away from her face. "It's true. He's ruined for all of us now."

"I'm surprised Tish ..." I trailed off, not totally sure how to finish that sentence. Both Laura and I had been surprised when Tish started dating Tony last year. He was what my dad would call a "big man on campus." Handsome, charming, and one of the chosen ones who had been accepted into the Delta fraternity freshman year. As much as I loved Tish, it was impossible to deny that she was Tony's polar opposite: quiet, shy, and maybe a little boring if I was being mean. Basically, she was like me. Laura had always been the designated social butterfly of our little cadre.

Laura giggled. "Hey, at least you've got *Ziggy*."

I snickered, but my stomach tightened at the mention of his name. "Stop it. We aren't discussing him tonight."

"Ziggy," which I now knew was short for "Zachariah," was the supremely awkward humanities TA who stared at me during class. Laura and I had found his Facebook profile one night and learned, to our horror and delight, that he was a member of the Pen and Quill Society: a LARPing group on campus. Ziggy was a "mage": which Laura and I had to Google. It meant he was some kind of magician.

Last week, in an effort to "put myself out there," I'd made the horrifying mistake of accepting a date with a cute guy I'd met on MySpace. His profile photo bore almost zero resemblance to the tall, painfully quiet, acne-covered senior who wrote things like "me likey" and "bomb diggity" on the margins of my papers. I didn't realize it was Ziggy until we met up for happy hour at SpaceBar that night. Things went from bad to worse when I learned he had recognized *me* from my profile photo. I'd made an excuse about a family emergency and booked it out of the bar, vowing to delete my profile the second I got back to the apartment to lick my wounds.

"Did you hear back from your professor?" Laura prodded.

I nodded slowly. Laura had convinced me to email my humanities professor about what had happened, but I still felt weird about the whole thing. "Yeah, forgot to tell you. He wrote back yesterday with a long apology about how this happened earlier in the semester to someone else. Long story short, Ziggy's not the humanities TA anymore."

Laura shot me an impressed look and took a turn in the road a little too fast. "Nice job, killer. What a creep."

I held my breath as our wheels edged toward the thin shoulder that petered off into the darkness beyond our headlights. I tugged on my seatbelt again, hoping it had been engineered to outlast the rest of the car despite its obvious fatigue. "I haven't been up to Coffee Creek in forever. How much farther is it to the reservoir?"

"Coffin Creek," Laura corrected me sternly.

I rolled my eyes. "I hate that name. Do we have to call it that? There's no coffin. Just muddy water and beer cans."

"Because it's fun. And because the freshman who went missing is buried there." She shrugged, then flashed me a wicked grin.

I sighed. "Her name is Ava Robles. And if they knew where she was buried, she wouldn't be missing, would she? If you had read *that* blog post, you'd know they never found her body."

Incoming freshman Ava Robles had gone missing near Coffin Creek three years earlier. The same year Laura and I had started at University of Idaho. I hadn't known her. Neither had Laura. We weren't on the guest list for that particular party.

Ava had been one of the few freshmen who attended the exclusive sorority party that night, at the end of Rush week. Her story had been firmly embedded in campus lore almost as soon as the news broke that she had gone missing. For weeks at the start of the semester, cops stalked sorority and frat houses to interview anyone who had attended the huge toga party.

When rumors—and a few bloggers—started to spread that her body had been dumped in Coffin Creek, the detectives even sent divers to troll the murky waters. They'd found absolutely nothing. From the blog I'd read, the police believed that the rumors might have been intentionally started as a way to throw off the investigation. It worked. And the rumors—as well as the unfortunate nickname—stuck like glue around campus ever since.

The only things they'd ever found of Ava's were her purse and phone, tossed into the sagebrush at the edge of the reservoir. They'd trolled it too, with zero success. All anyone really knew was that Ava had been at that party one minute—and the next she hadn't.

There were no traces of blood. No signs of a struggle. No witnesses who had noticed anything strange.

Everyone assumed she was dead. There was even some speculation that maybe she'd been pulled into the hills by a cougar. It wasn't likely, but it wasn't impossible. Despite the university nearby, this part of Idaho was mostly wild. The hills went on for miles and miles in all directions with sportsman's access.

I shivered. Thinking about Ava Robles was not helping my state of mind. "How much longer until we get there?" I asked.

Laura shrugged. "We'll be there in fifteen minutes, give or take. Is your stomach feeling better?"

"All good," I insisted, not counting the anxious bubbles. "But I'm freezing." I rubbed my arms, wishing again that I had brought my jacket. The last bonfire we'd attended—stoked by overeager freshmen— had burned so hot that somebody's bumper had melted by the end of the night.

"Me too, but this top looks like an old paper bag if I cover up my arms." She gestured to the high-neck cotton blouse that looked nothing like a paper bag. "I never learn. See if you can get the heater to work. Tish swore it did."

I turned my attention to the large knob next to the radio dial, cranking it all the way to the red side. It made a clicking noise, followed by a soft *pop*. "That's a no. It might be time to take the Volvo to a farm." I patted the window frame. "We love you, but you're falling apart."

Giving up on the heater, I settled against the bucket seat, reaching up to touch my hair. I'd cut it from waist-length to a trendy lob with bangs a few days earlier, and my head still felt weirdly untethered without the extra weight.

I shifted slightly to study Laura's long hair in my peripheral vision. It hung down her back and was such a pale white-blond that it seemed to glow against the gray seat. The summer before sixth grade, we'd both tried highlighting our hair with a combination of Sun-In and peroxide. Laura's hair had turned an ethereal white. My dark brown hair had turned Sunny-Delight orange in splotches I hadn't fully eradicated until eighth grade. I made a face and asked, "Was it a mistake to cut my hair?"

She smiled and tapped on the brakes as a deer's eyes glowed white near the side of the road before it bounded into the night. "Stop it right now. I keep telling you, it's gorgeous. And it makes your eyes look huge." She reached up to grab a hunk of her blond hair. "Mine feels like straw lately—how do you get yours so shiny?"

I flipped my short hair dramatically. "Thanks. It's probably from the Pie Hole. All that oil in the air—it's like pizza-scented deep conditioner."

Laura sighed loudly. "Another reason I should've taken summer semester off to get a job. I can't get over the idea that physical education is an *actual* college requirement. Are we not adults now? How am I being forced into running?"

I wound my cold hands into the soft underside of the halter top, keeping my gaze on the shoulder of the road to watch for more pairs of ghostly eyes. "Are you sure we took the right turnoff?"

I glanced at the Volvo's dash clock out of habit, even though I knew it would read 3:03 no matter how long we drove. This far into the hills, it felt like we'd been swallowed up by the night itself.

I didn't hear her response. As the dirt road crested a rise, we passed a skinny ATV trail ducking into the hills. A dark, hulking shape sat angled in the weeds like a black hole in the pale, dry grass.

A truck.

Everything is fine, I told myself firmly, channeling my inner Laura.

The moment we drove past, the truck's high beams blinked on, blazing into our rearview mirror as it roared to life and pulled behind us.

3

"It's the same car," I mumbled in disbelief.

"What? How can you tell?" Laura asked distractedly, navigating a pothole.

I squinted through the back windshield into the blinding headlights. "Same license plate: 2C GR275. I texted it to Tish earlier."

Laura shot me a look. "Liv, everything is okay. Even if it is the same car, it's fine. If they took this turnoff, they're definitely on their way to the bonfire. Maybe it's a couple that decided to mess around on the side of the road for a while." She grinned then cranked down the driver's side window, signaling for the other vehicle to pass us.

I stared at her in bewilderment as she calmly motioned out the window.

When the headlights in the rearview mirror didn't disappear after a few seconds, Laura slowed the Volvo to a crawl and motioned more dramatically, her pale skin illuminated in the foggy beams. "Go around, dumbass," she said in a soft singsong.

I quietly unzipped the travel pouch beneath my shorts and pulled out the flip phone with shaking hands. No service, as expected. And the battery had dipped to just five percent. Berating myself for not turning off roaming sooner, I quickly navigated to Settings then snapped the phone shut.

"Dick," Laura mumbled, her lips turned down in a frown. Her purple lipstick looked black in the darkness. "Why don't they turn off their brights, at least? They're blinding me. I'm going to find somewhere to pull over all the way. The road is super narrow here."

She hit the gas and brought the Volvo slowly back up to speed.

The other vehicle accelerated behind us.

"They could back off our ass a little," Laura grumbled, hunching in her seat so the glare of the headlights didn't hit her directly. "The good news is that if we get rear-ended, Tish's car won't be the one going in for repairs. It's probably been totaled for the past ten years."

The truck began flashing its brights on and off in rapid succession as if transmitting a message in Morse code.

"Give me a hot second," Laura exclaimed, tapping on the brakes as the road curved and emptied into another steep straightaway. The Volvo decelerated quickly, laboriously crawling up the incline.

"There should be—" I began as the other vehicle abruptly swerved left and pulled up alongside us on the narrow straightaway. It was so close to us that if Laura reached her hand out the window, she could have touched the passenger's side mirror.

"Who is it?" she asked, keeping her eyes glued to the road as we approached the next curve. "They're going to get plastered if they stay in the left lane and someone comes around that bend," she added lightly, as if that might be a favorable outcome.

I didn't answer right away as I stared into the darkness beyond Laura's open window. I had been secretly hoping to see someone we knew. Or at the very least, a car packed with random frat boys, their teeth flashing white as they laughed at our wide eyes. But as the truck came even with the Volvo for a brief moment, I could see the silhouettes of two men inside, facing forward. Each wore a dark-colored hoodie pulled up over his head, concealing all but the barest outline of his profile. Neither one turned to look at me.

I felt like I'd just been dunked in ice water, even though the cell phone in my hand was slippery with sweat. *This is bad,* my gut screamed. *Are you sure?* my brain fired back.

"Who is it?" Laura asked again as both vehicles crawled along in tandem. A hot trickle of adrenaline chipped away at the ice in my veins. "Do we know them or something? Maybe they recognize the Volvo. It's hard to miss."

"We don't know them," I whispered, clutching the seatbelt across my chest. Both men were still facing forward. Neither had even glanced in our direction. "Should ... I call the police?" I asked shakily, hoping Laura would reassure me that the answer was *no.* That there was some reasonable and innocuous reason these men were toying with us. For all the times I'd repeated the catchphrases from my favorite bloggers—"Be vigilant, stay alive," "Screw politeness," "Stay safe, get weird," I knew deep down I'd only call 9-1-1 if I was actually in the process of being murdered.

I moved one finger to hover over the Emergency Call button, glancing between the glowing red text and the headlights. Still no service.

"I—I don't know. What do they look like?" Laura demanded. For the first time, she sounded rattled.

The truck stayed alongside us a moment longer. Then it roared ahead violently, the smell of dust and rubber filling the air as it darted past the Volvo, moved into our lane and disappeared around the approaching bend with mere inches to spare.

I shook my head, already second-guessing what I'd seen. "I —I couldn't tell very much, but I really think we should turn around. There's two guys. Neither one of them would look at me, and they were both wearing hoodies pulled all the way up over their—"

Laura gasped as we took the curve.

Red brake lights blazed just a few yards away.

Made in the USA
Las Vegas, NV
24 October 2023

79667406R00198